EVERY MAN A KING

Anne Worboys

Every man a king

A NOVEL OF SUSPENSE BY THE AUTHOR OF
The Lion of Delos

CHARLES SCRIBNER'S SONS · NEW YORK

PR 6073 .O667 E9 1975

AUTHOR'S NOTE

Although real locations have been faithfully described, all the characters, with the exception of Odin, are wholly fictitious, as is the story.

I would like to acknowledge my debt to the people who helped me during the writing of this book and who, indeed, made the writing of it possible. Firstly, Diana and Bobby Hope-Falkner of Algeciras to whom I am especially grateful for the opening of doors I could never have seen, much less opened myself. To the Dowager Duchess of Bailen, Señor Don Erich Heberlein of Toledo, Mr. Humphrey Burkill of Kew Gardens Herbarium, Mr. Hugh Reynolds of Tunbridge Wells; to Miss Brenda Thexton who led me safely over the mighty Sierra Nevadas and last, but certainly not least, the beautiful Odin who carried me during two weeks of hair-raising fun.

1

WE CAME OUT of the airport carrying our bags and I said to the American who had sat beside me on the plane: "Perhaps you can tell me where the buses leave from."

"A bus? You won't get a bus to Toledo from here, but you'll easily hire a car. They're very cheap."

"What do you call cheap?"

"Around twenty dollars, I guess. That's about ten pounds English, isn't it?"

Of course I could afford it, now. There was my father's insurance, and the proceeds of the house sale. But it was blood money and I needed time to accustom myself to using it. "I'll get a taxi to Madrid," I said, compromising, "then a train. One sees more of the country that way."

The taxi-driver was fat and friendly. His English, meagre and uncertain as it was, was yet good enough to protest about going to Atocha station when he could drive me right to Toledo in an hour for a mere sixteen hundred pesetas. What was money, anyway, to an American? I explained I was English and he looked suitably sympathetic, not to say resigned. After a while he brightened, saying all those pesetas were only eleven pounds English. And besides, I would have to wait two—three hours for a train.

I moved so that he could see me easily in the driving mirror, shaking my head. I would go to the Prado and see the original of that framed print Antonia had given me years ago, Velasquez's *Adoration of the Magi* which she said could never be reproduced effectively and at least once in a lifetime had to be seen in the original.

At the traffic lights my taxi-driver took up a paper from the seat beside him, did some swift calculations with a ball point pen, then announced happily that he could run me all the way for nine pounds English. "No," I said firmly. The way I have been brought up, it looks morally wrong to take a taxi when one can catch a train.

Atocha was bedlam. A bored girl, glass-bound and labelled *Información*, making a liar of the taxi-driver, told me in impeccable English that the train for Toledo left in three minutes' time from platform 04, a hundred and fifty metres from that sign ahead. There was a moment of confusion while I weighed the Prado against a daylight arrival, then I picked up my bag and ran.

The American had been right, I should have taken a taxi. A noisy, boisterous crowd of Spanish youths, their hair neatly trimmed and black as tar in the sun, eyed me with detached interest as I struggled to place my bag safely and find standing room among them. It was a sort of cattle-truck lying between two carriages that were already full of plump, black-haired housewives with their shopping bags on their knees and a great deal to say to each other. I rested one leg against my bag, attached myself to a hanging strap and with a sinking heart faced up to the ninety-minute journey. With a bang, a crash and a series of bone-shaking jolts, we started on our way. The boys, taking lively advantage of me in this country where, I already knew, nice girls do not go unattended, flung themselves bonelessly to left and right, muttering wicked apologies in unintelligible Spanish. Hemmed in, embarrassed and helpless, I fixed my eyes on some non-existent skyline until, to my intense relief, a gypsy woman came through from the carriage in front and collecting a coin from each member of the crowd, set up some sort of draw, or lucky dip, so that for five minutes peace reigned. Then, as we rattled into a station, a ticket-inspector appeared and they all leaped to the

8

platform like startled rabbits. A fat, velvet-eyed woman in the carriage gathered up her belongings and heaved herself to her feet. I hurried in to take her place.

I remember every moment and every inch of that journey, for not only was it my first glimpse of the real Spain, but it was nearly the last day of my life. Certainly it was the last day of the old one, for afterwards everything was changed. The foreign look of Spain on that short afternoon, the surprise, even now, years later, is photo-etched on my brain.

There were tiny, square, white stations with romantic names like SAN CRISTOBAL DE LOS ANGELES; clean factories; a white obelisk on a distant hill. Railway tracks, disused, hemmed in by rough netting. Little dumps of metal. Untidy grass verges white with stones. A rubbish dump with the sign *No Fumar*. Emerald-green crops with the hard white soil showing. Ploughed fields, mole-brown. Two members of the Civil Guard walking through, guns in holsters, noting my presence, taking in every detail of my appearance with their critical black eyes, nodding at me gravely, granting me unspoken leave to stay so long as I behaved as their dictator would have me behave.

VALDEMORA. CIEMPOZUELOS. Two nuns with large plastic handbags, chewing gum. Hillsides tufted with dry grass. A black dog intent about his affairs. An olive grove. A fence like matchsticks on a low horizon. SESENA. A canal. Horned bulls in a field. A wide, glassy river. A market garden, grey-green with spring's first dust. A yellow-ochre station ARANJUEZ. Pot-bellied sheep with large udders and small floppy ears eating the tough grass. VILLAMEJE. ALGODOR. And then we arrived.

"It's a wonderful place," Antonia had said. "I'll never forget my first glimpse of it from the Madrid road. A great rock town, all apricot and grey, behind crenellated stone walls, and at the Puerta del Sol there is a square tower wearing a pixie hat of green and white tiles."

She had told us that much. She had been here. Not why. But today I saw none of what she had seen. Only a rather Victorian-looking station and TOLEDO in large print on a

9

sign. It was a let-down, and for one absurd moment disappointment warred in me with relief. I said to myself: *None of it is true. She made it all up.* And the American had been right. I should not have come in by the back door.

There were scarcely a dozen people left on the train now. All those stations along the way had swallowed them. I picked up my bag, went through the doorway to the station yard and asked a stocky little taxi-driver with a weather-stained face and evil moustache if he could take me to an hotel in the town. He nodded. "Hotel," he repeated, as though that was the only word he understood. Then he threw my bag into the boot and swaggered round to open the door.

"Do you speak English?" I asked.

He shrugged, moved his hands this way and that. "*Poco. Poco.* A leetle," he replied. And then I saw there was a card on his windscreen which read: *English spoken.*

"Do you know where *El Regalo del Rey* is situated?" I meant, just by the way, you might be able to tell me what route I must take tomorrow when I make my secret, spying trip into the hills beyond.

"The parador?" queried the driver. "*Alondra.*"

"No," I told him. "It is a castle. Or palace."

He nodded. "You stay at the parador *Alondra. El Regalo del Rey.*"

For a moment I stood there transfixed, staring at his faintly puzzled face, my head spinning, and then:

"*¿La reserva?*" he asked as he motioned to me to enter the car.

I am far from thick, but I could not seem to take in the unexpected and astonishing prospect that I might actually stay at the home of Antonia's ex-in-laws. At the back of my mind, my small knowledge of Spain whisked to the fore. In the interests of tourism, I knew, General Franco had asked the old families to oblige him by converting their castles, or part of them, into Government-run hotels called paradors. "*El Regalo del Rey* has a parador?" I asked, my voice rising with surprise.

"Sí, sí."

"Oh, then you must take me there." What luck! What fantastic, unbelievable luck!

The driver's expression had become one of doubt intermixed with a certain sympathy. *"¿Non reserva?"*

I puzzled that one out. "Oh, you mean, have I a reservation? No, I haven't. But you never know. They may have a vacancy." I seemed to remember there was a rule that one could stay only three nights in a parador. If this was true, people must be coming and going all the time.

"Dificil," said the man, shaking his head as he caught the drift of my meaning. "I take you. Maybe a room." He started the engine and we swept out of the yard.

Exultant, confused, totally thrown by this lightning strike of good fortune, I sat bolt upright now on the edge of my seat while we crawled along a winding scenic drive that encircled the town. Here and there at vantage points coaches stood empty, while tourists with cameras round their necks looked down into a dramatic rocky gorge, where the River Tagus swirled like grey silk beneath an ancient bridge. According to books I had consulted, the Tagus had served as a defence on three sides of the town and a formidable one it must have been in ancient times. Up on the hill against the pale sky of evening, dwarfing all round it, there stood a square building with four squat grey towers, vast, ugly, and somehow threatening. "Alcázar," my taxi-driver said, then went on, uselessly, in a flood of eloquent Spanish.

I could not see much of the town from this road on the opposite side of the river, only the close-packed little stone houses, pink, gold and brown, embedded into the granite cliff-top opposite, and we were driving away from it now, up the hill. We went over a rise and dipped down through an olive grove that bordered the road closely for a mile or so, then swung into a side lane turning back towards the river. Ahead now there was an archway built in soft apricot stone.

The driver swung in by an ancient lodge. A dusty hen sped from our path with a clutch of chickens in hot pursuit. I

11

leaned forward, looking puzzledly through the windscreen. Could this be the place where Antonia had come to give birth to her baby and abandon him? At the end of a baked earth drive as straight as a rod, there was another arched gateway set in the middle of two long, windowless buildings with tiled roofs. There were no towers, nor sign of grandeur. There must be some mistake, I remember saying to myself. This could not be the place of which Antonia wrote. She said it was a palace. Again I thought confusedly: *She made it all up!*

We went along the drive and through a second archway. I turned my head. The long buildings were apparently servants' quarters, or workmen's cottages painted white on the inner side and with doors and windows looking on to a dry grass slope. A black-haired boy in a scarlet jumper was throwing a ball to a thin dog. And there, in front of us now, was a third arch. We went through it into a huge courtyard, surrounded on three sides by a double-storied building, creeper-clad, and at the end an enormous, black-painted, arch-shaped double door, some low towers, and beyond, a grey dome and chimneys. Was that, then, the palace? I looked around me in bewilderment. Was this extraordinarily plebeian place the heritage of the great family to whom Antonia had given up her little son? The prison that had not, after all, been able to contain her wild spirit, her dreams, her passions and desiring?

I gathered my startled thoughts together and said in an embarrassed rush: "Is this the home of the Count de Merito?"

"*El Conde* de Merito," the driver agreed placidly, switching off the engine and settling down behind the wheel to wait. "Parador. *Sí, sí. Habitación.*" He pointed to a heavy, studded wooden door beside us in the creeper-clad wall. I climbed out, feeling rather like a spy, and uncomfortably exposed. The driver said: "¡*Mire!*" pointing to a notice on the wall which read: *English spoken. On parle Français.* I resisted the temptation to refer sardonically to the sign on his windscreen, and turned without much hope to the door. A sleek young man

12

in a white jacket had opened it and now inclined his head towards me in smiling silence.

"*Bonjour*," I greeted him, hopefully. He answered in Spanish and I gave him a rather blank smile before stepping uncertainly into the hall.

There was a vaulted ceiling, a wooden stairway, and to the right a door opening into an office. A man rose from behind a desk and came to meet me. He was young, strongly built, and with an air of such arrogance allied to tremendous vigour, tightly reined, that I thought, quixotically, running a parador was something he must steel himself to do as a penance and the rest of the time spend free with the elements. He looked like a horseman; a golfer; a climber; an adventurer, even. Anything but the manager of an hotel. His eyes were blue, a little paler than that Spanish blue I had seen with surprise within the demure dark lashes of nuns and those naughty young men on the train. His nose was high-bridged, his well-cut mouth both sensual and hard, his skin deep olive and his hair dark brown with a chestnut-kernel gloss. He looked, and no doubt he was, a totally different species from the gentle boy with the black satin hair and boot-black eyes who stood waiting patiently behind me now.

"Good afternoon. Do you speak English?" Out of the corner of my eye I had noted the presence of a framed card on the desk which read: *F. Lazaro. Administrador.*

That lively, handsome face closed. He looked at me without speaking for perhaps five seconds, not with dislike, but as though there was insolence behind his gravity in the same way as there was strength behind his stillness. I had a peculiar and very unpleasant sensation of being deliberately summed up. His eyes went coolly from my Saxon hair to the pale skin and obviously English clothes, too thin for a Spaniard to wear at this time of year, too pale for their strong summer sun. And then he asked coolly, without a trace of accent: "You are looking for a room? I am sorry, but we are full." He added with the casual disregard of one who knows his advice comes far too late: "It is usual to book in advance."

Somewhat taken aback by this blatant unfriendliness, I said: "I did not know. I thought paradors were for the use of passing tourists. When could you offer me a room? I shall be staying for a little while."

"Then it would be better for you to go to an hotel," the man replied with a minimum of courtesy. "You could stay here for only three days."

"Three days will do," I said, steeling myself to hold those highly-intelligent, cold blue eyes with mine. "Do you have a vacancy for tomorrow night?" I wondered with a dart of indignation if the Count de Merito interested himself in the parador sufficiently to find out that his administrator discouraged potential guests.

The man glanced down at a book on his desk, then with a flamboyant gesture, flipped some pages over and shrugged indifferently. "Perhaps you would like to telephone tomorrow."

I could not have said why I felt so certain he was lying. Did the indigenous population of Spain's interior think we English should stick to the Costa Brava and the Costa del Sol? For it was my Englishness he did not want, of that I was certain. I turned reluctantly towards the door, my mind churning against the insult, and not only that, but the impossibility, now, of visiting this place unobtrusively. I knew already from its situation, so far from the town, that the only hope I had of finding out what I wanted to know was to be in residence. There was a scuffling sound on the stairs, and because I was unwilling to go I turned, making an excuse of my idle curiosity, wanting to fight back, yet conscious that I had no weapon.

A short, bald man was descending at a run, his suitcase brushing and knocking the banister. Behind him, treading carefully but also with haste, came a middle-aged woman dressed for travelling. Señor Lazaro stepped forward with interest and alacrity. He spoke in rapid French: "There is something wrong, M'sieur?"

"I am sorry, M'sieur, but we must go," the Frenchman told

14

him anxiously. "I have had a telephone call. My mother is ill. We will pay for the room, of course."

"It is not necessary, M'sieur," I told him, speaking also in French, "for I am looking for a room. I will be happy to take yours."

His face lit up. "Ah! That is very convenient, Madame."

"It is nothing," I replied, avoiding the administrator's eyes. "I am only too pleased to oblige." Then I turned to Señor Lazaro. "It is as well to speak French, Señor," I said, demurely, in my own tongue.

He looked straight over my head. He was not more than five feet ten or eleven, but his extraordinary poise gave him extra stature. "It is a double room," he said, icy, final.

"I will pay the extra." I was suddenly nervous and felt it showed, but I spoke with all the authority I could muster.

"It is not our custom to rent a double room to a single guest." With a vigorous movement he managed to turn a contemptuous back on me whilst ushering the Frenchman with great consideration into his office.

But I had the bit between my teeth. I was determined, now, not to be thwarted by an arbitrary whim of one of the Count's anti-British employees who had grown too big for his boots. The two men proceeded to attend to the Frenchman's bill. The boy picked up the suitcase and the woman followed him out to a car. Showing more confidence than I felt, I followed the men into the office, took my passport from my handbag, laid it on the desk then went to pay the taxi-driver. He put my suitcase on the ground. *"Gracias. Adiós."* I stood waiting in a state of considerable uneasiness while he drove away, leaving me stranded.

2

THE SMILING BOY, having deposited the Frenchwoman's luggage in the boot of her car, picked up my bag and innocently led me back inside.

The administrator was smilingly handing the Frenchman his receipt and wishing him God speed. I waited. Deliberately ignoring me, he saw the family on their way, spoke at length to a servant who was crossing the courtyard, then returned casually to the foyer. I stood beside my bag, biting back my anger. After all, I said to myself, I have won. His rudeness does not matter. The boy spoke to him. I could tell he was talking about me, about whether the case was to go upstairs or stay here. Which room I was to inhabit, perhaps. F. Lazaro replied in Spanish, casually and kindly, then turning to me said in a voice that was at once cool and deliberately provocative: "It will be some time before the room is ready. The staff are on other duties."

"I will go for a walk," I said evenly, feeling certain he could have taken a maid off her 'other duties' had he wished. He went back to his desk. "But perhaps you would ask the boy to take my bag to my room now," I suggested, meeting those cold and rather beautiful eyes steadily. "I have come a long way and would like to wash my hands." Possession is nine points of the law, Antonia used to say. I wanted to lay claim to that room. To see my suitcase there. I waited nervously for him to tell me there was a cloakroom on the ground floor. He did not. He spoke to the boy in Spanish, the boy nodded to me and we went together up the stairs.

The room was purely functional. On the right there was a tiny bathroom and beyond, a small, neat, square bedroom with wooden beds and wrought-iron candle lights on the wall above; a small wardrobe with a distorting mirror and a marble floor in cinnamon and buff. There were glass doors opening on to a balcony enclosed by brick railings in V patterns; outside, a tree bursting into pale bud and through its frail branches a blinding, riveting view of the sun-drenched town, stark and treeless, with the great ugly *Alcázar* dominating it like a malevolent overlord.

I gave the boy some pesetas for his trouble and went to stand at the balcony railings. Below, there was a walled garden with vegetables in green rows on the brown soil, some apple trees powdered with fading blossom and on the rise beyond, an olive grove, its trees well groomed, elegant, like brown-green mushrooms. I did not like them particularly. They were too respectable. I love the Greek ones—light glinting on silver above a grotesque, contorted trunk. Perhaps these were younger, or merely Spanish, and therefore disciplined. Directed to grow neatly, I thought with amusement, by the *Guardia Civil*.

As I turned to come back inside, I saw that over to the right a crenellated tower jutted out towards a walled garden enclosing an area of unkempt grass and dry earth. Was there actually some sort of Spanish-style palace tucked away behind those walls? I could not see the dome because my view was blocked by a small raised roof. Well, I had a walk thrust upon me. Now was the moment to investigate. To find out about this extraordinary place that had sheltered my stepmother in her hour of need before I set myself to find out what had happened to her son.

I went back into my room, had a quick wash, picked up the key, and descended the stairs. The office, to my great relief, was empty. Swiftly I crossed the courtyard. Ahead of me as I paused beneath the pale arch looking out, the grey-green hills of Spain spread one beyond the other, purple-shadowed into the far distance. A wide, grand, spacious land that could be hostile to a stranger as it had so often been hostile to its own.

My mind was full of Antonia as I turned, glanced swiftly behind, noting that I had not been observed, then followed the wall that ran round the outside of the courtyard. Antonia must have walked over this dry, crusty earth a hundred times. A woman in black with a black headscarf came out of one of the cottages carrying a bucket. She paused when she saw me and stood staring, her face puckered against the brilliant rays of the setting sun.

The land rose here and as I turned at the corner of the wall I could see the towers and rooftops of what seemed to me a strange conglomeration of buildings on my left lying within an enormous square, for all the world, to my astonished English eyes, like a very miniature and ill-assorted town that had been squeezed up against itself. Huddled, no doubt, for protection against the enemies of the ages. The wall I was following had one or two small, barred windows but when I tried to see through them there was only darkness. A lizard, brown as the soil, slid jerkily across my path and disappeared behind some stones.

Ahead was a rough, grassy rise. Perhaps if I ascended that I might be able to see down into the Count's quarters. I went up some ragged stone steps practically obscured by overgrown grass and bordered by wild lilac and broom. The olives with their bunching foliage obscured my view, but the land rose, also, on the other side, and there the trees were a little more sparse. Perhaps I might see better from there. One of those brown dogs, coarse-haired, curious, came padding towards me from the outbuildings, then stopped, staring. I ran down the rough little slope and, following a dusty earth track, rounded the farthest corner, the dog following at a respectful distance. Here the hill rose straight up from a low wall. There were some jutting leaves that might be iris, and thistles a pale, soapy green.

Ah! Now I could see the side of the crenellated bastion that towered over the buildings at the back. There were two round turrets, a double row of enormous windows, and below, at ground level, impressive arches leading to a stone walk. I caught my breath. There it was, *El Conde*'s palace, cleverly tucked away, its grandeur totally hidden from the parador's guests. My heart beat a little faster with excitement as my eyes swept over the ochre stone. With its walls and hidden court-yards this hide-away was enclosed indeed, secret and to me exciting, with an air of grandeur and faint decay. Wickedness, I thought with a little shiver, might well be here, but somehow shackled with medieval chains.

Even now, I was well aware that a Spanish wife walked a very different path from ours, but all those years ago, Antonia had told me, a well-bred Spanish woman not only went closely escorted in public places, but never showed her bare arms, and was given in marriage *purísima*. As the Holy Virgin, Antonia said. But she had not been like that. Not *purísima* at all, after falling in love with Carlos. And anyway, not a Catholic. Antonia, the English girl, must have been more than a shock to the grand de Meritos of *El Regalo del Rey*. The dog came and sat near, watching me. I called to it and it approached reluctantly, then stopped a yard or so away, wanting this new company but faintly suspicious of it.

Ahead of me and a little further down there was a small wrought-iron gate in a wall and beyond was a riot of ivy, undernourished grass, shading pines growing out of stony, arid ground that would never make a garden as we knew it at home. The windows were all closed but where the light fell I could see the shape of an enormous chandelier in one of the rooms. There was no sign of life and yet the palace did not look deserted. Down in the garden an old man bent over a fork turned to stare up at me and I crept away, feeling guilty, like a peeping Tom. I went back up the hill, the dog following, and sat down beneath an olive tree to think.

Antonia was dead, and my father with her. It had been a combined, merciful, split-second death. If they saw the long, white, road-hugging killer car that leaped at them from the intersection then it must have been no more than a glimpse. I had that for comfort, if little else.

Antonia had married my father some years after my mother's death. Glamorous, and with a voracious zest for life, she flitted round my father like a purposeful, gaudy summer bee, doing over our faded and rather tired home; doing over my faded and rather tired father, so that one was suddenly conscious, as one had not been conscious for years, that he was six feet tall and wore clothes with an air. Antonia bought dresses from Fortnum and Mason. Semi-couture. At thirty-seven she had a figure as slim and lithe as my own. She spent my father's money lavishly, but she spent it well. We did not know, at that time, that we had been caught up in the gale of this new wife's frenzied forgetting.

By a bizarre stroke of fate, my father had chosen the French Basque country for their honeymoon and it was there that the bride had seen the black headlines in the paper. They passed my father by because he spoke no French. Besides, he had never heard of Carlos de Merito. Understandably, Antonia was not disposed to air her distant past, for she had been so sure that Carlos was dead, executed in the square of an ancient Spanish town almost immediately after their marriage sixteen years before.

"I haven't a clue about the contents of this letter," Mr. Pardoe, the family solicitor, had said to me as he handed over the envelope that was to send me from London to Toledo. "Your stepmother put it into my safe-keeping with her will. There's a covering note saying she leaves it to your discretion, Suzanne, as to whether you tell your father or not, but of course—" his tone dropped a decibel in respect for the dead, "she was not to know they would die together."

I carried home, unopened, the missive that was to intrigue and excite me, pull me out of despair, throw me into danger and change my entire life. Dry old Pardoe was thoughtful and extremely kind, but a communication from a departed relative is not one a girl would choose to read in company. I took it

20

back to the tree-girded home Antonia and my father had shared so happily for more than half my lifetime, opened the French windows, poured myself a very stiff whisky, lit a cigarette and, with an inevitably creepy sensation, sat down in the mellow glow of the setting sun to read the story my stepmother had wanted to tell me from the other side of the grave.

The near-deafening noise of cicadas starting up in an olive tree close by brought me back to the present. I took the letter out of my handbag and turned to the last page.

... I had given the child up, totally, as one does for adoption. It would not have been right to go back. Besides, they thought I was dead. The grandparents were marvellous people and I knew the child would fare well with them. I was perfectly happy about him until I found my husband, Carlos, might be living. I was never able to check because of your father. If you decide to tell Leo, break it gently. Make him understand I kept quiet for him. He had married me while my former husband was, or could be alive. Knowing him, you know he could not have coped with that. As to the child, I am sure it was only because the way was blocked that I felt apprehensive. And yet, I had this strange, recurring dream about the palace in Toledo. Could you go, Suzanne darling, and check on the boy? He won't be a boy now. He is older than you by four years. Born May 15, 1948. I always felt someone from my side ought to know what happened to the child ...

3

THERE WERE HALF-a-dozen cars, now, in the parador court-yard. I looked hopefully for a GB number plate and found none. Since paradors were set up for the express purpose of accommodating travellers, I said to myself, this time of evening one might expect people to start arriving. Six cars, and me. Even if all the cars were full, that added up to only twenty-five guests. Forget it, I said to myself. What did it matter whether or not the parador's administrator was lying when he said the place was full. I had a bed.

I went in at the front door and turned towards the office. He was there, behind his desk. I had a very certain feeling he recognised my footsteps, but he did not raise his head. Something inexplicable, perhaps mischievous, made me go to him. "May I have my passport back?" I asked.

He looked at me with blank eyes as though he had forgotten my existence which I knew very well he had not. Then he said: "It is the rule of the parador to keep the passports here."

"Very well. And by the way, does the owner of *El Regalo del Rey* live here?" I asked.

He put his pen down. Those eyes that could dance so rapidly from one mood to another were totally indifferent.

"Yes, he lives here. But he has an apartment in Madrid as well."

"I might see him, then?"

I saw the skin tighten across the man's cheekbones and round his mouth. He said with icy contempt: "The Count has been good enough to make this wing of his home into a parador to help promote tourism within the country. It does not mean that he wishes to turn himself into a public spectacle."

My face flamed and he smiled faintly, enjoying my discomfiture. An angry retort rose to my lips and stayed there. I was on very uncertain ground and had better keep my temper. There was a door standing open across the hall. I had to go somewhere so I went swiftly towards it, head held high. Here was a big lounge with high white ceiling and enormous windows leading to a balcony that must run directly under my own balcony upstairs. I went in.

At one end of the room there was a great stone fireplace where a log lay smouldering with smoke puffing lazily round it. There were heavy sofas and chairs with floral loose covers; some occasional tables on which lay little piles of magazines. I turned them over, flipping the pages noisily, angrily. *Paris Match, Vogue,* some local newspapers. I stood staring down at them, wondering what I was going to do, wondering why on earth I had come. A grown man of twenty-seven, and a Spaniard at that, was hardly likely to be in need of attention from me. *I always thought someone from our side ought to know what happened to the child.* For heavens' sake, my stepmother could have found a way of checking! People had no right to shelve their responsibilities then will them to someone else. Besides, if I found him, what could I say to him? "Are you all right? Your dead mother wanted to know."

Cool it, Suzanne. You know very well you came because you were curious. And lonely. Because, at home, this son of Antonia's had seemed like a sort of relation. You didn't think very much about it, did you? Well, start thinking now. Maybe you had better go home.

The heavy stillness of the room was broken by a friendly voice with a soft American accent. "Come over here and sit with me. I'll get you a drink."

23

I swung round, startled and pleased, thinking that against all the odds my companion on the flight had turned up here, but it was a stranger who spoke to me, a big man with untidy brown hair, a chin fringed with a reddish beard and oval grey eyes. He had been half obscured by a fluted stone column. Now he moved slightly to enter my view and was smiling up at me, glass in hand.

"How very nice of you," I replied. "Please don't get up." The first thing I noticed about him was that he was not dressed like a tourist. He wore very old, unpressed trousers, his shirt was open at the neck and not particularly clean and a creased red and white spotted scarf was knotted round his neck.

"Alonso!" In answer to his friendly roar the young Spanish boy appeared. "What would you like?" the American asked me as I settled in a chair beside him.

"I'll have sherry, please," I replied, "but there is no reason why you should pay for it."

"I never allow a lady to pay for herself," boomed my new friend cheerfully. He spoke to the boy in Spanish then turned back to me. "I'm Perry Ballisat. I've got a house in the town. What are you doing here all alone? I saw you come up in the taxi."

I ought to have been ready with an answer, but I was not. "I—er—I've come to look at Toledo," I said lamely. "My name is Suzanne Cole."

"From England?"

"Yes."

"I should think you'd do better to stay in the town, Suzie, if you haven't got a car," Perry Ballisat said. "This place is a hell of a long way out and you can never get a taxi anywhere but from Zocodover."

I really hate having my name shortened, but he was kind and I was feeling a little shaken and in need of a friend. "Zo—what?" I asked.

"That's the square. The centre. It's up by the Alcázar. Trouble is it's very tempting to trail off through the streets on

24

foot, but then you find yourself at one of the bridges and faced with this God-awful climb when it's too late for the taxi. You'll regret it, mark my words. This is no place to stay without transport. Well, cheers."

"I thought it would be interesting, just once, to stay at a palace."

His laugh was a small gale. "Sure, if your imagination stretches to that."

"What do you mean?"

"The palace is there all right, but it's tucked away behind that great black door you saw as you came in. You can't see it from any part of the parador. This wing we're in is comparatively new. I mean, new by their standards. Built about 1800 to house the olive presses and machinery. That wing over there—" he gestured beyond the windows that opened on the courtyard, "was the servants' quarters and stables. The Dowager Countess has a flat on the upper floor now, where the servants used to live, and the servants have taken over from the horses on the ground floor." He grinned. "You won't ever see the palace, Suzie. *El Conde*, as they call him, zooms through in his great Mercedes and the trap closes."

Boxed-up, Antonia had said in her letter. I could suddenly see. It is one thing to shut oneself off from tourists. It would be quite another to be, as this man suggested, trapped. My sherry arrived. In spite of my protests, Ballisat paid. "And what are you doing here," I asked, "since you have a house in Toledo?"

"Drinking a beer, that's all. And hoping the Count will turn up before I have to go. Say," he turned the full glow of his exuberance and warmth on me, "why don't I give you my address?" He fetched a stubby black pencil from a breast pocket in his shirt and wriggling his big, untidy body half out of the chair, found a notebook in a pocket in the seat of his trousers. "Come and see us when you get tired of the marathons. In fact," his face split into smile, "why don't you come and stay tomorrow? My wife Viola—"

I stopped him in mid-sentence, laughing, overwhelmed.

25

"Please, no, you're very kind, but—"

"But me no buts, wasn't that what your man Shakespeare said? I got a feeling you're not going to like it here. Why, there's no one to talk to for a start. People don't turn up until late and they're mostly tired and go straight to bed. The place is as dead as a dodo."

"I'll be all right, really I will. I am not one of those people who have to have company all the time. Besides couples tend to chat to a single woman in the dining room."

"What dining room?" I must have looked startled. "Didn't you know?" he asked. "Continental breakfast, that's all you'll get here." His concern was grave now, indeed. "Didn't Don Lazaro tell you when you booked in?"

I shook my head, not knowing what to say, or do. Suddenly, through the open windows came a swirling and crunching of tyres on gravel, then the sound of a door banging. Lively Spanish voices, raised in greeting. Chatter. Argument. "Ah!" said Perry Ballisat heaving himself out of the chair. "There's the Count now. You must excuse me while I speak to him." He bent down and patted my hand kindly. "Then I'll come back and take you into the town. I'll show you where you can get a good meal. I'm sorry I can't take you home right now. Viola would shoot me if I turned up with a friend tonight because it's our son's birthday. But think about coming to stay tomorrow. This is no place for you."

I was scarcely aware of what he was saying, or even that he had now left me and gone to speak to the Count. My eyes were riveted on the man who had entered the outer door and whom I could see talking animatedly to Lazaro. I blinked, stared, and shook my head. If Antonia's father-in-law was still alive, then he must be seventy at the very least. Seventy-five. Eighty. If he was dead, Carlos the revolutionary would be the Count. If Carlos was dead, Antonia's son. From where I sat I could see the new arrival quite clearly, standing as he was in a ray from the setting sun that shafted across the foyer from the wide open door.

I am good at guessing people's ages. This man whom the

26

American had identified as the Count, was somewhere in the vicinity of fifty. *He had to be Carlos!* Carlos, who was thought to have been executed in 1947, but who, that old headline said, escaped and settled among the Basques, stirring up anarchists, planning the downfall of *El Caudillo*, making such a dangerous nuisance of himself that he could never be allowed back into Spain while Franco lived. Carlos, my stepmother's real husband, and father of her son!

Across the length of the room and hall I stared at him. He was dressed in a well-cut dark suit and carried a briefcase. His Spanish-black hair was longish, turning attractively grey at the temples. He had moved a little my way and I could see him more clearly now. I wonder how you would react, I thought feverishly, if you knew Antonia, Countess de Merito, had not been blown up in that bus. That she had been living quietly in Surrey for the past twelve years as Mrs. Leo Cole. Perry Ballisat moved between the Count and me, obscuring him. I looked down at my hands. So, my mission had exploded into the air. There was no longer need to check on Antonia's son. I began to heave a little sigh of relief then caught my breath as the words of her letter flickered before my eyes.

... I had this strange, recurring dream about the palace in Toledo. Could you go, Suzanne darling, and check on the boy? And then, the part I had passed over because it had seemed unimportant. Carlos, after all, was supposed to be in exile. ... *I had felt everything was all right until I knew my husband Carlos was living.* I stared into space. There had been nothing in the rest of the letter to explain that fear. Was Antonia afraid her boy might be taken to the Basque country and brought up a revolutionary? Was she afraid he could be held hostage for his father's misdeeds? Or had she found this man she married to be truly bad? In which case, was she afraid for her son? Or afraid he might grow up like his father?

"Okay. That's settled." I had not heard the American cross the room. I jumped as he spoke. "There was some trouble

27

about your room. It's ready now, if you want to pop up. I'll wait here and drive you into town."

"No, please," I began to protest, but he would have none of it. "You'll thank me when you see how far it is. I'm only sorry I can't take you home—well, why not?" he asked himself genially. "Viola might—"

"No, no," I protested. "You're far too kind! I'll get my jacket, though, and drive back with you." I was in a hurry to cross that foyer to the stairs. I wanted to see Carlos, eye to eye. I wanted to see what style of man he was. He was still talking to Don Lazaro. My heart beat unsteadily as I went past them and looked into Carlos' face. And then I saw his eyes and something cold seemed to brush across me and gather in a prickling at the base of my spine.

I took the room key from the smiling boy and turned to look at Carlos again. He was looking back at me. They were both looking at me and their eyes followed me as I went up the first few stairs. The key was large with a cut-out at the end. In my confusion and embarrassment, I swung it in circles round my forefinger and it slipped, falling with a crack and rattle between the two men. Carlos bent to retrieve it. "I'm sorry," I said as I came back down the stairs, tripping a little on the lower step because I could not take my eyes from Carlos' face. He handed the key to me, inclining his head and smiling, a handsome man fading into middle-age. Not a demon after all.

I went back upstairs in a sort of daze. There had perhaps to be something in a man's face to show he had missed execution by a finger's breadth. Who knew what darkness a rabble-rouser and a fugitive experienced? Those years of exile could perhaps leave their mark on a man's soul.

All this I said to myself as I unlocked the door, yet it did not lighten my distress. In spite of the change of expression I could not rid myself of the feeling that I had looked into the eyes of a man I would not wish to know. An evil man. Forgetting for the moment that the American was waiting for me, I went through the glass doors and stood a

28

moment with my hands on the warm red bricks of the balcony outside my room, looking across at the hill-high town, a pile of disordered masonry with the cloak of dusky evening falling round it. What of the son, I asked myself, with such a man as father?

4

THE CAR WAS a Simca, ancient and dust-ridden, with dogs' hairs sprinkled liberally on the worn leather seats. Perry (he insisted I call him Perry because, as he said, we foreigners must stick together) heaved a rattling box into the back, gave the passenger seat a cursory flick with a paint-smudged rag, then with a cheerful: "Won't be a minute, I've got to pick up the picture," shot back inside. I turned curiously and lifted the lid of the box. It was full of brushes, small jars and tins of paint, and some oil-soaked rags. So Perry Ballisat was an artist! He came lumbering across the court-yard carrying a canvas.

"I'm just about going to get this in," he announced, hope-fully, I thought. "Mind your head." I ducked and he man-oeuvred the painting carefully through the door, over my head, and settled it with great care in a bridge position between the back of the front seat and the rear window. "All we need is a bit of careful driving," he commented as he climbed in. After half-a-dozen asthmatic whoops the engine started and we crunched slowly across the gravel.

"What are you painting?" I asked, thinking of Carlos still.

He grinned. "Get up on your knees and have a look."

I did so. It was a dark picture and I was far too close to see it properly. "It looks like a sad priest in an El Greco storm," I said. And then, mindful that he had been waiting to speak to Carlos when I came upon him: "Are you copying a picture in the palace?"

"Bright girl. Right first time. No one should copy an El Greco," Perry said, reproving himself, "but because I live in Toledo I get these commissions from nuts back home. They pay me well," he added laconically, "and we gotta eat. But between you and me, if the Greek is turning in his grave, I wouldn't blame him. No one, but no one, can capture the sheer bloody awfulness of his imagination."

"I'm sure you're far too modest," I replied, my mind racing, and not on the subject of art. "You must know the family, the de Meritos. The Count."

We crossed the courtyard and headed out through an arch on to the white dust drive. "By no means. I don't see him once in half-a-dozen visits to the *Finca*."

"Is that the name of the picture you're copying?"

He chuckled. "A *Finca* is a place. A farm. A set-up. Olive grove, outbuildings, parador, palace." He gave me a kindly, sideways look that reminded me of a friendly basset hound. "This is the *Finca Alondra*. *Alondra*—sky-lark, although you're not likely to see any because Spaniards are allowed to shoot song birds and eat them for dinner. They are served up as delicacies in restaurants."

I shuddered. "How horrible. So you don't know the Count at all? This is just a business arrangement?"

"Not even that," Perry assured me. "I wrote to ask him if I could copy the picture and he invited me over for a glass of wine. Then he said I could do the work, and Don Lazaro would see that I was let in and out. I wanted to see the Count today because I've nearly finished. I wanted to tell him I'd like to have one more session in a day or two, and that's the end."

"Have they got a lot of valuable pictures?"

"No, as a matter of fact, they haven't. The palace was sacked in the Civil War when the family were in exile. Things were pretty tough for them at one time. They had to get out in a hurry and exiled themselves in the French Basque

31

country until Franco allowed them back."

"When was that?"

"I don't know exactly. Before the end of the war I think, when the old Count sensibly changed his political leanings from Republican to Nationalist. The Countess found this picture in the Rastro—that's the flea market—in Madrid and bought it back."

We were running down the hill through the olive grove which was shadowed now by approaching night. "Is the Count de Merito anti-British?" I asked.

"Anti-British?" He took his eyes off the road to give me an astonished look, shaggy eyebrows swinging up to an enormous inverted V. "Why d'you ask that?"

"The administrator didn't want to give me a room."

"There's a sign outside saying they speak English," he pointed out, adding reasonably: "They wouldn't put that up, would they, if they didn't expect English people to stay?"

I was not sure. "Many Europeans use English as a common language."

"Yes," he acceded. "And of course there's one thing. Spanish women don't travel alone. You're likely to come up against one of two things with the men. They're hot-blooded and their own girls are still pretty inaccessible. On the other hand, if they weren't interested, they might take the prudish view that you're up to no good." I laughed, and he shot me a sideways look. "I wouldn't think Don Lazaro was a prude."

We went up and over the hill, then swung down towards the gorge. The whole valley had filled up with dusk.

"Why do you call him Don? His initial on the sign is F."

"It's a title, but don't ask me to explain. Everyone of any standing at all seems to have Don tacked on the front of their name. It's a sort of courtesy thing. I am sorry he's unfriendly. I don't really know him. He returned only recently from England. Perhaps it's personal. P'raps—no offence meant, Suzie—he didn't find you all that hospitable over there and came back with a chip on his shoulder. I wouldn't have

thought so, though. He's tough, and like all Castillians, arrogant and self-confident. They see black as black and white
as white. Maybe some English girl treated him badly. It
would be fairly typical if he were to take that out on the
whole nation."

"You're joking! Not when he has a business to run!"

"Oh, yes. Toledans' ancestors were heavily crossed with
the cruel Moors. You know about the Moors?"

"They invaded the south in the eighth century."

"Ha! Not only beautiful, but knowledgeable. Have you
heard about Florinda?"

I warmed to him. This open-hearted American was just
the man I needed for my morale. "Florinda who?"

"You obviously haven't. Her father was Governor of Ceuta
in Africa, and she had been sent here to be educated in the
household of Roderick, the last of the Gothic kings. She
used to bathe naked in the Tagus, down there between the
bridges. They didn't have bikinis in those days." He chuckled
earthily. "The king came on her one day, so the story goes,
and ravished her."

"I like that word," I said. "It sounds more fun than rape."

"That's right. She, Florinda, sent a messenger to Africa
and her father arrived to take her away. He was entertained
royally, and, ostensibly wanting to show his appreciation,
asked what gift Roderick would like from Africa. The king
asked for a particular breed of hawk to be sent and Florinda's
father agreed to send such hawks as the king had never
dreamed of. Then he went home and plotted with the governor
of Africa. The Arabs could never resist the bait of plunder,
and there was plenty to plunder in Southern Spain. They
and the Moors not only defeated Roderick, they stayed eight
centuries. That's why you get the eastern under-current in
the music of this area, and the dark eyes of many of the
people, and that very black hair. Those in the north aren't
nearly so dark. And I don't think they've got the streak of
cruelty that shows up here so often."

"I've always heard they're very fond of children," I said,

33

my mind obsessively on Antonia's son. "Florinda's story bears that out. I always thought they were far more family-minded than us English."

"Sure, I guess so. There's one thing you have to learn, though, Suzie. You can't lump them together as Spanish, as we say American or you say British. The people on the Costa Brava call themselves Catalans. The ones in the south, in the Costa del Sol area, call themselves Andalusians. The ones who live in Galicia call themselves Galicians, and so on. They're all as different as chalk from cheese."

"Tell me about the Basques." The people with whom Carlos was said to have joined up. "They're the revolutionary ones. The anarchists, the dissidents."

"With Franco's Fascist-type regime there are bound to be anarchists and dissidents in every province, all the time," he replied lightly. "And listen, you're not supposed to discuss politics in public."

But we weren't in public, we were in the car.

He laughed when I pointed that out and replied good-naturedly: "The Basques were Separatists in the Civil War. The Government had given them their independence some years earlier. Consequently, they fought for the Republicans. The Government was Republican. Franco defeated them."

"But I had an impression they didn't pack it in when the war ended officially."

"It's true trouble flares up in that area from time to time," Perry acceded. "They're very independent people and they don't give up easily. Believe me, Suzie, it's no sinecure, governing Spain. Franco is tough because he has to be. Every Spaniard is a king in his own eyes."

Don Lazaro looked like a king. I swung my thoughts away. And then Perry said: "Don't underestimate the Spanish. Some ghastly things happened in Toledo during the Civil War. Republicans were killing Conservatives; Franco's forces were killing the Liberals. You'll hear of the heroism of old Colonel Moscardo in the *Alcázar*, but let me tell you this: There was a Nationalist bombardier who baled out of his plane safely, then was dragged through the streets of Toledo by his parachute harness with his ears and tongue cut off and his crucifix stuffed in his mouth."

I shuddered, and changing the subject, in a way, commented: "Don Lazaro isn't so dark. Are the Castillians fair?"

He looked surprised, as well he might. "Lazaro is a fairly typical Castillian," he said. "Some are dark, some are fair. It's the way they speak that's important. They use Spanish in its purest form. Now here we are. I can't take the car any nearer because cars are not allowed in. But if you go up that cobbled lane in front and turn left you'll find the restaurant. And if you'd like to come and stay tomorrow, you're very welcome."

5

IT WAS A strange, lonely dinner in the small restaurant to which Perry Ballisat directed me. I would have preferred one of the bustling, tourist-ridden establishments on the Plaza de Zocodover but he had been insistent that I go to this little old beamed place with its tiled floor. Cool it would be in summer, but on this spring evening an oil fire stood between the white-clothed tables and I was glad of its warmth.

There was only one other couple in the restaurant. I did not know it then, but Spaniards spend the early evening in a *paseo*, a strolling up and down in public places, drinking an apéritif or a coffee, and waiting until the civilised hour of ten to dine. This recommended restaurant was so truly Spanish I could not read the menu. I did some rather untidy guessing and came up with melon, some very expensive lobster, and fresh fruit. *Fruta fresca.* One could scarcely go wrong there. Then I wandered back to the emptying square and sat down rather dismally in the cold to drink a cup of coffee I did not want, filling in time until I should get a taxi to take me back to the parador to bed.

I did not sleep very well that night. The lavatory in my tiny bathroom was a raging waterfall that eased off periodically to set up such a singing and whistling sequence as could not be shut out by the closed door. I lay on my bed gazing at a holy picture entitled neatly: *Le Baptême du Christ,* across which a shaft of moonlight lay.

After a while I sat up, looking apprehensively through the open door that led to the balcony, listening to the stillness of the night. Then I put my feet to the cold tiles and, shivering, tiptoed over to close it. I had never been abroad like this before. I could not even remember a time when I ate a meal in a restaurant by myself. The back-to-front business of the evening that had put me outside the life of the town, had certainly been unfortunate. But for the kindly if mistaken attentions of Perry Ballisat I might have run across some English-speaking tourists. I had been more thrown than I cared to admit by the inexplicable unfriendliness of the administrator who had so much charm in store for others. And I had been depressed by the total quiet of the shadowy *Finca* buildings on my return.

I crept back into bed and pulled the single blanket up to my chin. The roar of the plane's engines started faintly in my ears as they will when one is overtired after a flight, and in a confused dream-like sequence I saw the clouds parting as they had done when we were approaching the Iberian Peninsula, to expose the sea lying palely against a great curve of beach. I knew the Spanish Basque country lay beyond there and I had found myself wondering if it was through this wild country Antonia fled. The mountains had been tufted with snow and I actually asked myself if Carlos might conceivably be there, watching our vapour trail.

And yet, he was here, Antonia's husband. The man to whom she had been legally tied whilst married to my father, was half-a-dozen stone walls and a clutch of Spanish metres away. I turned restlessly over on to my back. The moonlight had moved down on the religious picture and the room was darker. "Are there any Republicans still in exile?" I had asked that American in the plane, before I knew Carlos was here. I remembered feeling faintly nervous as I said it, looking out of the window down on mountains that were flattening out into red earth humps, at a river the colour of pale jade winding sluggishly through a stretch of plain.

37

It had not looked the kind of country anyone would want to trek across alone. And twenty-eight years ago it could have been more desolate still.

"As a result of the Civil War?" the man had queried. "Oh, I shouldn't think so." He was speaking casually, not looking at me I remember, tearing the powdered milk packet open and tipping the contents into his second coffee. "About four hundred thousand went into exile in countries like Mexico and Basque France, but there was an amnesty a while ago. I should think anyone living in exile now would do so because he won't, rather than can't, return to Spain under a dictatorship."

I must go to sleep. In the faint light I could not see my watch clearly. Three o'clock? Four?

The New Universal Encyclopaedia had said, and it was written blackly across my brain: *In 1947 the number executed for activities against the régime was officially stated to be 252.* But Carlos was alive. The number had been 251.

*   *   *

It was true, what I had suspected, that there were not more than six lots of people booked into the parador that night. I saw again the six cars from the open doorway as I made my way into breakfast. There were still no GB plates. One German, two Swiss, and three French. The couple already seated were unmistakably German. I nodded to them as I sat down. The boy Alonso said: *"Buenas Días, Señorita,"* and brought me coffee with rolls. I lingered over breakfast hoping some of the French guests might arrive. I had been too long on my own. I was getting my problems out of proportion. I needed the normality of a casual conversation. The Germans, with a courteous nod in my direction, left, and eventually young Alonso came to see if I wanted more coffee. When I shook my head he removed my cup and plate so that I felt impelled to go.

Crossing the hall, I was arrested by the sound of Spanish

voices coming to me through the open door. There was the purr of an engine and crunch of wheels on gravel. I went with alacrity to stand in the doorway and my heart began to beat a little faster as I saw the Mercedes that had brought the Count last evening starting across the courtyard. The big, black arched door had split wide to expose, not the hall I expected, but another inner courtyard and from this the car had evidently emerged. It passed me, moving slowly, not more than four feet distant, and I had a chance to see a good-looking young Spaniard at the wheel. Antonia's son? Carlos' son?

My eyes darted to the very beautiful woman beside him. She had meticulously groomed black hair, an olive skin, and to my eyes she bore a very strong resemblance to the young man. As she turned to wave goodbye, she came full face. She had the gleaming dark eyes of her country's Moorish conquerors, and on her raised hand she wore several enormous and exotic-looking rings. The other passenger in the back seat was an elderly woman, very upright, with dark dyed hair, and she was dressed in black. The man Carlos stood in the courtyard waving them on their way.

Odd, that a whole life can turn on one small, unfriendly gesture. If I had been able to say to Don Lazaro: "Is that man, who is driving the car, the eldest or the only son of *El Conde* de Merito?" and if he had replied: "Yes", in spite of that black hair, those very dark eyes, that total look of Spain, I might have packed my bag and gone, thinking Carlos had inherited and was on good terms with his boy. But as I stepped back into the hall and took some strides towards the office that handsome, heart-moving devil deliberately turned his head away, and the die was cast. I shot out into the courtyard. After all, anything that passed between the two of us now was purely private. If Carlos did not wish it, neither his Countess nor the son need know.

"El Conde, por favor!" I had picked up that phrase the evening before in the restaurant. Everyone used it. I thought

it must be the equivalent of the French: *Attention!* or our: Excuse me.

He heard me as he turned to re-enter the palace. His face wore a faintly surprised smile.

"I assume you speak English?" I began. Antonia had said he did.

He nodded. "Can I help you?" he asked courteously. Now that I saw him in the bright light of morning he bore little resemblance to my tortured nightmare man. His eyes were black indeed and I found their darkness disconcerting, but the well-cut lips were turned up in a smile. His skin was considerably lighter than that of the Countess, if indeed it was she in the car, and he had a very straight, rather long nose with flaring nostrils that gave him, I thought, an exceptionally aristocratic look.

"I am Suzanne Cole," I said. "May I ask, was that your son driving the car?"

He nodded, affably enough. "My wife and mother are taking him to Madrid airport." He must have seen my face fall. "You wished to see him?"

"No," I said quickly. I had already decided not to speak to Antonia's son.

The look that had disturbed me so last night drew Carlos' features in. "Then what is it?"

"Is he your eldest son?"

His eyes flickered. "My only son. You have perhaps met him in England?"

"No," I replied. "Someone asked about him, that is all." I smiled. "He is well and happy. That is what she wanted to know. He came home for his birthday?"

"His birthday? My son's birthday is in November. Who is this person who is so interested in Damian?" He smiled, indulgently. "Obviously she does not know him very well." I could have walked away then and saved myself from all that was to follow. Perhaps I am more interfering than I realise. Antonia's boy, and at that time I did not know if

40

he was called Damian or not, had had a birthday the week before.

I said: "Perhaps you had another son who is now dead?" He did not move, and neither did he speak. "You see," I said, "my stepmother, who died recently, was Antonia Birtles. She wanted to know about the boy."

The smile stayed on his face. At least, the edges of his mouth remained upturned. The creases at the corners of those very dark and quite unreadable eyes seemed set, as on a wax image. I had a curious, rather frightening sensation of looking at a man who had receded from me in essence, leaving the body as an empty shell.

He said at last, in a deliberately steady voice: "I am sorry. You are suggesting I know the lady?"

Momentarily, I was at a loss for words. I have no way of knowing how a man should behave on hearing his first wife, whom he had thought long dead, had died only recently, but I had a very certain feeling this man's reaction was not the natural one.

"There was a letter," I said, "after she died, I mean — asking me to ensure your—her—son was—" I simply could not go on with the Count looking at me, totally still, and with that smile set like a mask upon his face.

At last he said coldly: "May I ask you, Miss, who you think I am?"

I licked my dry lips. "Carlos de Merito," I replied. There was such stillness as precedes an earthquake. Our eyes held, though I could read nothing from the baffling black of his.

"To the best of my knowledge," he said at last, "there is no one called Carlos de Merito. But please come in." He gestured towards the wide-open doorway. "Clearly, you are under a misapprehension, and perhaps I can help."

6

So MUST ANTONIA have felt when that great black door closed
behind her. For Antonia had been here. I was not fooled
by the mask he wore, and certainly not by the alacrity with
which he invited me into the palace.

Within the archway it was like a big, square room with
white-washed walls and stone-blocked floor. There were
double doors on either side. The one on the right was set
with glass and I could see through to an office-workroom
of sorts. There was a table on which stood a very ordinary
clock and a couple of candles. On the left there were two
glass cases containing hunting trophies standing on either
side of a white-painted wooden door.

The Count led me into a little entrance lobby with red
seats, then through another set of double doors into an
enormous hall from which a wide staircase led to the upper
floor. There were outsize portraits on the walls; soldiers in
splendid dress uniform; a lovely woman with a sad face; a
family group complete with dogs and a mural of the holy
family covering a good deal of the wall behind the stairs.
At the top, a thick rope hung from wall to banister like
those that cordon off rooms not open to the public in
stately homes. In the centre of the room there was an oblong
table on which stood a set of candlesticks made intriguingly
of stags' horns, and a pair of boxes with hand-embroidered

tapestry lids. On the floor, a carpet of Moorish colours and design.

I caught my own reflection in one of the ornate gilt mirrors and swiftly removed the mixture of awe and apprehension from my face. There were chairs in plenty here, big hard ones of green leather painted in flower designs, but my host led me through into a smaller room. This one also had the high ceiling but it had an air of warmth and relaxation, too. Here was the lower part of the tower I had glimpsed from my balcony, and within its recess those same red velvet seats I had seen in the entrance. The Count said: "Do sit down, Miss—"

"Suzanne Cole."

"Miss Cole. Not over there, if you don't mind," as I made for the turret embrasure that reminded me of the roundel within a Kentish oast-house at home. "I think we can talk more comfortably here." He gestured in the direction of a pair of small sofas facing each other near the centre of the room.

I sat down and he sat opposite. He had recovered his poise, now. He smiled and his smile was pleasant, except that I could not read the eyes.

"And now, Miss Cole. What is this about your friend and someone called Carlos de Merito? De Merito, of course, is my name."

"I thought," I said, shakily, "your name was Carlos."

He stiffened. Or was it my imagination. "Ernesto is my name."

Ernesto! Ernesto was the name of the younger brother who had on that last day escorted Antonia to the bus! The bus that she, miraculously, left before it was blown up by the bomb. Then where was Carlos? If he was dead, why did Ernesto not say so? And the child must be dead, too, or Ernesto could not have inherited the title. My mind spun.

He was looking at me, neither too closely nor too curiously, and certainly without suspicion. Perhaps that was what was

43

wrong. One ought to be suspicious of a foreign stranger who walks through one's door asking such questions.

"I have a letter—"

"You have it here?" he broke in quite gently looking at my handbag and half-extending his hand. "I would be glad to read it."

"No," I replied. "I left it in my room, but I can tell you what was in it, for I have read it so often I know it by heart."

"Do go on. Would you like an *apéritif*?" He looked round vaguely at a table containing half-a-dozen bottles. He was too cool, too deliberate by half. "Perhaps it is a little early." I thanked him and agreed. My hands were shaking. I placed them on the seat beside me and pressed down hard.

He put both of his hands into his pockets and looked up without expression at the ceiling. We sat a moment in silence, I was more than a little unnerved, not only by his deliberate calm but by the knowledge that there were three closed doors between the outside world and me. By the fact that he would not sit with me in the window but insisted on our being in the middle of the room where no one could see us from outside. I told myself I was being over-imaginative and rather ridiculous. I cleared my throat. "To start at the beginning, which was 1947," I said, "my stepmother was engaged to an English newspaper man who came over here to report on the Civil War."

"There was no Civil War in 1947." Ernesto looked me square in the eye. "It finished in 1939."

I found myself saying in a queerly calm voice: "Yes, I know. But there were troubles, uprisings, weren't there?"

He shook his head. "Not that I am aware of, Miss Cole." And then, patronisingly: "Perhaps in England you know more about our country than we do ourselves."

"Perhaps we do," I replied evenly. "There is censorship here." He did not acknowledge my comment, and I went on, telling him the story he must surely know only too well. "Antonia, who worked on the same paper as her fiancé,

44

got herself sent out to Madrid, but when she arrived she found this man involved with someone else. Carlos de Merito befriended her. She became pregnant."

"Oh," said Ernesto with some distaste and it was all I could do to suppress a nervous laugh.

"The letter said Carlos and Antonia were married by a priest, because of the baby—" I broke off. Ernesto had raised one hand and his lips were parted as though he was about to speak. Then apparently he changed his mind. A thought shot like fire through my mind. In France, for a marriage to be legal, one had to have a civil ceremony as well as the priest. Had he been going to point that out, then realised his mistake? Records would be kept, for proof. Suddenly I stopped being afraid. I had come here to find out about my stepmother's child. Now that I could see he must be dead, I had a sad and totally overwhelming desire to know what happened. On Antonia's behalf, I needed to know, if only to lay a small wreath of flowers on the grave.

"Go on," he said, coolly.

"Carlos was rounded up with several hundred anarchists for execution—"

"For *what*?"

I licked my dry lips. "I am telling you what my stepmother's letter said."

Ernesto rose. He took a cigarette from a painted leather box. "You smoke, Miss Cole?"

"No. No, I don't."

"I am sure you're wise." His mind was on more important matters.

Directly above me was a cupola painted in pale colours. Nymphs dancing hand-in-hand. This must be the grey dome I had seen from outside. It was very beautiful indeed. I kept my eyes on it, not wanting to look at this man. "Go on with your story, Miss Cole," Ernesto said. "This person you refer to as Carlos de Merito was executed?" Then, without waiting for my reply, went on: "Forgive me, but I really do not understand what all this is about. Someone

45

has told you a tale about a man who was executed twenty-eight years ago. Even the woman who told you the story is dead." He gave a sarcastic little laugh.

I took a deep breath. "Carlos was *thought* to be executed. Many years later, after Antonia had married my father, she heard her husband was alive and living in the Basque country."

Ernesto's lips turned down in a thin sneer. "But why? There was an amnesty years ago. *El Caudillo* forgave his enemies."

"Let's forget about Spanish politics," I said. "It really doesn't matter about Carlos, whether he was executed or not. I have come here, at my stepmother's request, to enquire about her son. I assume—" I stopped. I had been going to say: "I assume, since you have inherited the title, that he is dead," but something held me back. "She said she had the baby at the palace, this palace, because she was afraid to go home."

Ernesto seated himself opposite me again. I waited.

"I was here in 1947," he said, as though that proved my lie. As though there was nothing more to say.

I cleared my throat nervously again. "And who else?"

"My parents. You saw my mother leaving in the car. We lost my father several years ago." He leaned forward, looking hard at me. "But do go on with the story. I find it quite enthralling. What happens next?" He smiled, as though humouring a child.

My cheeks began to burn. "She said she could not face the enclosed life of a Spanish widow," I said. "She decided to leave the baby to be brought up by your family. Disguised as a peasant—"

"As a peasant?" he asked incredulously.

"She was the widow of a known anarchist, remember."

"Oh, of course." He smiled, humouring me once more.

"She took a bus—"

"From Toledo?"

"Yes, a bus for Madrid. It was blown up."

46

"This," put in the Count smoothly, "was presumably 1948?" He stared down firstly at his cigarette, then up at me.

"I suppose so."

"I do assure you, my dear Miss Cole, people were not blowing up buses in 1948. I have already told you the war was over."

I said carefully: "I have read the report of the Basque trials in 1970. You have a troubled and divided country, Count. A great many unpleasant incidents have happened here since 1939. The Basques don't like General Franco, do they?"

Ernesto smiled sardonically. "Of course they do not like him. But that is because he is Galician. The Basques do not like Galicians. I might add that Galicians do not like him either for no better reason than that he is one of them. The truth is, Miss Cole, that though I think every Spaniard must know in his heart that *El Caudillo* has made Spain what it is today, the Spaniard is not a grateful creature, and also, he is at heart a Monarchist. After Franco, we shall have a king, but every Spaniard considers himself a king," said Ernesto, underlining what Perry had told me, "and it remains to be seen whether King Juan Carlos is going to hold all the kings together the way *El Caudillo* has. Franco's problem is that he is a boss and my countrymen do not like to be bossed. Basques especially. There is an old Spanish saying: I obey, but I do not comply. Many Basques do not even obey. Among the Basque nationalists there are many with strong anti-Castillian feelings which are encouraged by the majority of Basque priests, in many cases Jesuits, who exert great influence. We, the de Meritos, are Castillian. To say that a Castillian is hiding in the Basque country ..." Ernesto threw out his hands in a dismissive gesture. "You are a foreigner. Nevertheless, I have tried to explain. It would not be possible, Miss Cole. You take my point?"

I certainly took the point that he was more concerned with ridding me of the possibility of Carlos' existence than that of the baby. "Can we go back to the bus?"

He inclined his head, but with a shrug and a gesture of disinterest.

I gave him a nervous smile. "Antonia had an attack of conscience after boarding the bus. She left it again, to rethink. Then she heard it had been blown up. She was as good as dead to the de Meritos and her child. She made her decision, then, to stay dead. And, incidentally, to stay off Spanish buses. She found her way back home by a hazardous route through the mountains to the French border."

"By herself?" There was that thin sneer again.

"No. She had help. She mentioned that there were other refugees. And a priest."

Ernesto was thoughtful for a moment. Then: "The family knew she was dead? I mean, they knew she was on—that— bus. That particular bus?" He was watching me carefully and I felt a prickling sensation at the back of my neck. *You, Ernesto, put her on that bus.* The words were there in my throat. I must go home, I said to myself, feeling cold in spite of the sunlight shafting in. This is none of my affair. And there is no Carlos. No child. Ernesto has his reasons for covering up. What should I know of Spanish politics, Spanish affairs? Yet I did say, in as even a voice as I could muster: "I presume so. That is the only way they would know she was dead. She never heard from them again."

Ernesto rose. He was smiling. "And now that the story is over you must have an *apéritif* with me, my dear," he said, "before you go away. This is a great work of imagination. We will celebrate it. Or perhaps," he turned to me, brows raised, "the story is not finished yet. Where is the child?"

I steeled myself to look at him. "That is why I came. Antonia asked me in her letter to find out what happened to him."

Ernesto put on a faintly bewildered expression. "And yet, she is dead. It is much too late for her. This sounds

48

like some strange sort of trick. Surely, if the story was true, she would have come back in her own lifetime to find out for herself?"

"She didn't want to know, at first. She thought he was in good hands, with the grandparents. She felt confident they would care for him. Then she married my father—that was about fourteen years later." I had to pause there, steeling myself to say what I had to say: "—and within a few weeks heard that Carlos was alive."

Ernesto had risen and gone over to the table on which the bottles stood. "Really, Miss Cole," he said with exasperation, "this is ridiculous. You are wasting both my time and yours. Not to mention your money in coming here." He picked up a glass and, holding it in one hand, turned to me. "What melodrama! She has to wait fourteen years, get married, and then—" he laid peculiar emphasis on the word 'then' "—find her husband is alive." Before I could answer, he said sarcastically: "How, since she presumably lived in England and was supposed to be dead, could she hear this man was alive, anyway?"

"It was in a French newspaper," I said. "She was on honeymoon with my father in the French Basque country when she read about him leading an uprising against the Government."

I was watching his back. He examined the labels of the bottles he must know well enough. "Sherry? Vodka? Whisky?" he asked. "What would you like to drink, Miss Cole?"

I did not want a drink at all. My heart was thundering in my breast. I had no wish to aggravate the discomfort of it. But I could scarcely turn down his hospitality. "Sherry, thank you," I said.

He took a glass from a very beautiful cabinet in a corner and uncorked a bottle. "And what did your father say to this interesting news?" Ernesto asked, carefully filling the glass, still standing with his back to me.

"He didn't know," I replied. "He didn't read French,

49

and anyway, he had never heard of Carlos. But my stepmother knew she had made a bigamous marriage. She had
to keep quiet, for my father's sake. But you see, she began
to worry about her child. As the son of a political expatriate,
she wondered what his situation might be."

Ernesto came back carrying two glasses. He put them down
carefully on either end of a long table between us. He
seemed to have himself well in hand. "If this were true," he
said lightly, "your stepmother must have been a very strange
woman. You are referring to the fact that the boy might be
held as hostage for his father? How unfortunate he would
be to have a mother who did not care to take him into her
protection?" His voice was thin with sarcasm. I did not
reply, for surely there was no retort I could offer.

"Miss Cole." I looked at him, at evil clouding up behind a
pleasant façade. Everything that went to make the second
Ernesto was there, in his black, cold eyes, in the set of
his cruel mouth. "I must ask you to forget this story," he
said. "I would certainly have to take steps—legal steps, I
mean—to stop you if you began to talk of such things in
public. There has been no de Merito scandal. No political
trouble. I am on good terms with my family, the church
and *El Caudillo*, the three essentials. I believe our leader
to have done a very great deal for Spain. Do you think I
would have a parador on my estate by choice and all these
foreigners coming and going? I have done that to oblige
the General," Ernesto said.

There was a sharp rap at the door. He spoke peremptorily,
in Spanish. It opened and Don Lazaro came in. He saw me
and stopped abruptly, brows raised in astonishment.

For a moment our eyes locked, then I looked away and
took up my glass of sherry.

"I met Miss Cole in the courtyard and invited her in."
My eyes flew back to Ernesto. Why should he find it necessary to explain my presence?

"I merely wanted to have a few words with you," Don
Lazaro, too, spoke in English. "It can wait, or—" he hesi-

tated, glancing pointedly with a half smile from my host's glass to mine. So he was clearly on good terms with his employer! Ernesto's words came hurrying one upon the other: "She was about to leave," he said, then turning to me with strained courtesy and suddenly blank eyes: "It was a pleasure, Miss Cole." He rose, and, caught unawares, I accidentally took a gulp of my sherry, gasped as the liquor stung my throat, and put the glass down on the table. I slid my bag over my arm and stood up.

With the dignity and discretion of a man of the world caught out in an amorous escapade, Ernesto led me swiftly through the big rooms and, opening the front door, stood aside for me to go. "You will understand that I do not want my administrator assuming I have taken to entertaining the parador's guests," he said, smoothly.

"Of course."

And then, to my utter disbelief, he shook my hand and without another word, left me on the doorstep.

7

As it was Don Lazaro's deliberate turning away that had governed my decision to speak to Ernesto, so it was the arrival of a taxi in the courtyard as I emerged from the palace that sent me directly into the town and inadvertently cleared the way for Ernesto to do what he had to do.

I was not thinking of the effect of my arrival on Carlos' brother as I emerged from the great door, only that I had to get away to think. I raised one arm as the car swung round. It came full circle and pulled up beside me. *"Toledo, por favor."*

"Sí, sí." We swept off into the tree-lined, arrow-straight drive, swung round the olive-skirted bends, past the neat, new, white-painted villas with their oleanders, over the Almantara bridge and up to the top of the town. He dropped me beneath the towering walls of the *Alcázar*.

I seated myself at one of the small iron tables in the square and when a black-haired waiter in a white coat came and stood over me I ordered coffee. There was animated chatter and a clamour of noise. Two ginger-haired dogs dashed among the tables chasing a large rubber ball, and a small girl in a tartan skirt ran boisterously after them.

I was glad of the hustle-bustle, and yet apart and unaffected by it. I sat staring at the tall, tatty buildings opposite with their dark blue awnings, their rusty, wrought-iron balconies and green window boxes waiting for summer flowers;

at the elegant cream façade of the Banco Español de Credito. The sun moved behind a roof top and somewhere in the back of my mind I registered the fact that the spring air was cold. A motor bike roared to a halt at the kerb and two khaki-clad soldiers walked away. Two members of the *Guardia Civil*, eyes watchful, made their way between the tables. There was not one other English person or American in sight. I must be mad, I said to myself, coming to an automatic unthought-out decision, to pry into this affair. There may well be a skeleton in the de Merito cupboard, but what right have I to rattle its foreign bones? I'll go now. I'll take a train or bus to Madrid.

I had finished the coffee and was paying my bill when it occurred to me that if I went straight back to Madrid now I was going to lay myself open to some awkward questions on reaching home. *You were in Toledo for a day and a night yet didn't see anything? El Greco's house, or the cathedral?* No, it would not do. I had to view at least one or two churches in this town that had been important enough to provide bishops who were the primates of Spain. There was the great Alcázar too, Toledo's awful jewel, and that historic bridge, San Martin. All right, I would pack as much as possible into the rest of the day, then collect my luggage and if there was no train or bus I would take a taxi to Madrid and stay there until I could get a flight home.

Having made up my mind, I bought a tourist guide entitled *A Day in Toledo* from the little kiosk on my right. I went to the Alcázar first because it was near to hand. I walked briskly from floor to floor, skimming through the handbook as best I could, stabbing into Spanish history with my mind elsewhere. And then, under those formidable eaves, I came to this citadel's number one hero who during the Civil War had sacrificed his own son for his beliefs—or desires.

"Father, they say they're going to shoot me if you don't surrender."

"Then commend your soul to God, shout *Viva España!* and die like a hero." I stood there with my guidebook in

53

my hand looking into the fanatical dark eyes of this Spanish soldier and feeling a little sick. Thinking, inevitably, of Carlos and Ernesto, of the young Antonia, and the bus that had been blown up outside of a war: of the child. *Forgive me, Antonia. I don't know what I am up against, either. I am running, just as you ran.*

I walked briskly to the Gate of the Sun, visited St. John of the Kings, and El Greco's house and museum. Then the morning was gone, and in English terms, a little of the afternoon, too. It was the Spanish lunch time. I found a restaurant that had been a Franciscan convent, with Toledan swords on the walls, banners hanging from rafters and wrought-iron bars set over the windows. I drank a carafe of red wine whilst trying to pluck up the courage to eat a partridge I had ordered on the waiter's advice.

"It is good."

"Yes."

"Speciality of Toledo."

"Yes. But it is strong. High. It has surely been hung for too long a time."

He did not understand. "Speciality of Toledo," he repeated, despising me because I was clearly not a connoisseur of good food. I finished the wine without plucking up enough courage to insult the management by ordering another dish, then left. In a little shop opposite I bought a very expensive box of almonds which my guidebook assured me was another speciality of the town. Then I set out down a series of narrow alleyways in search of Santo Tomo. Pride in the possession of El Greco's most famous painting: *The Burial of Count Orgaz*, had moved the town to provide chairs in the church on which tourists might sit to view this masterpiece at their leisure. I took my place. Perhaps it was the wine with so little food, perhaps the broken night, perhaps a combination of both. The next thing I knew was an attendant shaking my shoulder and I wakened to find my head down near my knees. Muttering an embarrassed apology, I staggered yawning to my feet and left to the titters of a coach-load

54

of tourists. That will teach me to drink wine at lunch, I said to myself wryly.

Heavens! It was after four and I had yet to see the cathedral. I gave myself an hour there, an hour to see one of the most famous cathedrals in Spain, itself the heart of Toledo, then wended my way down the hill towards the Tagus, looking in shop windows as I went at the displays of lovely Toledan jewellery, watching craftsmen beating gold and silver wires into fired steel for the handles of the famous Toledan swords. Too late, I remembered Perry Ballisat's warning that the taxis stayed in Zocodover Square.

I hesitated, retraced my steps a few yards, hesitated again. The walk to the parador I decided, mistakenly as it turned out, might not be much more trying than the climb back to the taxi-rank. I crossed the bridge and facing into the full glare of the afternoon sun, trudged up the winding road out of the gorge, sweat dampening my body and sucking my thin blouse against my skin. The road was narrow with only here and there a rough bit of waste ground beset with stones that I used reluctantly as a footpath in order to avoid the rushing traffic.

It was more than an hour later that I arrived, tired, dusty and footsore. I had been going to ask for my bill and a train timetable, but Don Felipe Lazaro was not in sight and I had no energy left with which to try to make Alonso understand. I took my passport from a pigeon hole behind the desk, picked up the key and went to my room. The administrator, I felt certain, would be only too pleased to make out my bill on the spot when I was packed and ready to go.

The bed was neatly made, the room tidy. I tried to run a bath but the taps seemed to have dried up. "Spanish plumbing is terrible" Antonia had said, but that was twenty-seven years ago. There had been time for improvement. I went dispiritedly back into my room and sat on the bed. It was then I saw the envelope leaning against the mirror. It was addressed in flourishing, attractive handwriting to Miss Suzanne Cole.

Curiously, I picked it up and turned it over. The flap was gummed lightly down. Inside was a single sheet of crested writing paper.

Dear Miss Cole,
"The Count has told me of your visit this morning. An extraordinary story, but of course we cannot help feeling intrigued. Alas, my son has flown to Paris on business so there are no young people here but if you would not think it too dull we would like you to dine with us this evening.
It will be quite informal. My mother-in-law will be the only other guest. Please come in by the back gate through the olive grove. As we are not in the habit of entertaining the parador's guests and do not wish to set a precedent, we would be pleased if you do not mention this invitation to our administrator.

Pilar Camino de Millas de Merito.

From the bathroom came a splashing and gushing noise. I dashed in to find the taps in full flood. They were both cold, but after the shock of my first abortive try, I was grateful to have any water at all. I returned to the bedroom and studied the letter again. The handwriting was strong, almost masculine, I noted in some surprise, remembering the beautiful and essentially feminine woman I had seen in the car this morning. Was it possible she did not know of an elder brother, allegedly executed before she joined the family? But the Dowager, Carlos' mother, certainly knew! Did Ernesto know of this invitation?

Baffled, and not a little distrait, I found myself going to re-read Antonia's letter. My suitcase lay on a wooden chair by the wardrobe. I slid my fingers into the pocket.

The letter had gone. I scrabbled round among the contents of the suitcase, tossing them on to the floor, shaking each garment as I put it back again, knowing I was wasting time. I went to the wardrobe and delved frantically into the pockets

56

of my coat, returned to my handbag and upended it on the bed, flicked through the pages of my passport, my travellers' cheques, returned to the suitcase, and when there was no more fooling myself I sat down on the bed and stared into space.

8

I DECIDED TO accept. Heaven knew what could come of this visit. My mind boggled at the possibilities. However, I had come on a long and expensive journey. It would be cowardly and futile to run. Besides, what could Ernesto do to me with his wife and elderly mother looking on?

The parador seemed deserted. There were no cars in the courtyard and the big door leading to the palace was shut. I went out through the main arch then turned left as I had done the evening before, following the wall round two sides where the olive grove nudged up against it and the big windows of the palace were visible. Here was the little wrought-iron gate set in a low stone wall. I opened it and went with some trepidation up a brick path bordered by low but unkempt box hedges and sheltered by an ancient grape vine twisting like a rope across an iron frame that must have supported it for a hundred years.

There was ivy growing thickly on the ground and running for several feet up the trunks of trees. The grass was long, rising dry and languid from hungry soil. On my left were the formal palace gardens, now only a pattern of small stone walls, roses running wild, an octagonal pond made of sand-coloured stone with an urn in the centre and the dry base full of dead leaves. It must have been very beautiful once, I thought, inevitably with a mixture of emotions, before *El Caudillo* demanded a living wage for peasant gardeners.

"Ah! There you are." I jumped. Ernesto, *El Conde* de Merito, was standing within an enormous and wildly overgrown circular summer house.

"You found your way all right. Forgive me for bringing you the long way round but I did not wish you to be seen by guests of the parador."

"I quite understand," I said, looking round urgently for his wife and mother.

"Do sit down."

There was a pair of pale marble seats and between them an oblong table beautifully ornamented with scrolls. One of the seats was almost entirely overgrown by ivy and roses, their stems as thick as young trees and twisted with age. There was ivy here, too. Its crawling tendrils had gone back and forth across the marble looking for footholds until there was very little of the seat showing. Were the four of us going to sit on this one seat? Were the de Meritos really in the habit of entertaining in this semi-wilderness? Or was I, as a mere parador guest, not to be asked into the palace? There was some fruit and a bowl of food at the far end of the table. A cold buffet in the garden?

"Do sit down," the Count repeated. There were bottles on the table and half-a-dozen glasses. Half-a-dozen, not two. And yet, I had a frightening feeling we were alone. Those six glasses were part of this very peculiar scene. Had someone cleared this seat today? A hack-saw, an axe and a pair of strong hands can undo years of growing in an hour. I racked my brains frantically for a reason for his keeping me out here. I would give him a few moments. If the ladies did not put in an appearance, I would run. I sat down gingerly on the edge of the clean seat. "Now, what would you like to drink?" Ernesto asked cordially.

"Shall we wait for the Countess?" A nervous tic began in my right eyelid and I pressed two fingers against it.

Ernesto glanced up ostentatiously, looking between two slim firs that stood on either side of the path that led to the inner palace courtyard. "She will be along at any

59

moment," he said. "She went to get my mother who may have overslept. My mother is an old lady now and her siestas grow longer." He turned back to me with an engaging smile. "This afternoon I have been working very hard. I need a drink. Do allow me to tempt you, Miss Cole, so that I may join you while we talk. I have consulted the ladies and we have decided to tell you about Carlos."

I blinked. He wore a curious, waiting expression, like a person taking a chance for sheer devilment. "Before they come, I want to tell you the essentials. My mother will explain in greater detail. Now, let's have a drink first. What may I offer you?"

"I'll have a gin," I said when I could get my breath.

"And what would you like in it?"

I was about to say tonic when I realised there was none in view. "What do you put in gin?"

He lifted up a small bottle containing a faintly yellowish liquid and having a Spanish label. "This is very good. It's a locally made cordial," he said. "We have excellent water in Toledo, you know. You've heard about the making of our famous swords? The waters of the Tagus are said to have special qualities from which the steel gets great resilience."

I gave him a strained look. "Am I to drink Tagus water?"

He laughed, brushing my question aside. "You will like this." He poured the drink and handed it to me, then poured his own. A whisky, I noticed, and he drank it neat. I sipped my gin. The cordial he had put in it was rather sweet. Not entirely to my taste, but palatable. And rather strong. I could scarcely taste the gin. Ernesto handed me a plate of tiny biscuits heaped with a cream that might have been goat's cheese. "Do take one. That spread is made from a very rare bean which you will see growing over there." He pointed and I saw against a wall just beyond the summer house a plant with papery green leaves and hung with light brown, roughish pods. "I found it on a visit to the West Coast of Africa some years ago. The part that used to be Spanish Guinea. They told me it would not grow here, but you see, it is thriving. We

60

pound the beans into this interesting cream and use it as a savoury. Taste."

I nibbled the biscuit. "It's very nice," I said politely. In fact, it tasted of nothing much at all. "About Carlos," I said.

"My elder brother, it's true, did marry this girl," Ernesto admitted, "and what you have said about the bus is true."

"Then why did you deny it this morning?"

He smiled. "I will explain. I put Antonia on the bus, and it's true we thought she was dead. Do have another biscuit, Miss Cole."

I've no doubt I was hungry, for I had been unable to stomach that partridge at lunch time but I only took another savoury because Ernesto proferred the plate so insistently. Taking another biscuit was an automatic reflex action while I waited for him to go on. I began to be aware of feeling distinctly odd. Perhaps it was the shock and apprehension.

"It's true, too, that my brother lived in exile for many years," Ernesto went on, "and that he led an uprising against the Government. I went myself to see if what the papers said was correct and found him hiding near a little place called Santo Domingo de la Calzada. It's up in the north, not far from Burgos. He was very irresponsible," said Ernesto, looking at me and smiling. "I asked him what his plans were for the future, because of course we had the *Finca* and the title to think of when our father died. He said he would never return home under a dictatorship. So I came home and talked to my father. I suggested he put the palace into my name."

"And he did this?"

"No," Ernesto shook his head. He handed me the biscuits. "Do have another one. And let me replenish your drink." I glanced down at the yellow liquid. "I have nearly finished, but I don't think I will have another," I said. "It is making my head feel a little woozy."

"What, one drink?" Ernesto was astonished. "What did you have for lunch? Some unaccustomed wine?"

"I did have some wine," I admitted. It seemed a long time ago, all the same.

"Just a small one," Ernesto conceded, and half-filled the glass. "My wife has just signalled from a window. She is coming. Neither of my ladies drink. We will have something to eat when they arrive."

"What happened?" I asked quickly, wanting to hear the rest of the story before they came. The words sounded thick. I had better not have any more to drink. I reached for another savoury, hoping it might have a sobering effect. That drink Ernesto poured must have been very strong.

"My father said the eldest son had to inherit the palace," Ernesto went on. "It had always gone to the eldest son. It came to the family in 1517 when Carlos V whom you know was not legally king, presented it to my ancestor General Perico de Merito. *El Regalo del Rey*, the King's gift. My ancestor won it for his part in proving Juana la Loca, Carlos' mother, mad, and having her put away so that Carlos could reign. Do you know your Spanish history, Miss Cole?"

"No, not really." I was very confused indeed. He was talking about Carlos being king. But he was not. He had been executed. Could I be drunk? Had I accepted more than one refill?

Ernesto said lightly: "To cut a long story short, as you say, it did not matter for there was an accident and my brother Carlos was then not in a position to inherit."

"Oh," I said stupidly. "He died."

Ernesto did not reply. He was staring at me, rather deliberately. "You don't look very well, Miss Cole. Perhaps you are unaccustomed to drink. The maid has laid out a little alfresco supper here." He stepped over to the far end of the table and produced a plate with that dish I had noticed earlier. It contained some whitish mixture like that on the savouries, or like fish. "Before the ladies come," Ernesto said, sounding anxious, "perhaps you had better have a little food, since obviously I cannot produce a sobering coffee in a hurry. You really do seem to have had a lot to drink, Miss Cole. Eat it quickly," he said. "They are coming down the path. I would not like you to appear inebriated before my lady mother."

I was baffled, embarrassed and confused. Was I drunk? I certainly felt that way. I took a large mouthful of the stuff Ernesto had served out to me. Like the savoury, it tasted of nothing at all. I swallowed it swiftly and took another forkful. I was, in a muddled sort of way, grateful to Ernesto. He was suddenly behaving in a concerned and fatherly manner. "What is this?" I asked between mouthfuls.

"It is the bean," he said. He sounded oddly smug. "The Ordeal Bean of Calabar. You may have the drink with it, if you wish."

But it was the drink that had made me feel peculiar. *Oh my God!* I thought. *He put something in it.* Hastily, I scooped up the rest of the mixture with the fork. Ernesto put another spoonful on my plate and I ate that. It did not matter that it tasted of nothing, and that I was not hungry. It ought to act as blotting paper. I put the plate down. Certainly I did feel a little better, now. I pushed the offending glass away and looked up the path towards the palace. There was no one coming! I swung back sharply towards Ernesto. He was looking down at me, smiling.

"They're not coming," I said. My voice had begun to rise on a note of fear but I clamped it firmly under control.

"No," he said gently, almost kindly. "They're not coming."

I tried to jump to my feet but my legs would not work and I sat down again. "It is the bean," Ernesto said smoothly. "It acts as a powerful sedative on the spinal cord." He sat down on the other end of the seat, resting one arm along the back, looking into my face and when he spoke again his voice seemed to be taunting me. "In the Cameroons these beans, crushed and mixed with palm oil, are used as a remedy for lice. And the Bakwiris use them with other drugs as a cure for rheumatism." He smiled again. "It is a very useful drug, Miss Cole."

Lice! Rheumatism! I must be going mad! "What have you done to me?" I asked hoarsely.

63

He took a long time to reply, and then he said, quite gently: "I am going to kill you, Miss Cole, because you are a very dangerous young lady."

Oddly, I did not think to scream. Looking back, I realise it would have been useless for he could so easily have clamped a hand over my mouth. I sat there on that marble seat looking down at my useless legs and thinking, ludicrously, that Fate had dealt me a bad hand, and that it was not fair. Why had I not recognised danger in this curious set-up of the overgrown arbour, the man alone? I could have run before it was too late. I was twenty-three years old, with all of life ahead of me. And I was going to die!

"You bastard!" I said. I managed that with venom, though my head was swimming.

Ernesto laughed. "It was not your business," he explained lightly. "Do you realise you were about to ruin the lives of four people?"

It was true, and I had only myself to blame. I felt a dreadful, black, consuming despair. *Antonia!* It had all been so unnecessary.

My mouth began to water, and I was suddenly unbearably thirsty. "Could you give me a drink? Some water," I said shakily.

Ernesto shook his head. "The thirst cannot be slaked," he said. "Let me tell you a little about this bean. A useful thing. Besides killing lice and curing rheumatism, the natives use it as a ritual poison. The thirst is the first symptom after the paralysis of the spinal cord. Water does one of two things. If it causes vomiting, then the victim is considered to be innocent. If it spreads the poison through the body, then he is guilty and deserves to die. I know you are guilty of interference, Miss Cole, so there is no point in giving you the water which anyway will not slake your thirst."

They were the last clear words I heard before I began to lose consciousness. After that I thought I heard a list of names, the words dancing up and down in my brain. "Liberia

64

... Ivory Coast ... Ghana ... Nigeria ... Cameroons ..."
And then, in the far distance: "I found it in Spanish
Guinea ..."

9

I WAKENED TO total blackness. My bed was smooth and hard and cold, like tiles. My clothes were damp, clinging to me as a very uncomfortable second skin. There was an unpleasant smell of vomit in the room. I lifted myself weakly on one elbow and immediately began to tremble, then shake uncontrollably. My whole body ached and there were little hammers battering in my head. I retched, but there was nothing more in my stomach. The dry retching tore at me and I fell back gasping. I lay on the cold tiles for some time before I could even bring myself to lift my head again.

There was nothing to see and all I could think of was the torment of dreams where strange objects circling round my head missed me by a hair's breadth. Demon cries. An overgrown marble seat with ivy—

The shock of memory brought me with a jerk to a sitting position and I had to wait for my head to stop swimming. Ernesto! I blinked, and blinked, and blinked again. Was I blind? Or incarcerated in total darkness? A dungeon. A dungeon beneath the old palace, from which there was no escape, ever? My mind zithered over horror stories I had read. A bricked-up room in which my bones might be discovered several lifetimes hence. Panic loaned me a little strength and I tried to clamber to my feet, fell back weakly, then tried again. This time my legs held. I shuffled forward in the inky darkness, hands outstretched, and came up against a wall. A papered wall! I leaned against it, tears of weakness and relief coursing down my face because I was not, after all, in a dungeon. I began to feel my way carefully along the wall. There was a picture, and then another; a corner to turn; a mirror; and then the cold frame of a door. I found the handle and in a panicky movement that was totally without hope, turned it.

To my utter disbelief the door opened and I fell out into a wide hall that was not dark, only shadowed, because the doors on either side were all closed. I looked at my watch. A quarter to five. Morning? Evening? To my left there was a large landing, a balcony rail and, across the top of the stairs, a thick rope. Behind that again, an enormous painting of the Holy family. Suddenly I knew where I was. On the roped-off upper floor of the palace where the windows looked out on the courtyard, except that they were closed and shuttered because no one came here, now. But the unlocked door? Momentarily, I was baffled and then it came to me, chillingly, that a dead girl does not turn door handles. Ernesto had the confidence not to use the key that would invite suspicion when the body was eventually found.

With the door open I now had a twilight view into the room. No, I had not been dumped unceremoniously on the floor. Ernesto had had the decency to put me on to a bed to die. Perhaps in a convulsion I had thrown myself off. The shuttered windows were so close that not a chink of light showed through. I crept fearfully back inside. My handbag might be here. Yes, here it was on the bed. Then I heard the sound of running water and, blinking in the faint light, I saw a small hand-basin in the corner of the room.

Memory came back, then. Memory of a terrifying fight against the paralysis of my legs. I remembered fighting my way off the bed and dragging myself across the floor, struggling to find an exit, determined not to die for a cause not my own. I remembered being consumed with anger and a desperate, all-pervading determination to live. I had to get to water. Ernesto, confident that he had done his job properly, had given me life because he had been unable to resist the temptation of verbal torture. Water, he had said, would give me a fifty-fifty chance, and I had been determined to drag my way to water. I had come up against the cold marble of a wash basin and somehow pulled myself up by a little stool—here it was, a small cushioned stool, painted blue. From there I had lurched across to the basin, drank until the force of my vomiting had thrown me back on to the floor, and into blessed unconsciousness.

I turned the tap off, closed the door carefully behind me and went shakily on legs that threatened to give way every step, towards the stairs.

The palace was silent as a tomb, and tomb-like. Surely it must be morning, for no afternoon could be as silent as now. Even with the family away there should be sounds as the servants moved around.

Slowly, step by step, I made my way down into the hall. At the foot of the stairs I caught sight of myself in the mirror, paper-white, with huge dark circles beneath my eyes. My hair sat wig-like on my head, unkempt, uncombed. I turned swiftly away, and labouring against my weakness, crossed the shadowy hall, stood a moment with held breath, listening, then tip-toed through the double doors into the entrance lobby. I stretched out an apprehensive hand. Yes! The door opened from the inside! Weak with relief, I stumbled through it, then with a nervous reflex action, pushed the door shut. Somehow, then, I knew I was alone and knew from the pale sky tinged with primrose that it was morning.

The fresh air revived me a little. I went down the shallow steps, looked left along the palace courtyard, then right at the big gate. I could make my way out via the gardens and round the outer wall. Or I could go through this big arch and take a chance on being seen by an early-rising member of the staff. I could just see the mat of high-built green that was the outer edge of the pergola. Memory flooded in, sickeningly, and I turned away. Did it matter if I was seen? Only Don Felipe Lazaro could question me, for only he spoke English. And

68

surely he was in bed at this hour of the morning. I would pack and pay my bill quietly, ask for a taxi and go straight to the British Embassy in Madrid.

The big doors were heavy but I managed to get one of them open. I stepped into the front courtyard and pushed it closed behind me. The door to the parador was shut. I crossed the gravel and without much hope, tried the handle. It did not move. I looked apprehensively at the bell, decided against it and knocked. Nothing happened. I waited a while. The whole place had an air of desertion. Then out of the corner of my eye I saw there were half-a-dozen cars parked in the courtyard. Of course the whole place could not have been evacuated. It was understandable that the palace would be empty at night, with the Dowager Countess and Ernesto and his wife in Madrid, and the servants in their wing opposite the parador.

Now I was faced with a decision. To stand out here until someone came to let me in. Or ring the bell. I looked at the bell. Well, why not? I raised my hand, and at that moment I caught a glimpse of daylight behind me where the palace door ought to be and realising it had swung open, I decided to go back and close it. If a servant suspected I had come from there, he might well waken Don Felipe. Even that short walk was exercise I could happily have done without. I retraced my shaky footsteps, pulled the door to, held it firmly for a moment, then let it go.

As I turned, the door to the parador swung open and the administrator stepped through. He was wearing riding breeches, an open-necked shirt, and carrying a crop in his hand. He saw me and stopped dead. His head had been high, his eyes sparkling. At that moment there was something curiously endearing and familiar about him, but the next, his face had closed. He stood quite still, waiting for me to come up to him. Waiting for me to explain why I was leaving the home of *El Conde* de Merito at daybreak when the family were patently not at home. He was not in on the poisoned food, that I knew most certainly. When a girl who is supposed

69

to be dead appears, one does not look angry and accusing like that. The relief in me was overwhelming.

"Kindly come into my office," Don Lazaro said, looking cold, and hard, and very deliberate.

I had intended to go on straight up the stairs to my room, but I had no key. Besides, there was something mesmeric in Don Felipe Lazaro's manner. I followed him and sat down in the chair that he pulled up to the corner of his desk.

"In the absence of the Count," the administrator said coldly, laying his riding crop across the corner of his desk, thrusting his hands into the pockets of his riding breeches and rocking back on the heels of his polished leather boots, "I am in charge of the *Finca*. May I ask what you were doing in the palace, Miss Cole?"

I felt very weak and really rather ill. As though I had been ill for some time and the walk down those stairs and across the yard had been too much for me.

"Where is the Count?" I asked.

There was a flicker of surprise in his eyes. "I will ask the questions, Miss Cole. What were you doing in the empty palace?"

How could I possibly tell this man that his employer had tried to poison me? "I went there," I began hesitantly, "because the Count invited me." I added swiftly: "You saw me there yesterday morning."

"I did indeed. He told me you had tricked him into asking you in. You told him some tale about knowing a relative, but he had a suspicion you were merely having a look. Perhaps I had better call the police now." He turned towards the telephone.

My heart began to pound. I had read enough in the press about tourists waiting over-long for their trials in Spanish jails to be certain I had to avoid an interview with the police. "Just a moment," I said. "Please don't ring yet." I went on unevenly: "When I returned to the parador yesterday—about five o'clock I think it was, there was a note in my room inviting me to the palace at six-thirty for dinner."

Those blue eyes flashed but Don Felipe spoke quietly: "The Count left for Madrid at mid-day. The others left in the morning. It is not the slightest use your telling me this story, Miss Cole. I saw him away myself."

"Funny," I said, not thinking it funny at all, "that he should come down on Friday evening and leave Saturday."

"The Countess was here all week with Damian, their son, who was on vacation. The Count was very busy in Madrid. He could come for only one night."

"And where has the Count gone now?"

"He is at work." Felipe glanced at his watch and a flicker of amusement touched his mouth. "At this hour I should think he would be asleep. Normally, he spends the weekdays at the flat. It will not be difficult for me to get him down here."

I began to feel terribly frightened. He was suddenly watching me very closely. I thought I saw his eyes soften a little and then he said: "You look rather unwell. Would you like me to call a doctor?"

Yes, I wanted a doctor, but not one of theirs. Somehow, I had to get to the British Embassy in Madrid.

His voice was unexpectedly gentle. "You have a—er—a health problem, Miss Cole?"

I took a deep breath. "No, Don Lazaro," I replied shakily. "I am not insane. And what is more, I can prove it." With trembling fingers I opened my handbag. "I have here an invitation from the Countess in her own handwriting—" I broke off, remembering that the Countess had not appeared, and remembering, also, the firm, very masculine style of the writing.

"Yes?" asked Don Felipe helpfully.

I put my handbag on the desk and felt inside. Travellers' cheques. Passport. Diary. Make-up. Comb. Everything was there but the letter. Sick with fright, I raised my eyes to his.

"It isn't there?" He spoke as though humouring a child.

"I may have left it in my room." I had not left the letter

in my room, that I knew for certain. "But I do assure you that I had an invitation to go to the palace at six-thirty last night."

"I was in my room at six-thirty," he said. "I saw you go out of the gate and turn towards the olive grove."

"Yes. I was asked to use the back gate." I said it with a terrified sort of defiance.

"The back gate," said Don Lazaro coldly, "has never, to my knowledge, been used for social calling."

"It was used for a social call last night," I said heatedly. "And now, if you please, I would like you to call a taxi. I think it would be better if I told my story at the British Embassy in Madrid."

Don Lazaro's eyes sharpened. Alarm? No, I did not think so, but he did seem as though he was beginning to recognise the fact that there was something here beyond his grasp. "Come, Miss Cole," he said briskly, "aren't you being rather ridiculous?"

"No," I replied. "Will you call a taxi?"

"I am sorry. But perhaps I will not call the police, either. I will call the Count in Madrid."

I was now in the grip of sheer, uncontrollable panic. What could I do if Ernesto returned? I could not even telephone the Embassy and get someone here unless Don Felipe chose to allow it. And what point was there in telling the truth? He could go up to the disused part of the palace, find a room with a rumpled bed and some vomit on the floor, and draw his own conclusions. Perhaps he would think the Count had returned to an assignation with me. Perhaps that was the way to play it. I said: "Why don't you go over there. Go to the top of the stairs and look in the—er—I think it is the second room on the right."

"I don't know what you are trying to tell me," Don Felipe said quietly, not looking at me now.

"I am suggesting you see proof I spent the night in that room, so eliminating from your mind the suspicion that I am a thief. I will go to my room and pack. Then, perhaps, if you still want to, we can talk again."

A mixture of emotions showed in his face. Puzzlement. Curiosity. "The upstairs rooms have not been used for some years, Miss Cole."

"I assure you, one of them was used last night."

"I think it would be better if you wait here until I return." He went out of the room.

I put my elbows on the desk, and closed my eyes against the palms of my hands. I already knew, or felt, there was no escape from the upper floor of the parador. If I decided to run, I had to do it from here, as soon as Don Felipe had gone from sight. After, when I was safely out of the way, there was Perry Ballisat. I still had his address. Or did I? Two letters had already disappeared. I opened my eyes and as I did so they fell on a white card standing open on a small shelf behind the desk. A birthday card with the date in large silver letters: 15 *Mayo. Felipe* in handwriting, some Spanish words and the signature, *Pilar.*

My eyes glazed over. My mind spun. Antonia's son had been born on the 15th May! Antonia, who had light blue eyes like his, a brilliance, a zest for life tightly reined but always ready to burst through. That same look, I saw in him. And now I knew the reason for that stab of memory as I saw him swing out of the door half-an-hour ago, eyes alight with the anticipation of an early morning ride. That look I had seen a hundred times on my stepmother's face. Felipe Lazaro, Antonia's son, employed as parador administrator by the Count de Merito. *We would be pleased if you do not mention this invitation to my administrator* the letter had read. My administrator! He who, if Carlos was really dead, was the rightful claimant to the title. No wonder Ernesto had got rid of me so fast yesterday morning when Felipe hinted he might join us in a drink. *I had this strange, recurring dream about the palace in Toledo,* Antonia had said. A sort of creeping terror came over me at the thought of what I would unleash by telling Felipe the truth. And yet, if I did

73

not, Ernesto would be back with a well-laid plot for my certain disposal. The police, perhaps, and his own marvellous alibi, that Felipe had seen him off the premises at mid-day on Saturday. I had to get out of here.

10

I LEAPED OUT of my seat, took my room key from the board and over-riding my weakness by sheer desperation took the stairs two at a time. I opened the wardrobe door and flung clothes and shoes haphazardly into my suitcase, jammed it shut and picked up my coat and handbag. According to a sign on my wall inside the door headed *Ministerio de información y turismo* one room for one person cost 230 pesetas. I counted the money out swiftly, added some more for the one breakfast I had eaten, opened the door warily, and came face to face with Alonso, gracefully relaxed against the corridor wall opposite.

"Buenos días," I said weakly, summoning up a panicky and idiotic smile.

"Buenos días, Señorita."

That I should underestimate a man of Felipe Lazaro's calibre! I moved tentatively towards the stairs, signing to Alonso to precede me. In silence we went downstairs together. The first thing I noticed was that the riding crop had gone from the desk. I looked enquiringly at the boy. He held his hands together, bent his knees and bounced up and down. "Oh," I said faintly, "riding." Worlds, it seemed, could turn upside down, but Don Felipe Lazaro, the parador administrator, would not miss his early morning ride. So, I was to be policed until his return!

Alonso opened the door, went outside and stood in the

courtyard revolving solemnly on one heel, scrunching the gravel with his polished shoes. I could see through into the lounge. The shutters were still closed. With despair in my heart, I went back up the stairs. From a landing window I saw the boy wander down to the great archway and look along the drive. I paced the length of the corridor, staring blankly at the row of plain doors, desperately seeking a plan of escape. At the top of the stairs there was one door standing alone and opening on a room towards the inner end of the wing. Carefully, silently, I turned the handle.

The door led into an enormous linen cupboard with shelves built on three sides. They were stacked with snowy piles of towels, sheets, pillow cases. There was a door in the opposite wall and my heart jolted as I saw a key in the lock. I darted across the little room, turned the key, and found myself looking down a narrow and precipitous stone stairway that must surely lead into the back of the parador courtyard. It was narrow and steep. I went down it as fast as I dared. At the bottom I came upon a little pile of logs and a coal bunker hidden from the courtyard by a head-high wall. Across the yard, not more than twenty paces distant, standing slightly ajar in spite of the extra push I had given it, was the big arched doorway leading to the palace.

I stumbled back up those stone stairs, fled through the linen room, fumbled the key in the lock, heaved my suitcase off the wooden chair and staying only to secure the door behind me and slide the key beneath it, sped back the way I had come. Now I was out in the open again. Depositing my bag beside the coal bunker, I edged very carefully out into the courtyard until I could see Alonso. He was wandering back, hands in pockets, from the arch. Moving behind the shelter of the stone structure, I waited, counting his slow footsteps as they crunched in the gravel, then miraculously, there was the sound of the heavy door closing. I picked up my bag and with long, tip-toeing strides crossed the intervening space, pushed open the big door of the palace proper, slipped through and pulled it firmly shut behind me.

It was adrenalin that took me down those stairs, across the courtyard and through the gate with that heavy bag in my grasp. It had to be adrenalin for certainly I had no strength. The perspiration was standing out on my forehead. I had to put my bag down in the inner courtyard while I wiped my face with my hand. My legs were shaking like aspen leaves, but they moved willingly and lightly, taking me along beneath the palace windows, round by the rose pergola and on to the little vine-enclosed path that ran to the gate. It was padlocked, but it was small. Groaning with weakness, I forced my bag up and over it, dropping it with a bump on the dry ground, then clambered swiftly after it, only faintly aware that I was scraping my legs on the wrought-iron, tearing my skirt. Then I lifted the bag and ran like a rabbit up the slope and into the olive grove.

The knowledge of partial safety brought back consciousness of self, and I stumbled and found myself gasping for air with noisy, shallow jerks that seemed to catch in my throat and leave my lungs empty. I stood, bent over, my heart pounding, feeling unable to go on. Then I saw that a little farther on the ground sloped away. I had to make another desperate effort. I did, but immediately I felt the ground sloping away beneath my feet, I stumbled and fell, to lie full length on the baked ground, my heart thundering its resentment at the treatment being metered out to a sick and exhausted body.

It had not occurred to me that Felipe might be riding through the olive grove until, in the hard earth by my ear, I felt the even vibrations of a horse cantering. My blood froze. There would be no way of hiding here within these serried ranks of neat grey trunks. If luck was with me, rider and horse might stay far enough from me for the trees to cluster and form a wall. If not, then I would be discovered.

I clambered to my feet and helped myself in the only way possible, by standing very straight on the off-side of the thickest trunk to hand with my case on its end beside me. The sweat of apprehension and fright coursed down my back as hoofbeats thundered nearer, passed agonisingly close, and pelted on their way. My knees gave then, and I dropped back to the ground in such a welter of sickening relief as a fox must feel, safe in its hole beyond the hunting field. Of course, if Antonia's son sat his horse the way he stood, with head high and eyes on the misty distance, he was unlikely to see a fugitive bolt upright on the wrong side of a tree trunk.

It was some time before I could muster the strength to go on. Now that the immediate danger was past, the adrenalin had gone from my veins. I rose shakily. My suitcase was now a dead weight three times as heavy as before. I could scarcely lift it, much less carry it. In desperation I swung it along a pace at a time, knowingly scraping the underside on the little stones that thrust up through the coarse grass, carelessly sliding it down slopes. The grove here, to my intense relief, had begun to run down-hill. I hoped it was falling away towards the gorge and the river, for that way I would eventually strike the road.

The ground beneath my feet grew harder as the slope steepened so that I had to brace my shoes against small, tough plants and bigger stones to prevent myself slipping. I did trip. My bag broke free, sliding and tumbling head-long, missing tree trunks by inches as it clattered and bumped for more than a hundred yards and I sat down sharply, holding a hand to either side of my face, closing my eyes, unwilling to face the moment when the bag should burst open, spilling my clothes on the ground.

Miraculously, the zip held. I slid down the slope and rescued it in a dry little gully that had long since lost its stream. Rock-scraped and dirty, I dragged it from beneath a fallen tree trunk, then sat down beside it, to rest. The silence was supreme. Occasionally a small grey lizard moved tentatively out from beneath a stone, then scuttled on its way, but there was no birdsong; no flutter of leaves or whirr of wings. I remembered with distaste what Perry had told me about them being served up as delicacies in restaurants.

Later, through the enveloping silence came the noise of a car engine. I raised my head, listening, and my heart lifted for traffic sounds would necessarily be muted by the olive trees, so perhaps the road was not so far away after all. Anyway, I told myself, I could not stay here for the rest of the day growing weaker all the time. I must somehow get to Zocodover Square. And then? A taxi direct to the airport. There would be a restaurant there and time enough to eat when I had booked a seat on the first available plane to London. I no longer wanted to go to the British Embassy. I began to wonder nervously if Ernesto cared enough to have me stopped. He had clearly taken some astonishing chances in the past. Could I count on his taking another in letting me go free?

I came to the road some twenty minutes and a long haul later. There were cars speeding by, nearly all of them going in the direction of the town. The bank was heavily overgrown with a coarse, dry broom. I tackled it gingerly, moving my case from hand to hand and bush to bush, using the foliage as a brake until, weak and trembling, I set foot at last on the narrow road. Almost immediately a car screeched to a stop and a young man leaned out. He spoke to me in Spanish. I shook my head. "I do not understand."

"Eengleesh?" I nodded. He jumped out, and, picking up my case, threw it with no more consideration than it appeared to warrant, into the back.

"Zocodover Square?"

"Ah! Zocodover!" He launched into a flood of Spanish which I suppose is better than two people facing each other in embarrassed silence.

"No comprendo," I replied. He shrugged. We slid into our seats and headed off down the winding road that led into the gorge, crossed beneath the gothic arches of the Almantara bridge and sped up the hill, the driver chatting companionably all the way, then patting my arm and shrugging smilingly when I could not understand. I dare say he was asking how I came to be in the road alone with a suitcase. For once I was rather glad of the language barrier.

If he had let me out at the taxi-rank I might have gone immediately on my way, but he pulled up on the corner where a waiter was already placing chairs and tables in front of his restaurant and it was there the devil caught me, seducing me with the heady scent of ambrosial coffee that even under normal conditions I am unable to resist. And there was nothing normal about my condition this morning. By a sort of reflex action I sank on to one of the little iron chairs. A waiter picked up my disgraceful looking bag and put it down beside me. *"Café, por favor."* The taxi-rank was not more than fifty yards away. In five minutes I would be speeding out of this town.

There was a hustling and bustling in the square. People came in from every side and as I sat there I began to wonder why most of them disappeared down the same alley which ran between two tall buildings. The warm scent of baking was everywhere, sharpening my hunger to urgency. And then I realised that all those black-clad housewives, those scurrying children, those striding men were on their way to collect their breakfast bread for they had begun to flow back through the alley again, carrying loaves beneath their arms. My stomach was groaning. I signalled to a waiter again. *"Pan, por favor."* I had learned by now the word for bread.

They were wonderful, those Spanish rolls. They tasted like no bread I had ever tasted before. Rich, and good, and strength-giving. The coffee was magnificent. The only trouble was, I knew I was not going to be able to keep any of it down. I sat hunched over the table in a fever of sickness and when I knew I could hold out no longer, looked round wildly for a way of escape. The vast untidy form of Perry Ballisat came at that moment swinging across the square with a couple of loaves of bread sticking out of a rope basket.

There could have been no doubt about my condition for he grabbed me by the arm, jerked me to my feet and pushed me unceremoniously towards the restaurant doorway. "In there you'll find a john. Ladies on the left."

There was not, after all, much to lose. A bit of bread and half a cup of coffee. Everything else had gone the night before. I emerged shaking to face the apprehensive stares of the staff. I gave them an apologetic look as I made my way out to the tables again. Perry was in my seat examining with interest my scraped and dirty bag. He was also finishing my rolls. "Didn't think you would want them," he boomed cheerfully. "Here, sit down. Been drinking the water, have you? It's dynamite. I should have warned you to stick to the bottled stuff. Viola cleaned her teeth in coke when we first came here, but you build up anti-bodies in time." He looked into my face, totally sympathetic but not a little amused. "How d'you feel? At least you're white instead of green, now."

I leaned my arms on the table and my tangled hair fell forward across my face. "I feel terrible," I said shakily.

His hound eyes twinkled. "Poor kid. Where are you going, anyway? You haven't seen Toledo yet, have you?"

"I—I saw quite a lot of it yesterday—"

"But what's the hurry? Viola's looking forward to meeting you. She will be tickled to death with that British accent of yours. You can't go without meeting Viola."

"I—er—I am not really feeling well enough for visiting."

"If you're not well enough for visiting, then you're sure not well enough for travelling. C'mon. I've paid your bill." He scraped his chair back.

"No, really, you're too kind—"

Perry swallowed the last crumbs of my breakfast, hoisted himself to his feet and looked down at my bag. "What have you been doing with that goddam suitcase?"

An elegantly uniformed policeman raised a white-gloved hand and the early morning traffic broke through with a whish and a roar, drowning any reply I might have thought up, reprieving me. "C'mon," said Perry, picking up the bag and taking my arm.

With a feeling of relief, I followed him.

11

THE BALLISATS LIVED, oddly, not far from the square. I say oddly because one does not expect to find large houses with leafy gardens so near the centre of a town, especially this town where spires and steeples, roofs and cliffs held sway. We came to it via an obscure little right-of-way round a corner and down half-a-dozen very wide granite steps edged by geraniums in big pots, past an art shop, a small church, then into a roughly-metalled road that narrowed to the width of a footpath. Suddenly, before us rose a stone wall quite ten feet high and in the middle, a blue-painted wooden door. Perry produced a key.

There was a small paved area with painted chairs and tables set under a trellised vine. Ahead, more steps leading down into a wide hall. We met Viola head on, carrying a tray. She was as pretty as a picture with short, dark hair, sparkling grey eyes and the tightest pair of frayed and washed-out jeans I had ever seen. She looked up admiringly at her large husband, nodded to me and said: "Well, well! The English girl! Hello, Suzanne. We're very glad to have you with us. If you'll just move those old papers off the table, darling, I'll put this tray down."

"Suzie's not well, honey," Perry said. "I'd suggest you show her the spare room and ask her what she wants most." Tactfully, his eyes avoided my torn skirt, my grubbiness.

"I would like to have a bath and change my clothes," I said.

They did not question me. Viola led me down some more steps into a big room that seemed to be part studio, part study. There was an easel in one corner, a desk in another, some old, worn but comfortable-looking furniture and a magnificent suit of armour. "My buddy," said Perry laconically as we passed. "He keeps me company when Viola runs home to mother every now and again."

His wife laughed. "He is our souvenir of Toledo, though what he is going to look like in a modern American house, I hate to think."

We went down some more steps and through a big sitting room with a grand piano and some better furniture, then round the corner into a narrow hall. At the end was a glass door opening on to a tiny porch and beyond that an elegant-looking garden with cypress trees rising like dark statues beside a stone path, and the familiar thin grass. Viola opened a door on the left showing me into a small, plain room. "It's not very glamorous," she apologised, "but the bed is comfortable, and the window looks out on a shrubbery. The bathroom is two doors along. I'll run a bath. In case you haven't discovered, the hot tap is marked C for *Caliente*." Perry came in with my bag. I noticed the dust had been wiped off. "If there is anything you want, just let me know. You'll find us out on the terrace."

I emerged an hour later towelling my hair to find a charming boy of seven, a little girl of three and a lively spaniel pup eagerly awaiting me. It was exactly the medicine I needed, well-adjusted, affectionate, humorous friends. I allowed them the premise that I had foolishly drunk the tap water, something no one with an English stomach and normal common sense ought to do, and I was paying the penalty.

"You got lovely golden hair," said little Marianne disarmingly. "Like my doll."

"That's what I can do with at the moment," I said, "a bit of flattery."

"The child will go a long way," commented her mother,

smiling. "Move into the sun, Suzanne. It's hot, but it will dry your hair quickly. Now what would you like to do? There is a hammock in the garden. Or would you like to go to bed? Or ..." She looked at me enquiringly.

They were marvellous, that American family. Of course I knew they must have been bristling with curiosity, yet they did not press me for an explanation. If my illness did not follow a totally familiar pattern, that also raised little surprise. They offered to telephone a doctor and I refused. I did not want to answer questions. Besides, a visit from a doctor was not necessary. I felt certain I was going to be all right. For the next two days I played with the children, learned a few words of Spanish so I could talk to Maria the maid, and gradually I was able to eat again and keep the food down.

On the third morning I was ready to tender my grateful thanks and go. They wanted me to stay and see some more of the town. I gave them my excuses, that after the beastliness of being ill, I wanted to go home. I could not say I was waking in the tiny guest room each night in a cold sweat that had nothing to do with the poison my stomach had so obligingly rejected. That the nightmare of Ernesto's face with its cruel lips, its malevolent eyes, lurked in the Spanish darkness, jolting me out of sleep into semi-consciousness. That his words came to me over and over, whispering, shouting, driving me mad: "Ghana, Nigeria, the Cameroons. Water ... Water ..." And then I would be dreaming of crawling across the floor, dragging my useless legs, clawing at the carpet, clawing at the wash basin, turning the tap with frenzied fingers. Gasping for water and all the time remembering: "Water does one of two things," Ernesto said. "And anyway, it will not slake your thirst." Chaos and blackness, until the dream began again. I had to get back to sane England, flying in on a prayer that all this might be left behind.

"You have been most frightfully kind," I said, "and I

cannot tell you how grateful I am. I do realise I owe you an explanation ..."

Perry's eyes twinkled. "Aw forget it. Spaniards can get tough. We guessed you had walked into something you couldn't handle. You don't have to go into details. They are great womanisers. And maybe *à propos* of that," he added, dropping his bombshell with a blast that hit my senses sickeningly, "Don Felipe Lazaro," he could not resist a lively look and questioning smile, "the chap you thought did not want you to stay, had a ghastly accident. His car went off the road and hurtled down into the gorge."

When I could find my voice I managed to say: "He's dead?"

"Dead? Oh no. He must have nine lives. He was actually thrown out, and survived. He said the brakes failed."

"When did it happen?" I asked, managing by a tremendous effort of will to keep my voice steady.

"Yesterday, apparently. I went up to the *Finca* this morning to take my last look at the El Greco and he was there, stretched out on a sofa in the room where I go to paint. He still looked rather shaken."

"In the palace?" I echoed. The administrator of the parador recuperating in the Count's home!

"Yes. There was another chap in the office. He didn't know anything about me but he asked Alonso and I was shown in by one of the maids. Lazaro told me about the car. It's down there, in the gorge. You can see it from the San Martin bridge. I came back that way to have a look. It's half under water," Perry said.

"He wasn't on his way into town then, when he had the accident?" Sharp with suspicion, I had to worm out the facts.

"No. He was on some errand for the Count. Of course, if he had been coming the other way, it might not have been so disastrous."

Perhaps I will never learn to stop and think. As we are born, so we act, and it may be that when I am ninety, if

86

I live that long, I will still be rushing head first into other people's affairs. I jumped up out of my chair. "Before I go, there's something I have to do."

"Can I do it for you?"

"No. You have done enough. Yes, perhaps you can. May I bring someone here? If necessary, I mean. There's someone I want to talk to, you see."

"Sure, sure. That's all right, Viola, isn't it?"

Viola nodded. "Who is this, Suzanne? I thought you didn't know anyone in Toledo."

"It's true, I don't. Perhaps there is something you can tell me. Do you know anything of the de Merito family?"

"They're one of the old families. We know what everybody else knows."

"Scandal, I mean."

"Carlos?"

My mouth fell open.

"Why, don't look so surprised," Perry said. "Everyone knows about Carlos. Nobody talks about him, though. He is their skeleton, or rather was. He's been dead for years."

"What do you know of him?"

"Nothing. Absolutely nothing. He was an anarchist, but he came to a sticky end. Some say he was shot way back in the 'forties. Others, that he got away and turned up somewhere near Burgos a few years ago. But it's generally thought some of the Basque Separatists resurrected his name to help their cause. Somebody is always starting trouble up there," Perry said laconically. "I think I told you, didn't I, that back in the nineteenth century the Basques got their independence from the rest of Spain, then they lost it again, and so it goes on. They're unsettled people."

"And you don't think Carlos ever had anything to do with them?"

"Hell, I dunno. I'm only repeating town gossip. The family were exiled in the Civil War you know, but they went to live in the French Basque country. French," he repeated. "He may have got some of his revolutionary ideas then."

87

"Is that all you know about Carlos?"

"There was Father Eladio," Viola put in.

"What about Father Eladio?"

Perry put an arm round his wife's shoulders and hugged her. "That's the Woman's Angle," he explained indulgently. "Viola's an incurable romantic. We had this old boy living in part of the house when we first came here. There's a sort of flat downstairs—well you've seen it, haven't you? You can see the windows from the garden." I nodded. "I wouldn't be surprised if he was senile—"

Viola broke in indignantly: "He was never senile, Perry. Just because he was old, there's no need to say that. He is a dear old man. I often meet him with the children on his evening stroll. We sometimes walk up the path to his house with him and once he invited us in. What he told us was rather a confidence, Suzanne, and we've never told anyone."

"He was boasting, honey. People like to pretend they've rubbed shoulders with the important folks. I didn't believe him for a moment but—"

"Well, I did," Viola broke in indignantly. "And I can't see any harm in telling Suzanne."

A priest! My heart was racing. "Tell me, Viola."

"He said he married Carlos. It's not that exciting really. It's just a romantic little secret, and whether it's true or not never bothered me. But you asked about the family, and really, that's all we know."

"Who was the girl?" I asked, my throat dry.

Viola shook her head. "Some foreigner, and anyway, she was killed too. It's rather a sad little tale, isn't it? The anarchist son making trouble for his aristocratic family. I would like to have known more about the girl. Anyway," she brushed the entire country and its political problems away with a cloud of smoke from her husband's cigarette, "this land must be full of tragic tales. I met an American who was going to write a funny book about Spain. Along the lines of *1066 And All That*. Have you read it?" I nodded. "Well, first of all he had to learn about the people, so he

88

read all the history books and at the end he decided there was nothing funny about the Spaniards, and the book never got written."

Perry laughed and patted his wife's shoulder. "She exaggerates."

I tried to summon a smile and could not. I rose. "I do owe you an explanation," I said, "and I am going to give it to you, just as soon as I can get a friend of mine here."

They looked up at me expectantly. "I have to go," I said. "Is it all right?"

"Any friend of yours is a friend of ours," said Perry in his lovely, expansive way. "Take my car."

I felt a lump come into my throat. "Thank you, but I haven't got an International Drivers' Licence." I had, but I had no intention of appearing at *El Regalo del Rey* in the easily identifiable Ballisat car. I was touching dynamite and if I had to be blown up I had no intention of taking my friends with me.

12

It was Alonso who met me at the door. His mouth fell open and he stared at me with saucer eyes. Had the circumstances warranted it, I might have laughed. Instead, I watched his back with apprehension as he shot inside.

It was not Felipe behind the desk. A stranger with a coarse and sallow skin, a thick bull neck and pouncing eyes watched my approach with vibrant concentration. "Is Don Lazaro here?"

He shook his head. "Don Lazaro has had an accident. Do you wish for a room, Señorita? I have taken over as administrator."

"No thank you," I replied. "I came to see him. Could you please tell me where he is?"

"I think it is possible he has gone to his uncle in Madrid." And again: "You would like to take a room?"

"I have not come to stay."

The man rose. "If you would care to step into the lounge," he said smoothly, "perhaps I will find him."

I did a double take. "But you said he is in Madrid."

"I mean, I will telephone and Don Lazaro may wish to return." He came forward as though to examine me more closely, his eyes leaping in a disturbingly urgent fashion from my person to the door as though in search of luggage he could confiscate.

I moved away, feeling chilled. "Thank you. I will call

another time." I went swiftly back to the taxi and climbed in. Perry had said Felipe was here so there was only one thing for me to do. Try to get into the palace by the back way, for I could scarcely stand at the big doors ringing the bell whilst this man or Alonso looked on. I watched out of the rear window until we had moved beyond the first archway and out of sight of the parador.

"*¡Para!*" It was one of the useful Spanish words I had learned during my stay with the Ballisats. The man braked and I opened the door. What on earth was 'wait'? *Pausa?* It seemed too easy, but some English words were very similar. "*Pausa,*" I said hopefully.

The driver nodded. "*Sí, sí.*" He leaned his head against the car door, closing his eyes. Any time, it seemed, was time for a Spaniard to doze. I ran up the dry grass slope, turned the corner of the wall, then sped over the rough ground down the side and across the back. I stopped, panting, at the little gate. It was unlocked. My hands tightened on the cool metal as I pushed it open, then hesitated as memory came clamouring back, dragging at my feet, drawing the dark vine around me, tugging the muscles of my throat against life and breath. If I turned my head away from that summer house, looming like a ghastly threat on the corner ahead ... I tiptoed along the path as though there were ears in the evil of that contorted mess of neglected vine and my heart nearly stopped when a voice said peremptorily: "Miss Cole!"

I swung round on a gasp.

"It does seem," commented Antonia's son, "that you are not easy to get rid of." Felipe was standing beneath an arch of green doorway, a newspaper in his hands, an expression of sheer incredulity on his handsome face. All the tension, all the fear fell away then and I came up to him, my heart and mind full of recognition and a tortured sort of love and sympathy. He was wearing a pair of neatly pressed trousers in a minute black and white check, a blue silk shirt open at the neck and a narrow, crocodile skin belt. Only perhaps because all my friends wear tatty old jeans and are never very tidy when they relax, I had a tentative and unnerving intuition of his acting the part of the son of the house. I should have remembered: Every man a king.

"I came here to see you."

His eyes flickered with something like amusement then he said sardonically: "Don't bother, Miss Cole. I will telephone my uncle, since it is his affair, and you may talk to him." He came a step nearer, within reaching distance, and I saw his hand was ready. "This time, I assure you, I will not be so careless."

At the word 'uncle' I had taken an involuntary step back. The new administrator had said: "His uncle in Madrid." His clothes ... his air of belonging in this, the palace garden ... I scarcely felt his grip on my arm. I said in disbelief: "Your *what*?"

"I beg your pardon, Miss Cole."

"You will telephone your—"

"The Count is my uncle."

I put a hand to my forehead. My head was swimming. So he had known all the time that Carlos was his father! Shock jerked me free of his restraining hand. What on earth had I got myself into? Some mind-bending plot hatched by Carlos' son and his brother, to keep Carlos out of the way? If this was so, I had to turn and run. I had to get out of here somehow. There was a noise close at hand and I jumped like a startled deer, but it was only some small animal scurrying through the long grasses at my feet. "Come on, Miss Cole."

"No!" I swung aside and sprang back to the path, avoiding Felipe's grasp by a hair's breadth, feeling the touch of his fingers as they grazed my shoulder, knowing the gate was shut, knowing I could not get away, yet running like a mad thing, wanting a miracle to save me from my folly, my nightmare.

In the event, Felipe with his long legs and swift stride

92

caught me before I reached the gate. He turned me round and stood looking down at me with a reluctant sort of compassion. "You are my uncle's business, Miss Cole, and I have promised to ring him and leave him to question you, but I must confess curiosity is getting the better of me. You did say you came to see me."

I was truly caught. The sharpness of fear went, to be replaced by a sickening acceptance of destiny. "There's not much point in talking to you now," I said, "since you're in it together. Just tell me one thing. I'll admit it's none of my affair, but I've come a long way and got myself into this. What have you done with Carlos?" I saw a sudden flinching in his eyes, a tightness round the well-cut mouth. He gave me a little push and I went back up the path. "Okay," I said despairingly, "don't tell me. I don't really give a damn. Carlos can roast in Hell, if that is what you want for him. He's not my business. You'll concede me that." I paused and he nudged me on again. "Why not just put me on a plane? I'll give you my absolute guarantee never to set foot in this dreadful country again, and never to mention anything of this to anyone."

I stopped so I could turn to look up at him. We were standing at the corner where the summer house lay. One more step and I would be on the straight path to the palace entrance, and the telephone. But he was not looking down at me. And neither was he holding my arm. His eyes were on the summer house where everything had so nearly finished for me. Someone had begun to cut the creeping vines and thick-stemmed roses from the overgrown seat. Felipe said in a strained but tightly controlled voice: "Would you care to sit down here for a moment?"

I would have given anything to say: No, not there, but obeying him meant staying away from the telephone and keeping Ernesto from the knowledge that I was here, a sitting duck. I went uncertainly over to the cleared seat. On it lay a book and a pair of sunglasses. A hacksaw and secateurs lay on the ground. Felipe stayed in the doorway.

93

His face was a mask but his eyes were infinitely disturbed. Someone had to speak and surprise was getting the better of me. "It is being cleared, after all? This summer house?"

He gave himself a little shake as though breaking a distant train of thought. "When nobody came back to finish the job I made a start but I was feeling shaky after the accident and had to give up." He leaned against the framework at the entrance, all aggression gone, and with a puzzled frown on his face. The neat hair fell softly forward on to his brow, giving him a boyish, vulnerable look.

"Who cleared the seat?" I asked, my mind skating back over what had been said, trying to find an explanation for this sudden change in him.

"I suppose one of the gardeners. Who else?"

Who else, indeed? Our eyes met, at the same moment as I realised Felipe's voice held a careful, straightforward question. I sat up straight, not on a spear thrust of hope. The feeling was too faint for that. But there was something. I said: "I think your uncle cleared this summer house himself."

"I never knew him tackle such work." But Felipe's words were not a denial.

"He did not want me in the palace, perhaps because of those large windows."

"Oh?"

"Anyone in the gardens or the olive grove might see a movement behind them. And your uncle was supposed to be in Madrid." He went on looking at me with that waiting air. "I am neither a thief nor a tart," I said.

"No," he replied. "I realise that. You gave me quite a shock, Miss Cole, when you said Carlos could roast in Hell. Have you come from him?"

So! I had a question from him, and until I answered it, I held the whip hand. I knew, with total certainty as one knows these things, that Felipe had nothing to do with, knew nothing about, Ernesto's attempt to murder me. This might be the chink in his armour and my way of escape if

94

I could convince him of the truth. "Before I answer that, I want to ask you a question," I said. "Do you know anything about a plant called the ordeal bean of Calabar?"

Felipe frowned. A thin, tortoiseshell cat came creeping through the bushes outside and peeped warily in. A brown butterfly made a fluttering, suicidal landing on a leaf and the killing paw struck. I looked away swiftly.

"Yes, my uncle brought one back from Guinea. It is growing—" Felipe turned, raised his hand to point, then allowed it to fall to his side. "It must have died. Pilar will be glad." He seemed to be speaking less to me than to himself. "She did not want him to plant it."

I looked out between the curling vines. Where the plant had been there was only a slight disturbance in the soil. "What was he doing in Guinea?" I asked.

"He went there to do a job for the Government. The Republic of Equatorial Guinea used to be Spanish."

"Why would he bring back such a plant? It is not attractive enough for the flower garden, and since it is poisonous, one would scarcely put it among vegetables."

Felipe did not reply at once and I had a queer feeling this was a question he had asked himself. At last he enquired: "What are you getting at, Miss Cole?" He said it quite straightforwardly, as the mask slid away. *What are you getting at? Just between you and me, I mean.* I knew I could tell him then, if I chose my words carefully. He had not come over to my side, but the cord between Ernesto and himself was not pulled tight.

"It is true, what I told you that morning, that I received an invitation from the Countess to come here via the back gate, but hindsight tells me it was written by your uncle. If you would care to show me some of his handwriting, I could tell. He gave me a drink here, where I am sitting now. The drink was drugged."

"This is a very serious accusation you are making, Miss Cole."

My mouth was dry. "I am afraid I am about to make a

95

much more serious one. By a very cunning bit of skull-
duggery, your uncle persuaded me to eat a mess of beans
from that plant which he has since uprooted."

Felipe's face was parchment white. "But why would my
uncle wish to harm you?"

"I will explain."

"Would you be prepared to tell your story to the police?"

That shook me. The Spanish police were not on my chosen
agenda. I wanted to say No, I would much rather go home,
for it was not up to me to see a Spanish killer put away
after I had got clear with my own life. *Foreign killers in
foreign countries are none of my affair, Felipe, although
you'd never know it from the idiotic way in which I have
busy-bodied my way in here.* But I had to say Yes, or he
would not believe me now. I chose a middle path. "I've
no proof," I said.

"Then why should I, or anyone else, believe you?"

There was a sort of proof I had not wanted to think about.
"I don't know if you went up to that room. If you did you
will know I was sick on the floor," I said. "I brought up
the beans. He told me, you see, when I became crazy with
thirst, that that was the way I might save my life. He said
water would either spread the poison swiftly through the
system, or make the victim sick. So he could not give me a
drink—in case I brought the beans up. I must have been
unconscious when he took me up to the room so I scarcely
remember anything else, but I have a faint recollection, like
a dream, of searching for water. It was in my unconscious,
or half-conscious mind, that I had a fifty-fifty chance if I
could get some water." The fevered memory brought beads
of perspiration out on my forehead. I wiped a hand across
it, and my voice trembled unconsciously as I went on. "He
really liked telling me there was a way out, but I could not
have it. I remember I was very angry about that. Scared
at the thought of dying, but perhaps I was more angry, and
perhaps it was the anger that gave me the impetus to live,
because that is what I remember, this determination to beat

96

him by finding water. And it was there. I must have recognised the feel of the cold base of the wash stand when I was crawling round the floor. My legs had been paralysed by the poison. That was the first sympton, Ernesto told me. I must have dragged myself up by my arms and turned the tap on and got my drink. The water was still running when I came to. And I had been sick on the floor."

"Would you be willing to have that—the vomit—analysed?"

"Of course. It is the proof, isn't it?" I added, trying to laugh about it: "The Count said, if the victim was innocent, the natives reckoned he would bring the beans up. Well...?"

Felipe said: "I thought you had too much to drink. I cleaned it up myself."

So there was no proof, now! My heart sank. "Are you going to believe me, then?"

He did not reply but I thought he felt it was in Ernesto to do this. He had not known his uncle all those years for nothing. He turned away. I watched him go along the overgrown path to where the bean plant had been growing. He stood looking down at the brown earth from which the root had been removed. Oddly, it did not occur to me then to try to run away. He came back and said to me in a queer, harsh voice: "Tell me why you came here."

I had shocked him into accepting the fact that Ernesto was a murderer. Something he had not known. I had given myself a chance of sorts. I was certain, in my own mind, that Felipe was basically a decent man. It was time to move ahead. To talk of Carlos, if Felipe was willing, and through this to somehow find a way of persuading him to allow me to go free. I said gently: "I came on an errand from your mother."

"Who has been dead for many years," Felipe replied. "If your passport is correct, the date of birth, I mean, then she died before you were born." He did not believe me, this time. Not one word. "I have a very excellent mother in the Dowager Countess de Merito. The other one did no more than produce

97

me and abandon me in a foreign country."

"That's why you don't like the English, isn't it?"

His mouth tightened. For the first time I saw very real vulnerability in this man. "All right," I said gently, "I suppose that was scarcely fair. But I assure you she did it for the best. In what appeared, at the time, to be in your best interests, I mean."

"My best interests," he replied, "were served by the kindly priest who brought me here."

A kindly priest! I said carefully: "Then when you say the Count is your uncle, you are merely using a courtesy title? If you were brought here by a priest, then the Count is no relation." Those blue eyes were brighter than the Spanish sky and there was alarm in them, and a burning look of half-knowledge touched with fear. "I thought, when you said Ernesto de Merito was your uncle, that you must have been adopted by his brother. You do know about him. You asked me if I had come from him. From Carlos?"

Felipe's intent expression told me he knew there was more behind my words than in them. He said without taking his eyes from my face: "I never met Carlos. I was adopted by his parents about the time he died. I believe the family took me to fill the gap he left." There was a waiting air to him, almost as though he knew some bizarre key was about to turn upon his past. In that moment when our eyes met and held, for the first time totally without hostility, I felt Antonia's ghost pass between us on a sigh. I said softly: "Carlos is, or was, your father, Felipe."

Felipe's relief somehow dispossessed him of everything I had seen in him before: arrogance; conceit; confidence. They slid away and I said to myself: *He somehow was aware.*

"I had a sort of proof," I said, "a letter from your mother, but your uncle stole it. Your mother did not die until a month ago. Thinking you were well looked after, she left you with your father's family so that you might inherit the title and the property. She married my father a long time later." I told him briefly about Antonia's hearing on her

98

honeymoon that Carlos was alive, and how she had worried about the child. "I came here to check on her behalf and seeing Damian in the car I assumed he was you. Thinking your uncle was Carlos, I spoke to him. That is why I was poisoned," I finished.

Felipe did not move a muscle, but I knew intuitively that his heart was racing. I knew because Antonia took shocks like this, with darkened eyes and hardened mouth. "You suspected this," I said. "In some way, you were aware."

He did not speak for a long time and then at last he said: "Once, I thought I knew. Damian, my cousin, also."

"Ernesto's son?"

He nodded. "It's a long story." And he was not going to tell it now, I could see. Well, there were more important issues.

"Who is the new administrator?"

"His name is Quiroga."

"Was he here before your accident?"

"He came that day."

"Do you think he could possibly have tampered with your car? He looks the sort of man who would kill his own grandmother for a few pesetas. Does it occur to you that Ernesto might have hired him to kill you in case I returned later?"

"Yes," said Felipe quite straightforwardly. "Yes, I think, considering all the circumstances, that you could be right."

"Tell me how it happened."

"I was going into town, but my car would not start. Quiroga said he knew something about engines. He came out with me, then sent me back into the office to pick up a parcel that was to be delivered to a place just over the San Martin bridge. That is how I happened to be on that steep road. When I returned with the parcel he had the car going and away I went." Felipe paused. "I shall have to get Ernesto down here, but not for the reason I wanted him before."

I suppose if one has lived with a man all one's life it would be difficult to suddenly accept the fact that circumstances could arise making him an enemy and a murderer. I could understand Felipe's hurt, his disbelief, his desire for a confrontation, his longing, perhaps, for Ernesto to come up with an explanation that would exonerate him.

"Don't underestimate Ernesto, Felipe," I said. "His entire future depends on getting you and me out of the way. He can shoot us right here in the palace garden, if he wants to. He's got the whole of Spain in which to hide our bodies."

He thrust his hands down into his pockets and took some steps across the interior of the summer house, turned and came back, head high, an aggressive, not a frightened man. "Run and hide? Where would that get me?"

"You won't get anywhere without arming yourself with a few facts," I said. "You're never going to get the truth out of your uncle. You have to find out for yourself what happened to your father. You know the artist, Perry Ballisat?" He nodded. "He and his wife have invited me to stay. They said I might bring you back. Why not come there with me, now, and draw breath? For all we know, Ernesto might even now be on the way here, because Quiroga, come to think of it, might have telephoned him when I turned up." I was suddenly very frightened. "Please come with me."

He said, as though any excuse would do for prevarication: "My car is at the bottom of the Tagus."

"But my taxi is waiting."

He stood looking thoughtfully down at me. At last he said: "We might go off into the town and get some lunch. It will give me time to think, anyway. I'll get a jacket."

"Where from?" I asked apprehensively, remembering he slept in the parador.

"From the office."

"I wish you wouldn't go there. Couldn't you creep out the back way with me?"

"No." I took it from the way he said No, quite categorically, that Felipe did not creep anywhere and made a note to choose my words more carefully in future.

13

HE ESCORTED ME to the little gate then went back alone towards the parador. I hurried round to the taxi, climbed into the back seat and made signs to the driver to wait. *"Pausa, gracias."*

Felipe came strolling through the big archway no more than five minutes later as casually as though he had not a care in the world. I had the door open and he slid in beside me.

He gave the man directions in Spanish then said to me: "You were right. Quiroga asked me where I was going and when I said into town he suggested I stay as my uncle was coming."

"What did you say?"

"That my business was rather urgent."

"He didn't mention me?"

"No."

We sat side-by-side in silence while the car sped down to the road. "Where did you learn your English, Felipe?"

"The de Meritos always have English nurses for their children, and an English tutor before school. We talk English a great deal in the family. Then at thirteen we go to school in England. It has always been done."

I said: "You were brought up totally as family, then?"

He gave me a twisted look, full of bitterness. "It is a pretty complicated crime."

It was indeed. "And by the way, where does the name Lazaro come from? Don't adopted children usually take on the parents' name?"

"That's right. It is the family name. My uncle is Ernesto Lazaro, El Conde de Merito. You have the same system with the nobility of England."

"Ah yes, of course," Ernesto had been prepared to live alongside his nephew right up to the moment when his own position was jeopardised. But what of the Dowager Countess whom Felipe thought of as mother? "Felipe, I have been wondering about your grandmother. She lives here, too."

In silence, he turned his head away. My mind turned unhappily to the little I knew of the Spanish. They were supposed to be kind to children. Did they feel less attached to that same child as he grew older? I remembered the story of Colonel Moscardo, the hero of the Alcázar, and his son. The boy was sixteen when he had been told to die like a hero so that the father might realise his own dream.

"Back in the summer house, you said you and Damian thought you knew about Carlos. What did you mean?"

"I will tell you. Not now. Perhaps over lunch." We swept out of the drive and turned into the olive-skirted road, the chickens from the gate house scattering and squawking as they ran. "You know, I find it very difficult to believe that my father should be alive and not trying to return after all this time. Many Spaniards who were in political trouble went to Mexico and South America after the Civil War and have never returned. That is a possibility, but a man of Carlos' type isn't going to stay in hiding around here for half a lifetime. And there is the situation of Ernesto assuming the title. I was ten when I knew Carlos to be alive, but my grandfather had the title then. He died when I was seventeen. Ten years ago."

Ten years ago, two years after the headlines saying Carlos was alive and Ernesto's visit to the Basque country, after which he was sufficiently confident to assume the title. I tried to remember what he had said when I asked him about his brother. The drug had been taking effect at the time and I may have got the facts mixed. I said: "I wouldn't guarantee to have it right, but I think your uncle told me he went to investigate when there was news that Carlos was stirring up trouble among the Basques and found him in a town with a very Spanish name that I would never recall, but I believe I remember what he said. That there was an accident. And then he said something about Carlos not being in a position to inherit. I thought he must have meant Carlos died. Yes, that's right, I asked if he had died in the accident. Ernesto just gave me a strange look."

In the shaded taxi Felipe turned to me and his face was alive with hope. "I know Ernesto. If he knew Carlos was dead, he would say so. Anyway, in this particular context it would be foolish to hide it."

"What do you suppose he meant, then, that Carlos was not in a position to inherit?"

"It's something we have to find out." Felipe spoke to the driver and a moment later we turned off the road, then began to climb up a slope that led northwards.

"Where are we going?"

"Over the San Martin bridge. It's a little early for lunch. I thought I would show you what happened to my car."

I stifled a shudder, thinking bleakly that I was responsible for that wreck and had Fate alone to thank for Felipe's miraculous survival. We sat quietly each with our own thoughts and a moment later swung over a high corner to see the gothic steeples of the town, slate-grey against a sun-bright sky, the apricot roofs below, and in front the Tagus swirling lazily round a bend where the cliff side rose sheer from the gorge. Felipe gestured to the driver and he pulled over to the side. He was curious, too. He came and stood beside us, firing staccato questions at Felipe, waving his arms in excitement.

Below us where the river broke from smooth silk to white lace froth the wreck of that small blue car lay half-

103

submerged. "Just think," said Felipe, tight-lipped. "I could have been part of that."

"I have suddenly become a fatalist," I said shakily. "One can only assume that you and I were not meant to die this week."

He turned, put a hand on my shoulder, looked down into my face and gave a lovely deep-throated burst of laughter. "You've brought me luck. I'll take you to my favourite bar to celebrate."

"I nearly brought you death," I retorted, "and I've no intention of doing it again. Isn't your favourite bar the place where Ernesto or Dracula Quiroga would come to look for you?"

His eyes glinted and he said with a lilt to his voice: "You may have been right about our getting shot in that enclosed garden, but no one is going to shoot us in a bar."

I said a little unhappily: "You like danger, don't you, Felipe?"

"Me? Danger?" My question seemed to amuse him. "Oh no!" He put an arm lightly across my shoulders. "This is a very historic spot where I so nearly said goodbye to everything." He gave me a queer, strained look. "Perhaps the unhappy ghosts down there didn't want me horning in on their martyrdom."

"What do you mean?"

"Way back, in 1405 I think, the locals dragged all the Jews they could find down to that bit of promenade opposite, slit their throats and threw them to those rocks below; then in the Civil War, Republican hotheads from Madrid rounded up all the Conservatives they could find and slaughtered them on the same spot."

I was shocked. "Why are you telling me this?"

He said, sounding vague and strange: "I just want you to know history tends to repeat itself in Spain."

"Is that a warning?"

"I am trying to be fair because I am about to ask you to stay and see this thing through with me."

I felt my stomach seize up with fright. I stared blindly down into the river where an angry swirl of brown waters hit a man-made dam and feathered out downstream, white as a bride's bouquet. He touched my elbow and together we moved back to the car.

Waiting at the traffic-lights for the single stream of traffic to come from the town, we were silent, my mind full of fear and indecision. Then he spoke, his voice brisk as though to take my thoughts from words he suddenly regretted. "Look out of the back window when we have crossed and you will see the Toledan coat-of-arms, two seated kings, given to us by the Emperor Alphonse II." Our eyes met. "All right, I'll put you on a train after lunch, if you really want to go," Felipe said gently, but he put a hand over mine and held it there.

We had a drink in a tiny bar in a narrow street where the barman greeted Felipe with a shout of pleasure and a handshake. We moved to a quiet end. "What sort of life have you had, Felipe? Were you happy as a boy?"

"Yes," he replied in his straightforward way. But there was nothing straightforward about his not wanting an Englishwoman to stay in his parador. I put aside my curiosity out of fear of touching that deep wound. In the event, he brought the subject up himself.

"I am sorry," he said, "about treating you the way I did when you wanted a bed. I'll tell you why. It doesn't amount to an excuse, I am afraid. You see, I thought I was an Englishman. I thought this girl, my mother, had come, pregnant, to Spain, and abandoned her English child in a foreign country. I never felt Spanish, until today, and I hated my mother for removing me from my heritage. Now I know Carlos was my father, it's quite different. It's like having a weight lifted off me. I told you Damian and I went to school in England. That clinched my Englishness. Damian used to feel a foreigner, but I did not. I loved England. I wanted to go back and live there. No, I don't dislike the English. But a lone English girl in Toledo struck me as

105

one of these repetitions of history I mentioned before. Think about it as a reaction from my own past. Why would a girl come here by herself and stay miles out of town without any transport? In some way I felt you were up to no good."

He rocked his glass one way then the other, and shrugged his shoulders expressively. Either Felipe was more Spanish than he knew, or else he was trying out his new native feelings. The sudden knowledge of being heir to an ancient Spanish title must be heady stuff indeed. We left the bar and he led me through high-walled streets and passageways, past enclosed gardens full of dusty pots of violets, a spider plant, Christmas roses, hydrangeas and once a startling red tulip standing high beside a huge clump of butter-yellow primroses. We went down a cobbled lane past a large black wrought-iron grille, illogically grand for the mean little dwelling it protected. There were windows covered by sacking, a torn green blind, a lace curtain, a tall lilac fragrant with flower and the grey skeleton of an ageing grape. Then there was a great stone arch, a courtyard and beyond that heavy wooden doors.

"This is a very good restaurant, and we can get a table here where we can talk," Felipe said. His rising pride had switched to a mood of gravity. He said, excusing himself: "I was a little drunk with shock for a while. It isn't going to be any fun."

No, it was not. There had never been any doubts in my mind about that.

There was a beamed ceiling in the restaurant and white stucco walls. Two steps led up on the right to a small open dining area for the owner's family, and a fat mamma was at that moment ecstatically embracing two small children who had rushed in from school. The floor was a pattern of marble pieces inter-set with stone. There were heavy, coarse linen curtains on the windows, brightly embroidered with cocks and stylised flowers. The head-waiter knew Felipe. We were shown to a table partially obscured from the rest of the room by a tall pot plant. "This will do very well," said

Felipe. "Please sit down, Miss Cole."

"Don't you think, under the circumstances, you might call me Suzanne?"

We looked across the table at each other and his eyes twinkled. "My mother was your stepmother. I don't think it makes us relations, but it could make us very good friends." It was not the most flattering comment that had ever come my way. Still, I thought, flipping a lock of rather clean and shining hair forward where he might notice it, I had to concede there was a good deal on his mind. "We'll talk about my mother some other time. Not now. She belongs to the past. But my father may belong to the present. Let's go into the background and see if we can come up with anything concrete."

"Let's start with your job. You haven't told me how Dracula came to take over the parador."

"I never wanted to work here," Felipe told me. "I had other plans. The family part-owns iron mines at the foot of the Sierra Nevada with the plain on one side and the great mountains on the other. I went there often as a boy. Damian and I used to ride up into the passes. There are wonderful horses there, half-Arab, half-Andalusian."

I said dryly: "Was it the work, or the horses and the countryside?"

He laughed. "Maybe that is why Ernesto kept prevaricating. Maybe he realised I would be out hunting or trekking all the time. Anyway, when I came down from the university in Madrid and suggested I go to Granada—that is where the offices are—he looked at me in astonishment. He said if he had known that was my ambition he would have kept a place for me."

"Had you not talked about it before?"

"Well, yes and no. He knew it was something I had always wanted. But he seemed surprised," said Felipe, looking puzzled, even now, at the memory. "He seemed to have forgotten. I was angry at first and I protested. Then he suggested I take over the parador, but I refused. Looking

107

back," he commented thoughtfully, "it is rather interesting. He went on a good deal about discipline, and doing what the family wanted, and so on. I remember thinking he was being tough with me because he didn't know what was in my forebears. But of course that was it. He *did* know, and that was why he was so tough. He must have been intent upon squeezing out any rebellious instincts I may have inherited from my father."

"And so what did you do?"

"I went off to Paris for a while, and Madrid, and even London for a spell, but without my uncle's blessing. Anyway, I didn't like any of the jobs I took so I came back and asked about the mines again. He suggested I take over the parador. Though it meant giving in and I hated the idea, I thought if I was on the spot for a while I might be able to talk him round."

The waiter came and Felipe translated the menu for me. "Are you adventurous?"

"No," I replied, thinking of the partridge.

"How about Gazpacho, then? Cold vegetable soup that couldn't offend even the most delicate English palate."

I nodded. "I don't want you to think I am difficult to please but—"

He stopped me with a peremptory little movement of the hand and a short laugh. "I know, I know. Don't forget I went to school in England. You shall have something that is light on oil, looks exciting and won't give you a tummy ache. Leave it to me."

Smiling, I agreed. "So, what about Dracula?"

"Oh yes. The day you disappeared, Ernesto brought up the subject of my work. Was I settling down, and so forth? I said I hated it, and to my astonishment he said there were to be some changes in the Granada business and if I was still interested he would look into it. The next day he telephoned from Madrid to say this chap Quiroga had experience of running hotels and was looking for a job. I was to show him the ropes, and Ernesto and I would drive down to Granada later in the week when Quiroga had settled in."

I picked up a hard little bread roll and broke off the end. "Later in the week you were supposed to be dead."

"So it seems." The wine arrived and Felipe tasted it. The restaurant was filling up, but the giant pot plant that stood between the other tables and ours ensured there was little chance of anyone overhearing us.

"Tell me, Felipe," I ventured when the waiter had gone, "what was Ernesto's explanation for my sleeping in that room which has been out of use for years?"

"He said he was just as bewildered as I was. Of course I always knew he brought women in when Pilar was away, but he uses his own room on the ground floor. It didn't make sense to me, to suddenly have you up there where the rooms hadn't been aired for years, and with nothing but a cover on the bed."

"That is what made you think I was a thief?"

He nodded. "And so, of course, I had no hesitation in telephoning him."

I suppressed a shiver. "How long would it have been before I was discovered?"

"Who knows? The staff don't go up there for quite long periods. There is no cleaning to be done."

"There would have been a hue and cry about a missing person."

"Yes. But why would anyone think to search the palace? He was really very safe indeed. It would be too late for conjectures by the time you were found."

"He is a man who takes chances, isn't he, Felipe?" The waiter brought our Gazpacho. Cold vegetable soup that tasted divine, all pink with tomato and dainty with a mysterious sprinkled green on top. "I mean, it is sheer tight-rope walking —having women in to sleep in one's own home, then his admitting to me the truth about Carlos and Antonia, then telling me water could make me vomit. Or was it cruelty? He really enjoyed telling me I was right at a time when I could not use the information." I was trying to close the gate between

Felipe and his uncle. I was afraid for him to face up to Ernesto.

"Yes," said Felipe. "He is a tight-rope walker. And that is why I was so excited when you told me he didn't actually say my father was alive. It would be like him to play such a game."

"You mean he would get the same sort of kick out of living with you and keeping Carlos somewhere, say a prisoner, as he got from telling me water could make me ill, then putting me into a room with a hand-basin?"

"Perhaps," Felipe conceded uncomfortably. "On the other hand, every bedroom in the palace has a tap. If he wanted your body or your skeleton to be found eventually in a bedroom, he had to take that chance. It was hardly a chance, anyway, if you were unconscious. He didn't even lock the door. The likelihood of your coming to must have been very remote. What he was not counting on was a miracle, or your tremendous will to live. No one could tell about that. Or as you suggested, Fate."

"He couldn't lock the door from the outside," I said. "It had to look as though I went there of my own accord."

14

"SPANIARDS DON'T EXPECT foreigners to understand about the Civil War. It was a mess by the standards of classic wars, with everyone fighting everyone else and each section with a cause of its own. Any excuse would do for blood letting," Felipe said. His voice had the sharp thrust of stinging anger and I felt he was thinking for the first time that as a true Spaniard the blood of Spain touched his hands, too. "Watching the war from the outside, the family came to recognise that General Franco was the right man to draw the warring factions together and the only person who was likely to restore peace. They sensibly went over to support him. Later, the old Count—" his eyes gleamed and his face softened with affection as memory flooded through him—"my honest-to-goodness grandfather, that is, took high office with *El Caudillo*'s Government, but I always understood it was no thanks to his eldest son that this came about. Carlos had remained a Republican."

I was looking for excuses for him. "Perhaps Carlos had become indoctrinated by the local point of view during the family's exile in Basque France."

Felipe shrugged. "He was pretty young at the time."

We were silent, each with our own thoughts. Then: "He must have been kind," I said. "He looked after Antonia when she was in trouble."

"Yes, didn't he!" Felipe agreed dryly, "And I am here to prove it."

The waiter came and took our plates away. "Perhaps Antonia was not so keen on him, in the end," I said thoughtfully. "There had to be a reason for her concern about you once she heard your father was alive."

"What woman wants her son brought up an anarchist? It was probably just that."

I was comforted by the thought. "Is it possible Ernesto put the bomb on that bus? Could he have been a killer even all those years ago?"

"You mean so that he could inherit in my place? There's a hurdle you haven't seen. My grandparents."

I was baffled by their part in it and so, I felt, was he. "That was your grandmother, I presume, in the car with Damian the morning after I arrived?"

"Yes."

I wanted to ask him if he felt she could be a party to such a plot, but his brow was clouded and: "I have a very excellent mother in the Dowager Countess de Merito," he had said. He put his elbows on the table, his chin in his upturned palms. "Did you ever put a stick in a wasp's nest?" he asked.

I shook my head.

"I did it once. I was just remembering."

"You're thinking it might be better to remain Señor Don Felipe Lazaro?"

"Yes," he said quite definitely. "Yes, I think it might be better. But it's too late. An attempt has been made on my life." He said with a sharp lift to his voice: "I might get one step nearer to heaven by not stirring up the wasp's nest, but I would certainly go one step back if I ignored the fact that my father might well be alive somewhere. Whatever he has done, he is a human being, and he has done me no harm."

"Tell me the long story you mentioned before, Felipe. You said both you and Damian knew."

"Yes," he said. "I'll tell you, now." He paused because a

112

great black cast-iron bowl was being set between us on the table. Prawns, mussels in their shells, pieces of chicken and lumps of meat, all arranged mouth-wateringly on a bed of saffron rice.

"Heavens! What is that?"

"A sort of national dish. Paella. You won't thank me when I tell you that both Gazpacho and Paella originated from thrifty cooks who used all the leftovers of the week for Sunday lunch." He noted my startled expression and his mouth twitched. "Don't worry. Things have changed. Besides, it isn't Sunday. Here, take this spoon and help yourself while I tell you my true fairy tale.

"There is a secret passage leading from some old store rooms over at the back of the garden at *El Regalo* on the corner where the wall joins the long low building that is really a continuation of the wing opposite the parador. No one goes there these days. There are olive presses and out-of-date machinery all piled in together. It was an interesting place for Damian and me to play as children. Sometimes, in the summer, we slept there. There was plenty of straw lying round." He smiled wryly: "Smoking ourselves dizzy. I suppose we must have spent a dozen or more nights there, over two or three summers. No one ever caught us because we always managed to wake up in time to get back into our beds.

"Then one night my uncle came. We thought he was looking for us so we lay low. He didn't search. He had a torch so he would have seen us if he had shone it round, but he went straight to the opposite corner and levered up a great flat bit of iron from the earth floor. It took him ages and when he had it up he sat down on a stool or something he must have brought with him. We were baffled. It seemed such an odd thing to do. In the end Damian fell asleep and I was on my own. I was just dropping off when I heard voices and my uncle calling softly that it was all right to come up. Three men came in through the hole he had uncovered. One was a very rough fellow they called Goizueta. One was a priest they called Father Eladio—"

113

I caught my breath and Felipe looked at me questioningly. "Viola Ballisat, the artist's wife, knows him. He told her he married Carlos."

"He is still alive?"

"I presume so. She might be able to find him. She said he is very old."

"This man seemed old to me then," Felipe said, "but of course that doesn't mean anything. Anyone over twenty-five is old to a ten-year-old."

"Go on with your story. And the third man?"

"He was Carlos."

"How do you know?"

"They called him Carlos."

"And what was the meeting about?"

"It was more of an argument than a meeting. One of the men said: *You'll see I don't get back,* and my uncle agreed, quite coolly. He said: *Not while Franco is in power. I will kill you first.* And then he added: *We are all safe while you stay out of Spain.* That was what intrigued Damian and me. The fact that we were all safe while this man stayed away. It was quite scary to small boys, and we saw Ernesto as a sort of hero who was going to kill him to ensure our safety. I've remembered those four sentences over seventeen years because Damian and I used them in our war games. They were more dramatic than anything we could invent and they had the romantic authority of having come from an adult."

"Did you speak to your uncle about it? After you grew up, I mean?"

"Damian said he would ask his father one day but before he was old enough we were both aware of the precarious situation of the old families. We knew, without discussing it, the whole thing was better forgotten. But to return to that night. Ernesto and his visitors were arguing about someone called 'the boy'. *Chico.* Suddenly Damian turned over, muttering. He chose his moment badly when there was no one speaking and you can imagine the consternation. They swung a torch over. I shut my eyes, pretending to be asleep, but I

114

heard them come across and then I could hear them muttering to each other.

"I don't know how I pretended successfully to be asleep, but I did. The torch, of course, was not on my face. Then I heard a man's breathing coming nearer, and a little rustling sound in the straw as he went down on his knees. Because he smelled of tobacco, I assumed it was my uncle. He kissed me, and I assumed he kissed Damian, too. Children don't query what appears exceptional to an adult—that my uncle would discover us asleep out there and kiss us. I was only too glad not to be dragged out and punished. It was not until much later that I realised it could have been Carlos kissing me, and as he had to lean over me to kiss Damian, the chances were he had not kissed him. I decided then I could have been *Chico*."

"What is *Chico*."

"The boy. Little boy."

"And you said Damian knew."

"Yes. As an adopted child, naturally I always had my real parents in mind. In some muddled way I knew there was a Carlos somewhere because the Countess spoke of him occasionally when she thought we were not around. Naturally, I assumed the two Carlos' were one and the same. I never told Damian about Carlos kissing me but that summer I fought my battles as Carlos' son against Damian, *El Conde* de Merito's son. By the following summer we had grown out of it."

"And didn't anyone ever overhear?"

"I don't think so. We played war in the outbuildings and the olive grove."

"Perhaps your uncle did know. He may have brought the bean back for you if you should ever prove a problem."

"He has other poisonous plants growing," Felipe replied thoughtfully, staring down at his plate. He had eaten very little. "The Apple of Sodom, for instance. That grows near the Mediterranean coast. He brought it back after a visit to the iron works in the Sierra Nevada. No one could poison anyone with it because of the exceptionally bitter taste."

115

"Might not keeping a collection of poisonous plants be his cover-up for having the useful, tasteless one?"

"Who knows? My aunt made a fuss about this plant when it came up because the flower is rather like that of a runner bean. I remember the argument, and my uncle pointing out that the pod was quite different. He also made the excuse that it would take about thirty to make a fatal dose and one could hardly eat that many out of curiosity."

Felipe pushed his half-empty plate away. "So where does that get us? Oh, by the way, would you like some ice cream or fruit?" I shook my head. "Coffee comes from coffee bars, I am afraid."

"Yes, I have already discovered that. But don't let's go." I felt safe here. By this time Ernesto and his sinister henchman would certainly be looking for us. I did not want to move until Felipe had decided on a plan that did not involve facing up to his uncle. "I'll have an ice cream after all," I said. "Mocha, if you please." I could make that last a while.

"What would Damian's attitude be," I asked, "to your emerging as the Count? I mean, it is usurping him, isn't it?"

"I don't honestly think he would care," Felipe replied. "We are very close. Always have been. He never wanted the *Finca*. He is a financier. He works on the *Bourse* in Paris. But there is something you've forgotten, Suzanne."

Felipe's face was sombre indeed. Of course I had not forgotten that Damian was Ernesto's son and the Dowager, who might be delighted at the resurrection of her eldest child, was also the murdering Ernesto's mother. At last I came out with it. "Do you feel able to ask your grandmother, Felipe?" She had to be safe, for surely a mother and grandmother would not touch blood.

He did not reply but I could see he knew now that this had to be the beginning of the trail back. And I knew that if he offered to put me on that train now, I would not go.

In the event, he did not make the offer. We hired a car and drove straight to Madrid. Felipe said the hour of the siesta would be over by the time we reached the old Countess'

116

flat. I had the impression one did not disturb a Spaniard's siesta.

We drove up a wide street lined with small and very expensive-looking shops. "This is where the big designers are," Felipe told me. "The Prado is over there beyond the most beautiful post-office in the world."

I laughed. "Is that national pride?"

"We'll drive past it later, and you will see."

We did drive by it later. It was grand and exquisite indeed with its fluted marble columns and its statuary, but by then there was too much in our minds and hearts.

"Antonia (your mother? my mother? It seemed wise to say 'Antonia') told me everyone should go to the Prado if only to see *The Adoration of the Magi*."

"Then I shall take you," said Felipe. "Here on our right, is the *Parque Conde de Orgaz*."

"The Count Orgaz who was buried?" It is worth making an idiot remark sometimes. I felt the tension slide out of him and he laughed, too.

"You went to Santo Tomo then?"

I wiped my eyes. It had not been that funny, but perhaps, as a woman, I was even more emotionally disturbed over the coming confrontation than Felipe. A man approaching thirty scarcely needs a mother. I was to find later that a Spaniard, though he may not need one, appreciates her rather more than a young Englishman. "To my eternal shame," I replied, "I went to sleep in front of that picture. The Burial of Count Orgaz."

"Barbarian."

"Yes." We drove into the courtyard of a rather grand block of stone-built flats and went up in a clanking iron lift to the first floor. We had not spoken since we stepped out of the car.

We were shown in by a maid in the kind of neat black uniform dress one does not see in England now, with a little white apron gathered at the waist. She greeted Felipe warmly and showed us into a very grand room with white cherubs

117

flying above the cornice of a high ceiling, a great deal of heavily carved furniture, and rugs in the Moorish style, richly coloured and looking more like coarse tapestry than carpet. Felipe indicated a chair by a window. I sat down. He lit a cigarette, stubbed it out then went to the piano. I did not know what it was he played, only that the music seemed to hold the visions, dreams and longing of his past and that those dark angry chords had to have come from Wagner. He played them with all the intensity and emotion of these last few dreadful days, with anger in his fingertips and a ram-rod back. I sat by myself in the window thinking with rising despair of my own insolent folly that had brought him to this. He must have been happy enough, before, and he had been safe. Heaven alone knew what we were coming upon now.

15

I DID NOT see her come into the room. The music ended on a deafening crash of chords and Felipe swung round on the stool. She was standing in the doorway and my back was half turned to her. "Well, Felipe, my son."

He jumped up and kissed her, then introduced me. "Miss Suzanne Cole, from England."

She was a tall woman with snapping brown eyes set in sockets wrinkled like fine crepe, and hair that was elegant and glossy but, to my English eyes, too black for her years. She stood surprisingly erect, for she must have been over seventy, but when I clasped the hand she held out to me I felt the bones beneath the dry, parchment skin. "I am very pleased to welcome you here, Miss Cole," she said, but her unsmiling eyes were on Felipe and there was anxiety in the set of her mouth. She said: "Tell me quickly, Felipe, and let's have done with it."

He led her to a high-backed chair. "Oh no, *Abuela*, this is not a quick matter."

She said peremptorily: "You know I do not like to be kept waiting for unpleasantness."

I have always been intrigued by the complex study of heredity and environment. Antonia had her signals, too. Whilst Felipe played grand, sad music, his mother would pour us each a glass of wine before breaking bad news.

"Who is Carlos, *Abuelita*?"

The Countess flinched, shot a piercing look at me, then back to Felipe. "But you know very well."

"I am not sure that I do," Felipe replied steadily.

She said: "I really do not think Miss Cole—"

His eyes met hers swiftly with a glimmer of a smile. "Miss Cole—Suzanne—must stay. She is concerned."

"Concerned with *Carlos*?" The Countess's voice rose.

As though needing to hold the moment at arm's length, she said to me: "My eldest son." Her eyes lingered on my face.

I nodded.

"What I need to know," Felipe said, "is whether Carlos ever married."

I saw a flash of fear in those dark eyes, and then she seemed to pull herself together on taut strings. "I do not know," she said in a brittle voice. "At one point I was told he married, but there was no proof."

"No certificate? No church record?"

She knew. The coming of this question had always been an anticipation, lying close beneath the thin surface of her existence. It had come and she was as much prepared for it as she had ever hoped to be. "Ernesto searched," she said simply. "There was no proof." She turned to me. "Please tell me, Miss Cole, why are you here, for this is a very delicate and very private family matter."

Felipe said: "Let me answer. Ernesto put a girl called Antonia on a bus?" The Countess flinched again and to my astonishment I saw tears in her eyes. After nearly thirty years, she could weep! "Antonia, it seems, left that bus. She had second thoughts about me," Felipe went on. "She did not die until very recently. Suzanne is her stepdaughter."

The Countess rose and came shakily towards me. I jumped up to take her hands, astonishment warring with pleasure and dismay. "You must tell me about Antonia. I only knew her for a year. She was a flower in our lives. A lovely English rose. I had been despairing of Carlos. I had said a Novina to Saint Anthony in whom I always had great faith. On the ninth day Antonia came with news of Carlos' death, and carrying his

120

child." The Countess must have seen a blank expression on my face for she said: "You are not a Catholic, Miss Cole?"

"No."

"For a Novina there are nine days of prayer or going to Mass. Antonia came in answer to my prayers. How could I doubt what she said, that the baby was our grandchild? I never knew where she came from or even very much about her, but I loved her like my own daughter. Ernesto knew this, and he knew we needed a child for comfort at that time, so he did not tell me," she looked straight at Felipe, "what he suspected, that there had been no marriage. When she left, he searched for proof and there was none. It is a fact, my dear," the Countess reiterated earnestly, "that there is no record anywhere of Carlos' marriage to anyone. Ernesto was given access to registers, civil and church, but there was nothing."

The old eyes clouded. "Antonia would be forty-nine now," she said with certainty, as though she carried my stepmother's age in her mind, adding on each year as it came, grieving in her heart. "I am glad she had all that time. Twenty-seven more years. Were they happy ones?"

Deeply touched by the power of the old Countess's emotion, I had to swallow hard before I could speak. "I think so. Certainly the last twelve, when I knew her, she was very happy indeed."

"I am glad." She let my hands go and turned to Felipe. "You want to know, at this late date, if you are Carlos' son." It was a statement, not a question, and she was not even looking at him. She went over to one of the big windows and stood gazing down into the courtyard below, that unexpected hair pitch black against the gold of the brocade. Felipe had returned to the piano. He was still as a statue with one hand resting lightly on the polished surface, his eyes on his grandmother's back. Her shoulders lifted, then in the deep silence I heard the long, muted sigh of her breath. She turned to face Felipe. "When you first came I believed you to be my grandson," she said. "Antonia told me she and Carlos were married. Why should I not believe her? Why should I ask for proof?" She spoke defensively as though, ever since, she had blamed herself for not doing so. "Antonia went, suddenly, without saying goodbye, and without leaving an address.

"She had persuaded Ernesto that this was right and he and she arranged it between them. She told him to tell me she had lied about Carlos. That the child was from an English newspaper man who had come over to Madrid on a job. That she had been engaged to marry him but that he had gone off with someone else. She had met Carlos and he told her to offer the child to us, to take his place, if he should be killed. He was killed, and because, Ernesto said, she wanted a good home for the baby, and because she could not go to England and face her family with an illegitimate child, she did as Carlos suggested. She bought a wedding ring and came to me."

"Then why did you tell me I was brought to the *Finca* by a priest?" Felipe asked quietly.

"It was decided that way. Forgive me, *Querido*, but we did not want to tell you the truth. You would not have liked it. And it was painful to us, too. We were very pleased indeed when Antonia came to tell us she carried Carlos' baby and that they had married. Then, when she left and we knew—" The Countess broke off and corrected herself, "—when Ernesto said she had been on that bus and we assumed she was dead, we thanked God we had you. Even after Ernesto told us you were not Carlos' child we thanked God for you. We had lost two children."

Felipe was watching his grandmother closely. I could see he believed she was telling the truth as she knew it. "We brought you up, *Querido*, as our own son, or grandson. You know that. We could not have loved you more. You realise this, don't you?"

"Of course *Mamita*. Only I think you might not have been so quick to believe Ernesto when he said I was not your grandson."

She threw out her hands in a despairing gesture. "There

was no proof! And no resemblance! Felipe dear, in many ways you resemble your dear mother, but I have never really seen anything of Carlos in you. Truly, my dear. I would not say so if it were not so. And Ernesto would not lie. That he should do so is unthinkable. He is my son."

"Perhaps he would lie so that he could inherit," Felipe replied baldly.

I found myself glancing swiftly round the walls, looking for a photograph, but there was no one who could have been Carlos. An old man in a lace cravat, a lady in a crinoline. Pilar and Ernesto in bridal finery. Felipe as an English schoolboy.

"Felipe!" The Countess was saying, truly shocked, "Felipe! That is unworthy of you, and I am very surprised that you should say such a thing."

He said gently: "I am sorry, *Abuela.* Ernesto is subject to the same human aims and weaknesses as the rest of us. Do you think he is an angel?"

"I certainly do not think he is a devil." She said: *Diablo!* but I knew what she meant. "Perhaps you do not remember, it was eleven—twelve years ago—when Carlos was said to have appeared near Burgos. The papers were full of it. Carlos de Merito was said to be leading an uprising."

"I remember," said Felipe quietly. He looked down at the piano, stroked the keys.

"Ernesto rushed to Burgos. Or not Burgos—it was a place called Santo Domingo de la Calzada where Carlos was supposed to be hiding. He was very excited. Oh, *pequeñito,*" the Countess' face was suddenly ravaged with pain, "you hurt me when you say Ernesto would want to take Carlos' place. The eldest son has always inherited, and of course Ernesto accepted that. When it seemed Carlos might be alive we could scarcely eat or sleep for days with the excitement of it. And Ernesto was the same. He acted quickly. He drove straight to Santo Domingo. But it was not so. The anarchists had resurrected our son's name to lend weight to their cause. Ernesto was very depressed on his return. It was a cruel experience. It is unfortunate," the Countess said sadly, "that no one actually saw—" she bit her lower lip and turned her head away. "So many dreadful things have happened in Spain. Where does one find proof of anything?"

There was proof of a kind in the story Felipe had told me of Carlos coming up the secret passage and kissing him, but I could see he had too much compassion to tell of that now. The Countess had been through a good deal. If she had to know about Ernesto's duplicity, then she would know when it was inevitable that the facts be released. It was not inevitable yet.

She turned to me, her eyes moist. The old face looked older now than when I first came in for memory had dragged at the lines. "Tell me about Antonia," she said.

I glanced across at Felipe. He had gone to sit on the edge of a large, heavy brocade chair, his long legs bent, the knees high. He was staring at the carpet between his feet. I wanted very much to say Antonia would not have gone willingly without saying goodbye. Ernesto had more than his attempt on my life and Felipe's to answer for, I was sure.

The old Countess and I talked for five, perhaps ten minutes. Then Felipe stood up with a jerk and said we must go. They spoke briefly of his accident then Felipe said: "Ernesto has told me I may work at the mines. But I have been badly shaken. I would like to go somewhere for a few days."

"Poor boy. And now this! Go to Damian. Paris will cheer you."

"Perhaps."

"I am pleased about the mines. Ernesto told me he did not intend to have any of the family working there. I am glad he has changed his mind. You will have an *apéritif* now?"

"No, thank you. We must be off."

The Countess and I parted with warmth and affection. "Come and see me again, my dear Miss Cole."

"Thank you." My heart was heavy for her.

I could feel Felipe's tension as we stood waiting for the ancient lift. He did not speak but as we came out into the big, elegant hall his energy burst like shock waves, thrusting me along with him as he ran for the entrance and down the steps into the cool evening. The sun had gone but the sky was still light from the city's glow. I looked at him with apprehension across the roof of the car as he unlocked the door. "What are we going to do now?"

"Drive to Santo Domingo de la Calzada. Do you want to come? Or shall I drop you at the airport first?"

Momentarily, I was engulfed by a wave of sheer panic. "I can't go to the airport. I haven't got my luggage," I said idiotically, shying away from the issue.

He grinned. "I wouldn't have made the offer if I hadn't known. Come on." He slid behind the wheel.

"Oughtn't you to think about this for a while?" I asked as I jumped in and looked round for the seat belt.

"Santo Domingo is at the core of things. We can do our thinking there." He pulled out the choke, switched on the engine, put the car into gear.

"Yes, of course. But if Carlos is there and your uncle realises you have disappeared, who knows what sort of trap you're going to step into?"

"Ernesto won't know I have disappeared. My grandmother will tell him I was with her until seven."

But this was madness! I was sitting bolt upright against the leather seat as the car swept out into the traffic then stopped dead against the lights. There was breathing space before he slid into the fast route. I had to think of the right way to stop him, and I had to do it fast. It was too impulsive. I knew well enough it was no use pointing out that he had had an accident and ought to be taking things easy. I was not even certain the fact that this was my own first day on my feet would impress him over-much, but I could try.

"I don't want you to think I am chickening out," I said, "but frankly I feel done. Is there really any advantage in going tonight?"

He looked at me with quick concern, then the lights

changed and the car shot ahead. "It's only about three hundred kilometres," he said.

I calculated swiftly. "A hundred and ninety miles? It seems a very long way in the dark. No dinner, and a midnight arrival. What do we do then? We've no lead."

We swung round an enormous fountain flamboyant with statuary and into a flying stream of traffic, then up a boulevard lined with vast beds of tulips in military rows.

"No, that's the hell of it. But," he added dryly, "where do we get a lead here, short of asking Uncle Ernesto?"

"Where are you going to get one in Santo Domingo? You can't waltz up the main street at midnight yelling: 'Anybody know the whereabouts of Carlos de Merito?' And do you know what he looks like? Your houses seem singularly devoid of pictures of him."

"There are none," agreed Felipe. "Ernesto would see to that, of course. And my grandmother would feel it was hardly the thing to expose a likeness of the family black sheep. Of course," he added reasonably, "one could hardly say to visitors: 'That is my son who was executed ...'"

And then I had an idea. I jerked round in my seat. "Oh Felipe, I've suddenly realised! Pull over! Pull over to the right. You can get out at the next intersection! Remember I told you Father Eladio said he married Antonia and Carlos! Viola Ballisat might know where he lives—" I stopped on a gasp. Felipe had swung the car round at a terrifying angle and we were shooting up a side street. "Lord! If you drive like this all the time it's no wonder your car ended up in the Tagus!"

Only by a faint uplift of his mouth did Felipe show my admonition had registered. He said urgently. "Are you sure the priest is still alive?" He had braked down to a reasonable pace and was cruising back towards the park.

"I don't think the Ballisats have been in Toledo more than a couple of years so he was certainly alive fairly recently. If he came to the palace with Carlos, then the chances are he knew where Carlos came from, and would certainly know his

126

associates." I was suddenly very excited. "Come on, let's get back on to the Toledo road. And please, please try not to drive like a madman. My nerves are sticking out like organ stops already, without that."

Felipe laughed. "Hang on to your seat belt. You don't look like a girl who is scared of a bit of speed."

"I am not. But ..." I stopped, knowing there was no rein that would hold Felipe now. He was on the wings of a dream —or a nightmare. The best or the worst I could do was go along with him and help where I could. And then I remembered that I, too, had been a long way off the ground today. I had forgotten all about the Ballisats.

"Felipe, stop at a bar or kiosk, somewhere with a telephone, will you please? Perry and Viola must be worried out of their minds about me. I left them this morning saying I would bring you back, and here it is nearly dark and I haven't even been in touch."

"You're going to tell them about this?" Felipe's glance was sharp, uncertain.

"I—I did say I would explain on my return. But it's not fair to them, is it? To involve them, I mean."

"The fewer people who know the better."

"Yet we can't find Father Eladio without Viola's assistance. Unless you want to ask some other priest. Do they all know each other? I mean, Toledo isn't such a big place."

We were moving into another traffic lane, dashing between the lights. "That way is slow, and it's public," said Felipe. "I agree that it's not fair to involve the Ballisats, especially when they have been so good to you. And he has occasional contact with my uncle over the painting. It's awkward. I am thinking out the alternative." Felipe was heading up another main road, his foot hard on the accelerator, his face strained. "The trouble is, it's not unreasonable to assume that my uncle is looking for me now. Let's ask your friends," he suggested optimistically, "and see if we can manage to get their help without giving an explanation in return."

16

IT WAS NIGHT in Toledo. The crenellated city walls were just a blur against the sky and the magnificent Gate of the Sun a mere granite tunnel splashed with car lights as we whipped through. Felipe drove as near to the Ballisats' house as the rough cobblestones and width of the road would allow. We locked the car and walked to the blue gate. Viola came in answer to our bell. "Thank goodness!" she exclaimed in very real relief. I introduced Felipe. "The friend you said you would bring?" she asked, her eyes enormous.

"That's right." They shook hands, and she led us with more than one intrigued backward glance across the flagged terrace beneath the trellised vine, then down the steps into the studio. Felipe glanced round in that quick way he had then went over and stood looking at the suit of armour.

"Perry likes it," said Viola defensively.

"And so do I." Felipe gave it a swift, cursory examination. "This is a good one. They're turning out a lot of rubbish now for the tourists. I commend your taste."

Gratified by Felipe's sincere flattery, Viola flushed charmingly. Perry shambled into the room and did a double take when he saw Felipe. Then he grinned. "You said—a friend."

"Felipe is a friend."

"Women," said Perry good-humouredly, "I will never understand. I went down to the Tagus to see your car. Apparently they're not going to haul it up?"

"I dare say they will, for the sake of tidiness if nothing else, but you should know Spain by now. Anything that can be put off until tomorrow will not be done today."

"That's right." Perry looked questioningly at me. "And now? Do sit down, both of you. Can I get you a drink?"

Felipe thanked him.

"Scotch?" asked Perry genially.

"Thank you very much." Our host went to a cupboard in the corner. "What about you, Suzie?"

My head was beginning to ache with the strain. I would have loved a cup of tea but that meant Viola going out of the room to make it. But of course! That was what I must do! Get Viola on her own. "At the risk of being laughed at for being a creature of unbreakable habit," I said wanly, "I need a cup of English tea."

Viola rose to the bait like a hungry minnow. Or so it seemed. I had not reckoned with the fact that she had her questions, too. I caught Felipe's eyes with a warning look as we rose. We went through to the kitchen together and she shut the door then turned to me. "What goes, Suzanne?" she demanded excitedly. "One minute you're telling Perry Señor Lazaro doesn't want you to stay at the parador, then you walk in with the same Señor Lazaro, practically hand-in-hand!"

I picked up the kettle and filled it. "Can I ask you a question first?"

"Sure."

"Where does Father Eladio live?"

She stared at me, her eyes wide and questioning. The kettle began to purr on the gas. Then she said suspiciously: "What are you up to?"

"Something frightfully personal, I am afraid."

She reached for the teapot. "Is it? Is it really? Because I am going to need an explanation. You see, I am responsible for telling you about Father Eladio saying Carlos de Merito was married. That is what it is about, isn't it?"

"I am afraid so. Yes."

"Then I am bound to ask you why you have taken up with their parador manager."

I could have flung my arms round her and kissed her for that gift of safe ground. "Did you not know," I asked innocently, "that Felipe is a member of the family? The Count's nephew."

"Is he?"

"Indeed."

The kettle was boiling. She reached for the tea bags. "I am going to send you a pound of lovely loose tea when I go home," I said.

She laughed. "You may as well not. It sounds rather messy to me. So why do you have to see Father Eladio?"

"Do you mind if I don't tell you, just now? I mean, not until after I have seen him?"

"I don't know," Viola replied unhappily. "I feel so responsible. Perry was right when he told me not to gossip."

"Viola," I said, "Felipe is family. Felipe Lazaro. Lazaro is the family name."

"Is it?" She shrugged. "I don't understand these things. Titles are so complicated. Of course, I don't say I don't believe you. I just wish . . . Couldn't we talk to Perry about it?"

"I'd rather not. Really. Just in case he gets talking to anyone from *El Regalo del Rey* I don't want him to be involved. I want him to be able to say honestly he doesn't know what we are doing. Don't you see it's not fair to involve him?"

"What about me?"

"You're not on chatting terms with anyone from the *Finca*. It's different for you," I said coaxingly.

"But Perry will ask me."

"Couldn't you tell him what we're doing is a secret between you and me for the moment?"

"You said you would tell us when you came back."

"I'll tell you in the morning," I promised in desperation. Heaven alone knew what the morning would bring.

Waiting nervously for her to make up her mind, I lifted the teapot lid and mashed the tea bag absently with a spoon.

"I don't know Father Eladio's address," Viola began reluctantly, "because I meet him sort of accidentally on his walks. He walks where I walk the children."

"Where is that?"

"As regularly as clockwork, he goes down a little path by his house at seven o'clock every morning and again at five in the evening—just as far as a look-out spot on the cliff above the Tagus. He took us—the children and I—back to his house one afternoon and we sat in the garden. But I couldn't for the life of me tell you the address. And it's far too late to meet up with him at the lookout."

"Could you draw me a little map?"

"I suppose so," Viola said. "You had better go in the morning, though. There wouldn't be any street lights."

"We have to go tonight. Perhaps you could lend us a torch?"

She looked at me in silence for a moment, her mouth buttoned up in an expression of worried dismay. "Are you coming back again?"

"Yes. If you will allow me to stay. If you'd rather not—"

"Oh no, no, no. Please, I want you to stay. Don't think I am inquisitive, Suzanne," she said contritely. "But it's my information you're using, and I feel dreadfully responsible."

"I understand." It occurred to me then that I could pack my bag in the morning and take it with me to Santo Domingo, thereby clearing these kind people of any implication in my affairs. I said: "You have been very kind to me, Viola. You and Perry. Don't think I'm not grateful. If it hadn't been for his rescuing me I would be back in England now, leaving this job undone."

"Job?" she echoed.

"You could call it that. And when you hear what it is, I am sure you will be glad you have been able to help."

"Is it concerned with your—the way you turned up here—I mean, looking as though you'd come through a hedge backwards?"

"Yes."

131

Partially mollified, Viola reached up to a shelf for pencil and paper. "I'll draw the map."

We took the cup of tea out into the studio. Perry looked at me questioningly and I smiled guiltily in return.

Felipe was standing with the glass of whisky in his hand. His eyes were startlingly blue in that arrogant face and he was holding himself tall and alert in the oddly dramatic stance, now familiar to me, as though he must be away to greater things. He tossed off the remains of his drink and I found myself gulping my tea, pushed into hurrying by the electric urgency in him. I tried to ignore him. I tried to chat normally but found myself growing more sharply on edge and soon I was making our excuses. Felipe's: "We haven't had dinner, you know," brought forth the dry comment from our host that eight-thirty in the evening was a long way short of the Spanish dining time.

"That was awkward," said Felipe lightly as the big door closed behind us. "You've got the address?" It was difficult to recall, at such a moment, his curious gentleness with his grandmother or the French family who had been in trouble the night I arrived at the parador.

"I've got a map and a torch in my handbag. I hope you don't mind, but I had to promise to tell them in the morning."

"Tomorrow," said Felipe, flinging the day recklessly into the future, "can look after itself."

17

As Viola had warned me, it was dark down here where the cobblestoned streets threaded in and around the cliff-top. The moon had not yet risen and there were few stars. The houses, for the most part, were built close against one another but here a stone wall stood before a low building blackly clouded with trees. We found the path that ran in from the cliff-edge, bordered on one side by an old wall cloaked with some creeping vine and broken here and there to reveal rank grass and weeds. On the other side the bank fell away and when Felipe swung his torch over the slope a little group of cats snaked back from some small carcass, then crouched watching us with green glass eyes. For the most part the slope was rock-strewn and the path unfenced.

"There has to be a better way in than this," I commented as I stubbed my toe for the third time.

"Not necessarily. Some of these old places are very much tucked away. On the other hand, we may be going to a garden entrance. The front of the house may be flush with a street." He slipped an arm through mine. "You'll be all right, so long as the torch battery doesn't run out."

We turned a hair-pin bend, went up a slope, doubled back towards the cliff, then through a very dark tunnel where trees grew overhead, and out once more on a straight track.

We did indeed come to a garden entrance, a small wooden gate, unpainted and overhung with an ancient wisteria vine

133

whose gnarled and twisted trunk ran along the top of a tall stone wall. There was a bell chain that came through a narrow slit in the stone work. Felipe pulled it. "Can't hear a thing. I hope it works." A moment later a light flashed on in the wall above our heads, there was an answering shout and then footsteps on stone and the sound of a key groaning in a lock. The door opened a little way and an old woman peered out at us.

Felipe spoke to her in Spanish. Her thin grey hair was scraped back from a low forehead into a tight little twist at the back of her head, the eyes black currants in a dried skin as wrinkled as crepe. She shook her head in reply to Felipe's question, rattled off a brief answer, then made as if to close the door, but Felipe was too quick for her. With one foot in the opening he spoke to her again, his tone polite and apologetic, but firm. The woman backed away, eyes flashing angrily. I saw now that she wore a black apron, not particularly clean, and grey ankle socks with heavy black shoes.

"She says the priest doesn't see anyone at night," Felipe said, turning to me. The woman was suddenly still, staring at me sullenly and suspiciously, waiting for my reaction.

"What shall we do?"

"It can't wait." He spoke gently, pleadingly, in Spanish and pushed the gate wide. Suddenly and unexpectedly the servant capitulated, locked the gate and marched fussily ahead of us along the path towards the house, scolding us loudly as she went.

"Father Eladio obviously speaks English," I remarked to Felipe, "because Viola's Spanish is pretty limited. Kitchen and marketing variety. It is terribly frustrating not knowing what that woman is saying."

"Mostly abuse."

Someone inside evidently heard our footsteps for a flood of golden light came through a wide window on to a stone terrace pointing up some plain wooden seats, a slat table and a lot of geraniums in leaf-green bud. A heavy wooden door led into an unpretentious little stone house. A man's voice called: *"Qué es eso,* Gertrudis?" and Felipe answered but the servant's shrill reply drowned his words. The door was open and with a toss of her head she marched straight through. After a second's hesitation, we followed.

Father Eladio, dressed in his priest's gown, was seated on a hard chair at a plain wood table. He had been reading and his spectacles had slipped down his long nose. He looked over the top of them, not angrily, but certainly in some surprise, as the servant explained our presence loudly, and with many gesticulations.

The priest addressed us also in his own tongue and Felipe replied: "My friend does not understand Spanish. May we speak in English? I am sorry, Father, but I had to see you. It could not wait until morning."

He replied with a mild rebuke: "Everything is urgent to the young. What do you want, my son?" He was very thin, very bald, and what hair he had, growing in a straggly fringe round the back of his head, was the murky white of city snow. He had strange eyes, dark and heavy-lidded, but the eyes themselves, set deeply in a face that was cobwebbed with life, were sharp and bright as black diamonds.

"I want to talk to you. This is a friend of mine, Suzanne Cole. You don't know me, do you? But I realise now I do know you, by sight," Felipe told him.

Father Eladio nodded to me, rose from his chair, settled his spectacles back in their rightful position and came to look into Felipe's face. "Yes," he said, his eyes unblinking, "yes, I do know you." He turned away, seeming to draw into himself, into a silence that had weight and depth and a curious sort of intensity. I glanced nervously round the small room with its white-washed walls, its cheap furniture, its fire set with sticks that would gather dust through the summer, its bare tiled floor; at the religious pictures on the walls, a dying Christ over the fire and a small vase of pale daisies beneath a little statue of Mary and the Child. The room smelled stale and musty. Somewhere a tap trickled noisily on stones. The servant suddenly left the room.

135

The priest looked round vaguely, almost as though he had lost his way. Felipe went to him, took his arm and with that surprising gentleness that never failed to touch me, helped him back to his chair. I stood, looking down into the dead fireplace, knowing that we had not come in vain, feeling elated for Felipe and a little frightened for myself, knowing that the moment to pull out and go home had long passed and knowing too with a sort of dread that what was to come could be infinitely more terrifying than anything I had been through so far.

"Gertrudis! *Vino tinto, por favor.*" The priest seemed to have recovered from his initial shock. He was looking reasonably calm, though two dark spots burned in his pallid cheeks. His command brought a snapped reply from the next room and the servant came in carrying a bottle which she put down on the table with an ungracious thump. Equally ungraciously, she took some small, plain glasses from a shelf. Father Eladio poured some wine into each and signed to us with thin, gnarled hands to take one. Felipe pulled out a chair for me then one for himself. The old man looked at us gravely. "Who sent you here?"

"Nobody."

His voice sharpened. "Then how did you know where I lived?"

"It was not difficult," Felipe replied. "You have lived here for some time."

The priest pondered on the words, patently aware of their ambiguity.

"You have had an accident. Are you all right?"

"Yes, thank you. I do not think it was an accident. That is why I have come to you. You know about my father."

The old man stiffened, but not with shock. He had known immediately he recognised Felipe, why he had come. He turned to me. "Who are you, my child?"

"Afterwards—Carlos' wife married my father."

"The girl was said to have died."

"Not then. She did not travel on the bus that blew up. Only recently she died and this story was among her papers."

136

His spectacles had slipped again. He looked sharply at me over them, then back with concern to Felipe. "Where is Carlos now, Father?" I asked.

"I do not know. When I saw him last he came from somewhere near Burgos but the friends he brought with him were Basques."

"Seventeen years ago?" Felipe asked. He was thinking about the meeting in the barn.

"Perhaps. It was about then."

"You married my parents."

Those deep-set eyes were momentarily full of compassion, then he turned slightly away saying: "I am a very old man and I have not much longer to go. I have prayed for guidance on this matter, and made my decision. In the chapel at the *Finca Alondra* there is a safe. In it you will find your parents' marriage lines and note of your own birth."

"There is no safe in the chapel, Father," said Felipe with conviction.

"It is hidden. It is behind a plaque over the altar."

Over against the wall the old woman started, scratched her head then was still again. I looked at her apprehensively. I had a queer feeling she understood English, or at least some of what we were saying. The priest followed my eyes, turned his head and spoke to her, sharply, in Spanish. She went silently out of the room.

I said: "She was listening!"

Father Eladio shook his head. "She is uneducated. A peasant. She speaks only Spanish."

Felipe asked: "Who put the certificate in the safe, Father?"

"I did. Your mother gave it to me for safe keeping. I had access to the palace in those days. I took Mass and heard confessions there."

"But surely other people know about the safe? My grandmother? My uncle?"

The priest inclined his head. "Your grandmother knows. She left the family jewels there when they went into exile. I knew because I was entrusted to put them there. The old

137

Count, the Countess, and I. We did it together."

"But surely she would have told my uncle, on his inheriting the title and the *Finca*?"

"I do not know," replied Father Eladio. "Perhaps she has. But if so, she would have told him it was empty, because she believes it to be so. I doubt very much if he would have it broken open. As you will see when you go there, it is not a task to undertake out of ordinary curiosity. But who knows ... In order to get to it one has to move the heavy altar. The plaque itself is extremely heavy and it is screwed fast into the wall. Your mother, being a Protestant, never used the chapel, so it was a good place to hide the papers, for Ernesto would never have thought of looking there. I believe he was under the impression she took them with her."

I suddenly felt sick. "Is that why the bus blew up?" I asked baldly.

He put the palms of his hands together, the fingertips under his chin in an attitude of prayer. "What's done is done."

I felt cold to my very heart. No wonder Ernesto searched my suitcase. Perhaps it was not only Antonia's letter he hoped to find there.

Felipe said: "You have the key of the safe?"

The priest shook his head. "The key is at the bottom of the Tagus. I did not want the paper to be found until the old Count died. It is not an impossible task to find a locksmith."

"Why did you not interfere when my grandfather died? Why did you not get in touch with me then?"

The old man's eyes clouded over. "That is my greatest sin. Cowardice. Your uncle had convinced everybody your father was dead. I decided it must be so for your grandfather's death was no secret and if Carlos had been alive he would have heard. I knew how badly your uncle wished to inherit, and I wanted to live. There was much work for me to do among the poor, the sick." He added apologetically: "It seemed to me more important than your inheriting the title. But I am glad to have been able to put things right for you before I die." He added very gravely: "I have also, and I do not need to tell you this, put an immense burden of decision on you."

Felipe's face was dark and strained. "And if I had not come?"

The old man hesitated. "You did come. You made it easy for me. Leave it at that!" He rose. "I do not wish to be discourteous but I must ask you to go now."

Felipe and I rose also. "Thank you, Father. I am very grateful." And he was angry, too. Felipe would not easily forgive this man for what he had left undone until now. "Have you any idea if my father could possibly be still alive?"

"None. You would have to make enquiries among the Basques who live, or anyway visit, near Santo Domingo de la Calzada, for Carlos was there when the last news of him came. I am sorry you have to go by the back way because it is very dark but my front door opens on a brightly-lit street and I do not want to take a chance on your being seen leaving."

"We do not mind," I said.

"You will not, in any circumstances, tell anyone you have been here?"

"Of course."

The moon had risen and a faint opal light lay over the garden. I could see the sloping lines of roofs and the lifted spear of a young cypress against the sky. We went silently across the stones to the gate, opened it with the key and pulled it noisily closed behind us. The path was gloomy. Felipe switched the torch on so that we could avoid the loose stones on the earth track.

"Where to?" I asked.

"The safe. I shan't be able to sleep until I know if the proof of my parents' marriage is there."

"What if your uncle is at tne palace?"

"I'll have to find out where he is. The chapel is situated diagonally across the courtyard from his rooms. The stained glass windows look onto the courtyard. He would see a light."

139

"So?"

"I think it might be a good idea to ring my grandmother. That's the most innocent way of ascertaining my uncle's whereabouts. She is very fond of me. We left her genuinely disturbed."

We had indeed.

"She may well have sent for my uncle to talk about our visit. Or at least telephoned him. I might be able to find out where he has gone without actually asking him. I hardly think he will stay at *Alondra* tonight, anyway. It's eight or nine hours since Quiroga told him of your appearance and he dashed down from Madrid. When he found I had gone he was bound to put two and two together. If he has broken the safe open and therefore knows about Father Eladio's secret, then the papers will have been destroyed long ago. That brings us back more urgently to Santo Domingo."

"You'll need an alibi, if you're going to disappear up there."

"That's just what I was thinking. Now, here's the river wall. We turn round and go down some steps into the little square. Remember? Can you see?"

I understood his reluctance to switch the torch on. We were somehow more anonymous in the dark. "You told your grandmother you were going to visit Damian."

"Yes. But it won't work for tomorrow. I've got to set up a series of small day-alibis. When I see how things go I might pretend to go to Paris. The trouble with Paris is they can check. They can ring Damian. Turn left here. Do you know where we are now? Remember this steep little street?"

"Yes, I do. And then we turn down into the Ballisats' road."

"Top marks."

"Let's face it," I muttered. "I didn't do much to earn them. It's the easiest place in the world to find your way round. The lit-up Alcázar at the top of the hill, the Tagus running a half-circle round the bottom. Simple!" As I spoke I was thinking of the blind alley of Santo Domingo de la Calzada. Felipe had never been there. I did not even know where the town lay. Where did one start looking for a man who had not been

140

heard of for twelve years, in a strange place among strange people? And then I remembered that Felipe, when telling me the story of Carlos' visit to the outbuildings at the *Finca Alondra*, had said two men came up the tunnel with him. I had been alerted by the mention of Father Eladio's name because I had already heard it from Viola, and consequently had passed over the other one. But: "Stop, Felipe," I said urgently now. "That night in the barn, who was the third man? Father Eladio, Carlos, and...?"

Felipe gave a startled exclamation. "Goizueta?"

"Why didn't we think to ask Father Eladio about him? He said Carlos came with *some* Basques. These men might still be around. They might know what happened to Carlos."

We were standing stock still in the steep little street, the darkness lightened by the faint glow of a white-painted wall. Felipe grasped my hand and turned me round. "Let's go back. Maybe he can tell us the names of the others. We'll be better off with three, or four, than one. Anyway, I can't be sure I haven't got that name wrong, after all these years. It won't hurt to check."

We ran back the way we had come, up the precipitous little lane with its rough cobblestones, round by the white building with the low black roof, across the tiny square and up the steps. In our urgent rush we had to use the torch now. The light flashed in stabbing beams from path to wall and wall to path as we ran. "Are you all right?"

I needed my breath so I nodded without speaking. We climbed some more steps, crossed a shuttered square and up that last scented lane. He slowed a little as we turned on to the rough earth path that led in from the bank above the gorge. Even so, I found myself sliding on loose stones, tripping on those embedded in the earth track and once would have fallen headlong if Felipe had not held my hand. My other hand was pressed against my rib cage on a pain. My legs had begun to tremble by the time we came to the high stone wall outside the priest's garden and the dragging memory of my illness was born in upon me. Even for a girl on top

141

form it would be no picnic keeping up with Felipe.

He said: "We can go right in without ringing the bell if the old witch hasn't been along to lock the gate."

But Gertrudis had already done her duty. Felipe reached for the bell chain and pulled. "It scarcely seems fair," I said breathlessly, "upsetting the poor old boy again."

"One disturbed evening is a very small price to pay for what he has left undone," Felipe retorted curtly. He tugged at the bell again, and again there was silence. We waited in the darkness by the gate and I was glad of the respite. A moment later we heard the priest's voice calling faintly: "Gertrudis!"

We heard him call again, and again. Cold fingers crept along my spine. I said: "She *was* listening, Felipe. I know it. And now she has gone."

He was still holding my hand. I felt his fingers tighten, heard the sharp intake of his breath. "Gertrudis! Gertrudis!" The cry was without hope. Father Eladio, too, it seemed, now realised the woman had left.

18

"IT MAY BE that you were right about that woman," said Felipe worriedly as we hurried back down the path, the torchlight dancing on the ground ahead of us, the darkness crowding round. "But if she is an old retainer of Father Eladio's, and the chances are she is, taking everything into consideration— her familiar manner with him and churlish behaviour when some extra work came up—he would be bound to know whether she speaks English or not. A woman of that type doesn't start learning a foreign language all of a sudden. I think the answer to her curiosity is more likely to be the fact that she recognised me. If she has gone off to make a report it's possible she is reporting on my visit itself, rather than the substance of it."

"It's a comforting theory and I hope you're right."

"Don't worry," he replied grimly, "it isn't going to lull me into a false sense of security. The sooner we get up to the chapel with a locksmith the better. Let's make for Zocodover. I'll ring my grandmother from a kiosk. We had better pinpoint Ernesto's whereabouts before we start thinking about that safe."

We were hurrying up a flight of narrow steps. "Where will you get a locksmith at this hour? And a discreet one at that?"

He did not answer immediately. We went across a little square decorated with pots of geraniums and into a narrow

143

alleyway that was so black Felipe needed the torch again. "Don't think I am on social terms with local criminals," he said with a smile in his voice, "but I do happen to know a fellow who will do anything for a price. If he can produce a locksmith we'll bundle him into the car immediately."

"And creep up through the olive grove?"

I ought to have known better. He said brusquely: "If it's my palace, it's my safe. Am I asking the man to commit a crime? Anyone can lose a key. I shall drive in through the main door."

"Even if Ernesto is there?"

"We-ll ..." His laugh was brisk and brittle. "I'll answer that one when I find out where he is."

The square was crowded as always at this, the hour of the *paseo*. Young men and girls, old people, whole families all well turned out, walked up and down eyeing each other, seeing and being seen. Here was that restaurant where Perry had found me earlier in the week pausing for breakfast on my rush to Madrid. The tables on the pavement outside were filled with chattering groups and white-coated waiters strolled in and out among them serving ice creams, *apéritifs*, coffee. "Look!" said Felipe, "there is a vacant seat. I'll go and telephone."

I sat down gratefully on the hard little metal chair with its orange plastic seat, stretching my aching legs out before me. A waiter came and gave me his insistent attention until I was forced to say: *"Dos* whisky, *por favor."*

Felipe came striding through the tables just as the drinks were being served, and I knew from the expression of relief on his face that his uncle must have left Toledo. He pulled out a chair opposite, then noting the glasses said, "Thanks. That's a good idea."

"I was embarrassed into it. Rent for the chair. Anyway, I am sure a drink will do you good."

"You're probably right. Drink yours fast then. We're on our way." He picked up his glass, tossed the whisky down straight and producing some notes from his trousers' pocket, signed to the waiter. When the man did not come immediately he left some money on the table and, taking my arm, guided me impatiently through the tables to the edge of the square. "Sorry about that," he said apologetically. "I'll buy you another one day and give you time to enjoy it."

I had not minded leaving most of the drink, but I could have done with some more rest. "Do you always move at this pace?"

"There's nothing I like better than sitting round with my feet up and my eyes closed, but you'll admit this is urgent business."

"Oh sure." And it was. Anyway, I was a little uncertain as to whether the quivering of my legs was due to weakness and fatigue, or to my apprehension about the disappearance of Father Eladio's servant.

"You don't mind another walk?"

"No—er—no. I love walking."

He chuckled. "You're tougher than you look. This isn't far. About three or four alleyways and a few steps. That's all."

"You haven't told me about your telephoning," I said as he hustled me down a narrow walk between two tall buildings on the opposite side of the square.

"Sorry. Ernesto is safely on his way to my grandmother's. I've no doubt she asked him to come and talk about our visit, although she didn't admit to it. She said he had been at the *Finca* all day."

"Why?"

"That's anybody's guess."

We hurried through the dark streets lit only here and there where a side road broke in or a tiny square lay open to the sky.

"Where are we now?" There was a series of those beautiful arches that I had come to recognise as of Arab construction with their alternate bands of masonry and brick.

"That's Santiago del Arrabal. One of the oldest churches in Toledo and full of beautiful Mudejar work. I'll bring you back to see it some time," Felipe promised, then without

145

pausing for breath: "We're looking for a tiny alley—Ah! This might be it."

We went uncertainly down a very narrow cobbled lane that smelled strongly of onions and garbage and dogs. Felipe counted the doors. He paused before one that was painted in a strange greenish colour. The house itself was squeezed in between two taller buildings. There was one narrow window protected by a grille, and two similar windows above. A woman opened the door a few inches and looked at us with suspicion. After a short exchange with Felipe she reluctantly drew the door in and stepped back.

We were in a narrow, unlit hall which led to a bare kitchen. A man rose from a hard chair and came forward to shake Felipe's hand. He did not introduce me. While they talked I looked round. There was little enough to see. A small blackened stove, a wooden bench, a tap with an enamel basin standing below, another kitchen chair, a very small window curtained with torn lace, a scrubbed table and on the walls some colourful pictures from calendars. There was one photo in the hall, that of a fierce-looking bridegroom in an ill-fitting suit and a worried bride in a white gown, innocent of shape or style.

The woman spoke to me. I shook my head. *"No comprendo."* I pointed to the photograph on the wall and then to her. She smiled and nodded. It was really as far as we could go. Felipe and the man seemed to have come to an agreement. Felipe took out his wallet and handed over some notes, then the two men shook hands again. *"Adios,"* I said to the woman. She smiled faintly, murmuring something I did not understand.

"We'll get the car now," Felipe said. "He is going to bring the locksmith and meet us down near the Alcantara bridge. His name is Blas."

"I suppose his sort of man doesn't use a surname?" I commented dryly.

"No need to. He is paid in cash and I suppose one is expected to forget his face and his name." I gave an involuntary

146

little shiver and he said concernedly: "Are you scared? You don't have to come."

"I am scared out of my wits," I replied as I tripped on one of the rough cobblestones and recovered my balance by grabbing his hand, "but don't let that bother you. I wouldn't miss it for anything."

Blas and his agent were standing in the shadow of a wall close by the road that ran up from the gorge. Felipe stopped the car. The man we had interviewed stepped forward to identify us, signed to his friend, then melted away. Blas opened the back door and slid into the car. *"Noches,"* he greeted us briefly.

"He doesn't speak any English," said Felipe.

"Buenas noches," I replied, happy to air my phrase-book Spanish and giving myself an excuse to turn my head and look at him. He was an unprepossessing little man with a small, wizened face and sunken dark eyes set close to an exceptionally long nose. His black hair grew forward from a low brow like a thick black mat. He was not more than five feet three or four and with the tough, wiry thinness of a small animal which knows how to fend for itself in adversity.

We crossed the bridge and speeded up the hill in silence. As we approached the entrance to the *Finca Alondra* Felipe said: "Be ready to slide down on to the floor as we come in to the courtyard." He spoke to Blas in Spanish and the locksmith replied with a brief: *"Sí, sí."* I turned my head in time to see him disappear on to the floor. No doubt, I thought dryly and a little nervously, he has had plenty of practice at this sort of thing. As we approached the big arches Felipe said; "Okay, better go down now," and I bent forward from the waist, pressing my face against my knees. A moment later the car stopped and Felipe jumped out. I heard the big doors creak, then he was back in the driving seat and we slid through into the palace courtyard. "Stay where you are," he said, "while I shut the door." At the gentle thud of wood on wood I raised my head, opened the car door and stepped out. Blas joined me, carrying a businesslike holdall.

147

The palace was in darkness, the courtyard black beneath the night sky. There was no moon and only a sprinkling of stars. Felipe said: "Follow me," and went across the intervening space, his feet inevitably making an unnerving Crunch! Crunch! sound in the loose gravel. Through the gloom I could just make out a tall gothic arch that I had not noticed on the two occasions on which I had visited the palace before. It was set into the side of a wall that jutted out from the bricks and masonry of the main inner structure and would have been fairly obvious to anyone not in a rushing panic to get away as I had been.

Felipe produced a bunch of keys from his pocket. We entered in silence. "If you don't mind I'll close the door before I turn on the light," he said. Darkness closed around us, suffocatingly. Then a small chandelier flared into light and I breathed again. The two men conversed quietly in Spanish.

It was a small and quite simple chapel with wooden forms to accommodate perhaps twenty people. At the side of the altar were chairs with tapestry seats that would be for the use of the family, each with its own silken hassock. In the high roof there were vaulting criss-crosses formed from wooden beams, and in the outer wall some beautiful stained glass windows. The altar was made of heavy carved wood and above it on the wall was fixed a golden sunburst with the family's coat-of-arms at the base. There were half-a-dozen religious pictures round the walls. A small but very beautiful wooden statue of Mary and the Child stood in a niche on one side of the altar, and on the other, a shepherd cradling a lamb in his arms. The locksmith went up to the altar and, laying down his bag of tools, began ferreting through them.

"Is that the plaque? With the coat-of-arms?"

"Yes. It's going to be a mammoth task, getting that down." Felipe looked worried.

"Father Eladio was right, then, when he said no one would look in the safe out of curiosity." When Felipe did not answer I realised he was taking nothing for granted and superstitiously, I touched the back of one of the wooden forms.

"Blas looks tough, but he hasn't much weight," Felipe said, looking critically at the little Spaniard.

"I'll help."

"Will you? It isn't exactly a woman's work."

"You can scarcely ask Quiroga."

"Scarcely!"

"Well," I added, "I am strong. At any rate, I was before I made a glutton of myself on your uncle's ordeal beans. Come on. Let's have a go at it."

We moved the heavy altar, inch by inch, until it was far enough away from the wall for Felipe to push a form behind it. The wooden plaque that held the sunburst and coat-of-arms was fixed to the wall by screws. Blas produced a large screwdriver and with swift, small animal movements like a beaver building its nest, he piled up the lovely hassocks and standing on them undid the screws at the bottom. Felipe said: "There are two more we're not going to reach. Suzanne, do you think you can find your way out to the gate in the dark? Right opposite the palace entrance—the door with the glass show cases and wrought-iron—there is a door leading into a guard room."

"Yes, I noticed it before. A guard room, is it?"

"Don't turn on the lights if you can help it. The room beyond that is a work room. There should be a small ladder leaning against a wall."

The courtyard was a little lighter now for the moon had risen behind the turrets and ghostly shadows fell from jutting roofs and chimneys. I tiptoed across the few yards of gravel that separated the door of the chapel from the main door, the crunch of my footsteps nerve-rackingly noisy in the silence. The entrance was a black patch of nothingness. I stretched out a tentative arm and found the wall, then felt my way along it, fell up some steps, and recovering my feet again found a door standing ajar. I pushed it open and switched on the torch.

A ray of light leaped across the room. There was a scuffle and rush of tiny feet. I stifled a scream, and then something

149

small and furry dashed past my ankles. Cats! There was a window looking on to the palace courtyard and in the light of the torch's beam I saw a small table on which lay a note pad, some pencils, a candle stick. With fast beating heart I shone the torch on a second doorway and through that into what looked like the store room. There was indeed a ladder against the wall.

Transferring the torch to my left hand, I picked the ladder up, then paused for a moment, listening. The night was very still but there was a sound, faint, shuffling, almost obscured by the lively panic beating of my heart. I switched the torch off, moved the ladder soundlessly towards the door and my nerves screamed as it scraped against wood. There were footsteps, yes, coming from I knew not where, but coming nearer, and then, over on my right on the other side of the room from which I had taken the ladder, a cord of light fell at the foot of a wide door, and I held my breath. The footsteps slowed, stilled, and a shadow fell across the centre of the cord. I nearly ran. With all the strength in me I forced myself to stand still, not breathing, knowing that to get out of the room undetected I would have to somehow evade in sooty darkness the leaning ladder, the table and the chair. I shrank back against the wall, knowing it was useless, knowing myself to be totally exposed.

And then the cord of light re-formed, the footsteps shuffled a moment, moved away, hastened, and suddenly the light was gone. I wiped a hand across my brow and found it wet. Of course this room led on to the servants' quarters, and anyone might come through at any time. I felt for the ladder again, grasping the rungs clumsily in my panic to be gone, with the torch held awkwardly against my thumb, the torchlight leaping and sliding across walls and floor. Somehow I managed to struggle through the two doors and out into the yard. I switched off the torch and left it on the step, then carried the ladder across to the chapel door.

Felipe came down the aisle to meet me. "Good girl," he said absently as though speaking to an obedient dog. "Here,

150

let me take it. You didn't see any sign of life?"

"No." It seemed the right reply. He had more than enough on his mind.

Blas pulled the form away and they set the ladder against the altar wall. "Now, if you don't mind, I'd like you to stand on the other side," said Felipe, businesslike, absorbed. "You and I have to support this thing when the screws are released. We don't want it toppling to the ground."

Blas went up like a monkey and removed the top screws, then we slid the ladder across and he mounted again to deal with the other side. With our feet firmly braced against the altar, the three of us inched the heavy plaque down the wall until the base touched the floor. Then he and the locksmith lifted it carefully away to lay it flat on the floor so that the rays of the sunburst would not be damaged.

Because they had concentrated all their attention on the safe removal of the plaque it was I who saw the blank wall first and caught my breath in shock. Surely a priest would not lie! Surely he would not send Felipe on a wild goose chase! Felipe finished the job he was doing, straightened, then looked up. I wanted to go to him but my feet were like lead. For what seemed like hours he stood staring at the wall, and Blas too. You could have heard a pin drop in the silence of the chapel. Then, still without speaking, Felipe went down the length of the aisle and switched on the second chandelier that hung nearer the altar. It cast a glow of light on the wall from which the plaque had been removed. We all stared at it in this terrible silence, the pale clean square the exact size of the plaque where the wall had been protected from light and dust.

I could not believe it. I would not believe it. Scarcely knowing what I was doing, I went to the ladder and put one foot on the bottom rung. And then I gave an involuntary little cry, for above me on the wall I saw something, I scarcely knew what, but something that sent the faintest shot of hope through me. I said: "Felipe!" and swiftly, without pausing to check the ladder's foot, climbed up and reached out to touch

151

that tiny, slightly darker patch I had seen on the wall. The ladder rocked dangerously.

The Spaniard gave a warning cry and Felipe leaped forward. I made a wild and useless grab at the wall and my hand slid across something wet, my nails clawing at paper that came away loosely against my hand and at that moment the two men caught the ladder and I, floundering, regained my balance. "Look!" I exclaimed breathlessly, excitedly. "Look! There is a door here, but it's covered with paper." I tore some more of the paper away and as I did so I realised the significance of the wetness, the sticky wetness on my palm, and all the despair I had felt when I first saw that blank patch came flooding back. "I am sorry," I said as I came down the ladder again. I could have cried. "I'm sorry, Felipe. That square of paper has been put there very recently. It is still wet. The paste! The paste is wet."

Felipe's face was stricken. "That is what Ernesto was doing here today! He did know! Or guessed."

Blas said something in Spanish and Felipe answered him, gesturing to him to climb the ladder. He went up in his monkey fashion, tools in his hands, and tore the rest of the paper away to expose a flat door with recessed key hole. Felipe's face was marble white, the eyes suddenly haggard, and there were deep lines of anger round his mouth. I said with the utmost compassion: "I'm sorry. I am so sorry. What can I say?"

The Spaniard, unaware of our distress, was working on the lock. "He may as well open it," Felipe said hopelessly. He was steadying the ladder, head bent, his shoulders slumped. Unable to bear the sight of his disappointment, I went back down the aisle and sat on the end of one of the forms staring at the floor. The two men began to talk in Spanish and I looked up. Blas had the door open and had thrust one arm in up to the elbow. He searched round inside and brought his hand out, empty. He looked from Felipe to me then back again, black eyes drawn into pinpoints, his sharp face blade narrow now, alert.

There was nothing to be done but put everything back where we had found it. We worked in silence. The queer little Spaniard saw our despair. He cast rat-like inquisitive looks at both of us. I did not like his interest. I did not trust him, but I could not say so to Felipe for it was far too late. Besides, did it matter that Ernesto should hear of the night's doings? It would give him a laugh.

Felipe returned the ladder to the work room, I scrunched the torn paper up and pushed it into my pocket, then collected the torch.

We left the way we had come, with Blas and me down on the floor and the headlights switched off. We drove through the parador courtyard and therefore past its front door but the door was closed against the night and curtains drawn. We had left everything in the chapel as it had been before our coming and the ladder leaning innocently once more against the wall of the work room.

"What are you going to do?" I asked.

"Drop our friend, buy you some dinner then—"

"I really could not eat. Come back to the Ballisats. I am sure Viola would be only too happy to give you a bed. Then we can get an early start in the morning."

We ran down the dark drive towards the front gate. "I propose to sleep here," Felipe said.

I swung round in alarm. "In the parador?"

"No. Quiroga has that. In the palace, in my own room."

"You cannot!" Even in the darkness of the car I could see, or perhaps it was mostly that I felt, he was terribly angry.

"No one will try to kill me in Toledo again. That would be too obvious altogether."

"Felipe! You could be killed here and your body taken somewhere else so that it looked like an accident. Or you could just disappear, if Ernesto was desperate enough."

"He's not desperate," replied Felipe with cool certainty, "because he holds the proof of my parents' marriage. Either that, or he has destroyed it. We're not to know if he looked

153

in the safe today because it suddenly occurred to him that since he didn't find the papers in your possession when he took Antonia's letter, they might be there. Or if he knew all the time, and decided to find a new hiding place. After all, he would know that Antonia could not put them there all by herself. He may even be aware that Father Eladio helped. That would account for the old man's anxiety to get rid of us tonight."

"Please, Felipe, stay at the Ballisats' tonight."

He touched my hand briefly. "It's not fair to involve them. Besides, Ernesto won't be in a hurry. He has time on his side, now. My grandmother will have told him of my plans for tomorrow. Therefore she will know I would not have gone off to Lisbon or Barcelona or wherever Ernesto might think to set up an accident, since, as we said before, he can't reasonably make another attempt on my life in Toledo."

"What did you tell her?" We were speeding at Felipe's natural crazy pace round the bends in the hills and heading off towards the town that glittered like a fairy castle each time we came over a rise, then disappeared as we leaped into a fold in the hills.

"I told her I will go to Paris the day after tomorrow. It would be quite acceptable for me to meet with an accident there. But tomorrow, in the morning I am to visit the doctor who saw me after the accident, keep a luncheon engagement in Madrid, then do some shopping and visit my tailor. I managed to bring all this out quite casually. Then I said I might call on my uncle in Madrid tomorrow night to talk about work at the iron mines, but if by any chance he or I was not able to make it, I would see him the next day and go to Paris the day after. It's enough to keep him off the Santo Domingo route tomorrow. Iron mines!" exclaimed Felipe, taking one hand off the wheel to slap his thigh. "That's it! He could have me disposed of without any trouble at all down there. A riding accident in the Sierras would be a most natural thing. The clouds can come down in those passes with extraordinary speed. If the weather cracks up and you're

154

caught there at three thousand metres, believe me, you're in trouble."

"Three thousand metres?"

"Over nine thousand feet. The Puerto de Jeres pass is ten thousand six hundred feet, in fact."

"And everyone knows you're just the man to take a chance. Maybe you're right. But Felipe, please don't go back to the palace." He did not reply and I knew it was useless to try to persuade him. I felt, too, that in spite of my near exhaustion, if he returned to the *Finca Alondra* tonight I was not going to find much rest.

We stopped on the town side of the Alcantara bridge where we had picked up our locksmith. Felipe brought a bundle of pesetas out of his pocket and handed them to him. With a *Gracias, Señor*, Blas disappeared into the night as swiftly and silently as he had come.

"Isn't there a chance that he might sell his information?" I asked nervously. "He is a queer, silent fish."

"By the time he sells it I hope it will be useless," Felipe replied. "And anyway, I doubt very much that he would. Where is he going to find more jobs if he gets a reputation for ratting?"

What really mattered was that Ernesto should not know from whom we acquired our information. I thought of the servant woman and Father Eladio's: "Gertrudis!" like the cry of a lost bird. And where were we to find the marriage certificate now? The proclamation that Felipe was the rightful *Conde* de Merito?

His voice broke roughly into my thoughts: "Hell, who cares about that bit of paper! If we find Carlos we find all the proof we need."

155

19

HE GAVE ME the palace telephone number before he went on his way. "Besides, I've got to pack a bag," he said. "Heaven knows whether we will get back from Santo Domingo tomorrow. We may have to shoot right up into the Basque country for the information we need. And if we do get back, there is this Paris question ..."

"You're actually going?"

"No. But it could be useful as a temporary alibi." We were approaching the Ballisats' house. Felipe braked at the head of the narrow little lane that led to the wooden gate in the stone wall. "I'll be here early in the morning. We have to see Father Eladio before we go."

Then suddenly I had an idea. "Viola said he takes a walk, regularly as clockwork, early in the morning. I'll put a scarf over this rather obvious hair of mine, borrow a black coat, and meet him on the path. I've forgotten exactly what time Viola said, but I can check with her."

Felipe hesitated.

"Please. He was really very disturbed about your going to his house last night." And there was more to my plan than that. I was still remembering the fact of the servant's clearly unorthodox disappearance. I did not want Felipe to go into that little blind alley and find someone waiting for him at the house. I did not particularly want to go myself.

"All right," he said reluctantly. "But take a notebook and

pencil. If these chaps are Basques their names are liable to be a metre long. They can be dossiers of their owner's identity. I'll be here at eight o'clock. If you're not back, I'll wait, and then we can set off. And you had best bring an overnight bag. But warn your hostess you may be back tomorrow night and need a bed."

We sat a moment in silence in the darkness of the car. His hands were on the wheel, his mind, I felt, a mile away from me. I touched his fingers with my own and he turned sharply. "Won't you change your mind? About sleeping here? Please, Felipe."

He only said, distantly, "I'll see you to the gate. You have the key?"

"Yes."

Still he did not move. "I've been trying to say you needn't come tomorrow."

"You know I have to go," I told him gently.

"It could be dangerous."

My hand closed over his. "I owe Antonia a great deal. For her—I have to go." But it was not entirely for her, and even then I think I knew it. I was looking out into the darkness of the lane so I did not see him move and he caught me by surprise. His kiss was an imprint of himself—heady, quick, thoughtless perhaps. Certainly it held no promise. It might even have been a farewell, but I felt it might be a gesture of gratitude. My eyes misted over and I fumbled for the door handle. "Good night, Felipe. I'll be ready at eight."

They were waiting for me, two worried-looking people sitting on either side of a small fire in the studio. At the sound of my footsteps on the tiled floor Viola jumped up. "Suzanne!" Her pretty face was flushed with relief.

Perry rose heavily and crossed the room, took me by the hand and led me to the sofa. I knew then I had to tell them. There is no shielding by an imagined protective silence those who are already worried.

"Coffee?"

"No, thank you."

157

"Drink? Whisky? Gin? Wine?" He was standing over me, his brown hair untidy where he had run his hands through it, his chin with his reddish beard thrust out with a near-belligerency I had not seen before, but there was compassion in his oval grey eyes.

"Okay," he said, "so you don't want anything. I'll give the fire a poke and you start shooting."

I dropped into the seat with an enormous sigh. "We didn't want you involved," I said apologetically, "because you have to live here."

"It's because I live here that I have to know. I find," said my host slowly and very, very thoughtfully, "that I have given house room to a stranger who is mixed up in Spanish politics. Right, start at the beginning, if you please."

In the event, I was rather glad for them to know. I recounted the whole story. It was incredibly easy to talk to this kind American couple. There was scarcely a movement between the three of us. A twig fell upon the hearth and Perry kicked it in with his toe. The clock ticked loudly and once it struck the hour. Midnight.

"Felipe is mad to go back to the *Finca* tonight," said Viola at the end.

"Not mad," I said. "Certainly very, very brave. I think you'll find he has to do it." Viola lifted enquiring brows. "Because it's his," I told her simply. "I don't think you can protect men like Felipe."

She smiled faintly, her eyes on my face. "Are you in love with him?"

"Now that would be taking on something, wouldn't it!" I bent over the fire for, idiotically, the colour was flaring in my cheeks. "Besides, I scarcely know him."

"It doesn't matter sometimes."

I went over to the desk and took one of Perry's cigarettes then sat down beside her again. It was a smoking occasion.

"I'll go with you to meet Father Eladio tomorrow. I'm practically certain he said he has his early morning walk at seven o'clock. I am always up at that time, anyway."

"No, please. That is why we didn't want to tell you. We felt you ought not to be involved."

"That's right," said Perry. "And if I were you, I'd do that little chore, then get back home as fast as I could go, Suzie love. You've done your bit. You've spilt the beans. Now it's up to Lazaro. Honestly, if you knew a bit more about what went on in the Civil War—"

I held up a hand to stop him and though I laughed my laugh was very shaky indeed. "I think I know all I want to know about that. I've got to follow this through to the end. Will you be here to let me in if I come back tomorrow night?"

Perry raised his thick, bushy brows. "And if you don't?"

"I may only have gone on, following clues northwards into the Basque country. I'll send you a telegram to say so."

"And if you don't return, and we don't get a telegram? Don't think I'm trying to frighten you," said Perry making no attempt to hide the fact that he was indeed trying to frighten me, "but do you have a next-of-kin?"

For the first time, then, I realised that there was really no one at home whose life would be markedly affected by my death. "It occurs to me now," I said wryly, "that Felipe Lazaro must be the nearest relation I could produce. Quixotic, isn't it? You see my point? I have to help him."

"I don't like it," said Perry. "I was going to send you packing, but—" he broke off, resting a gentle hand on my shoulder.

There was silence for a long moment, then Viola said briskly: "Let's cross our fingers for Felipe, and go to bed."

*   *   *

Curiously, I slept. Youth and exhaustion proved a good match for my apprehensions. Perry had given me an alarm clock but I wakened at six forty-five and was able to turn it off before the ringing disturbed the household. Viola had given me a plain and rather worn black coat belonging to Maria, her daily maid. I tied a scarf over my hair, put the coat on and

159

crept quietly along the tiled corridor in my stockinged feet, across the two big living rooms and up the steps to the outer door. The key was in the lock. I paused to put my shoes on then went out into the cool morning. Dewy cobwebs were strung prettily across the vines on the terrace and the wooden chairs glistened with moisture.

The sun rose over the back of the town so it was not yet visible behind the rising spires and roof-tops above the Ballisat house. I shut the gate in the wall carefully behind me and made my way swiftly up the steep, cobbled lane to where Felipe had left his car last night, rounded the white building then turned down an alleyway that led into the tiny square. Two black-clad housewives with hair scraped away from their drab brown faces were shaking mats from upper windows. My watch said nearly a quarter past seven. I had been longer than I realised. Confident of my directions, I began to run up the steps, my feet clattering over-loudly on the granite. I sped down that high walled lane, up the other flight of steps, across the tiny square where a dozen small and rather dirty cars now stood parked nose to wall, past three workmen in blue overalls with shovels over their shoulders, and up the steep little lane where the scent of honeysuckle floated lightly on the air.

I came out panting at the cliff-top. Two old women in shawls and headscarves lumbered past, deep in conversation. Here, near the edge of the gorge, the houses were shuttered tight, asleep in their walled gardens. A car engine burst to life close by and because I had not seen the car, or even a lane wide enough for a car, I started and turned to look. Beyond a broken wall there was a little clump of acacia trees and beneath them a small car was reversing in a dirt lane. The driver saw me and immediately turned his head away as though he did not wish to be recognised. A Spanish Romeo, I thought with dry amusement, getting out early, and inevitably my mind flew to Ernesto who brought his ladies, audaciously, to Pilar's home. I turned down the path that led to the priest's house, then swung back. Some tiny cog in my

160

memory had spun, alerting me. I ran back to the wall but the car was already on its way, jolting and bumping across the rough turf. There was something familiar about the set of the driver's head. Only that. And yet ... I am jumpy, I said to myself. I'm seeing bogeys behind every bush.

I turned back into the path that led to Father Eladio's house. As I had suspected, it looked a good deal better in the daylight. A rough track, to be sure, and more enclosed than I had thought, but with nothing sinister about it. Wild clematis grew over the earth slope, and some stunted lilac, jumbled in among thistles and vetch, spurge and juniper. There were also a good many discarded plastic bottles and some torn newspapers. And then I heard voices, not far ahead, and my heart sank for I realised it was possible the old priest had met a friend. It had not occurred to me that he might not be alone, might not, in fact, even walk alone at all in case of a fall. I hesitated, went on, hesitated again.

But I had to speak to him. Felipe could not set out on this long journey without any lead at all. And anyway, I was jumping to conclusions. That was a woman's voice, and then another man who did not sound at all like Father Eladio. The voices came to me across the stunted bushes on the hair-pin bend so that they were quite close, though I could not see the speakers. I paused at the corner, uncertain, for it had begun to bear in upon me that these people were not engaged in ordinary conversation. That they were in fact distressed, and there were considerably more than one or two. I heard a woman's shrill cry. A wail, or lament. I felt my muscles tense and the small hairs prickling on the back of my neck. Something was wrong. The black, currant eyes, the surly face of the woman Gertrudis flashed before me and without stopping to think further, I sprinted round the blind corner ahead.

He was lying where they had put him, toes turned to heaven, and they had crossed his hands on his breast. I could see that much as the two men and the woman hung over him on the dark part of the path where the trees met overhead, gesticulating, uttering cries of anguish into the morning air.

And one of the women was Gertrudis, flailing the air with her arms, crying her despair. A man spoke to her sharply and she turned away towards the house, walking, then jogging as fast as her old, bent, black-stockinged legs would carry her, crying as she went.

Scarcely realising what I was doing, I approached the men. They were rough fellows in workmen's overalls. They eyed me in sullen silence. I said: "What happened? An accident?"

They did not reply. I think they might have understood from my distressed, enquiring manner, but they did not want me here, a stranger. One of them took a patterned kerchief from his neck and draped it over the grey face as though they did not wish a foreigner even to look on one of their own in death. I turned away. He could have fallen, I said to myself, unconvincingly. Old men are not very steady on their feet and this path is very rough. He was well over eighty, I added, compulsively putting off the evil moment until I had to face facts. Compulsively thrusting from my mind's eye the picture of the man I had seen starting up the car in the lane just a few moments ago and knowing now that his swift and heavy pouncing movement as he turned away had reminded me of Quiroga. Trying not to accept the fact that I had brought about Father Eladio's death just as surely as I had brought about Felipe's accident and Ernesto's attempt to poison me. Third time unlucky.

20

ALL MY LIFE I shall remember that dash to Burgos and then off down the winding road to Santo Domingo with the agony of guilt in my heart and Felipe driving like a madman, lashing at Fate. I had told the Ballisats I would not return to their house. Viola was upset, Perry silent, guilty. They did not want me to stay, I knew that, and yet neither did they want to let me go. But one cannot involve totally innocent strangers in the sort of black deeds that had come our way. I brought my bag, packed, into the studio and Felipe carried it, in silence, to the car. I kissed them both, and the children, patted the dog, and listened wistfully to Viola's explanation that was a pattern of my own thoughts. Old men have to die. Does one shut the stable door after the horse has gone? Why should the servant Gertrudis be upset if she had indeed conveyed to Quiroga the news of Felipe's visit?

"Because she did not know what would come of it," Felipe had replied and could have guessed correctly. "She might be given money to spy on visitors. How would she know it was her master who was being watched? Besides, there was Blas."

"You were so certain he could do no harm."

"I am not certain about anything any more," Felipe stated angrily, "except that there are too many people who know now, and we must hurry before it snowballs further. Before my father, if he is alive, can be moved somewhere where I might never find him."

From Madrid we drove along a straight, smooth road that allowed Felipe to have his head, through the silver shades of olive groves for mile after mile with the breeze rippling the sharp little leaves into billowing curtains of silk.

We talked desultorily. "Are the Basques really a race apart?"

"Certainly they don't consider themselves to be a part of Spain."

"Perry says none of you do. He says you're a Castillian, rather than a Spaniard."

"That's right."

We passed spring vineyards, the plants cut back to their tiny twisted stems, in neatly regimented rows like a battalion of small, black, indignant hens. We tore through treeless acres where mud-coloured villages lay flat against the red soil and vast churches stood pointing their spires into the sky. We flinched as we rushed past those great juggernauts that pound through the country at a terrifying pace, rocking our car with the impact of the air sandwiched protestingly between us.

I turned to Felipe. "Is it possible to tell me, explicitly, what makes the Basques more separate than the rest?"

He laughed. "You're still worrying that bone."

"I've time on my hands. I've been thinking. I seem to remember reading, when I was trying to get a bit of information prior to my coming here, that they claim to be the oldest race in Europe."

"That's right. They're pure descendants of pre-Aryan aborigines. They speak Euscara, a language that is a riddle to students of philology."

"Well," I said, "I reckon that makes them different." I pondered in silence on Carlos' perfidy as we crossed the great plains of Castile where black forested hills lay outlined starkly against the powder blue of distance; as we swept by pale trees, dainty with spring against the brick red soil; sprouting fields green-washed beneath the sun; low hills purple-black as grapes against an apricot sky; a gay red tractor in a bright green field like a child's toy unfolded from its emerald wrapper; fat-topped umbrella pines balanced precariously against small hills on thin, bent stems; sandy hills, flat swamp land.

"I've just remembered something," offered Felipe. "Have you heard of the Infante Don Juan?"

"Who later became Juan I, King of Castile?"

"That's him. In 1371, if I remember rightly, he swore the *fueros*, special privileges which gave the Basques immunity from taxes and military service."

"Then he made them into a separate country?"

"I suppose you could say that."

"And do they still pay no taxes?"

"The *fueros* were almost wholly abrogated in 1876 by Alfonso XII, but Basque Nationalists resent it to this day."

"I should think so. They had been on to a good thing for five hundred years. But Perry Ballisat said the Government gave them their independence not long before the Civil War."

"That's why they fought with the Republicans."

I turned my attention back to the countryside. We fled down into a valley where a snow-fed river, olive-green, was split into white foam by the decaying pylons of a slate-grey bridge and then on softer terrain we passed poplars in Indian file stalking with solemn dignity down to a wide, calm river bunched with willows.

It was nearly mid-day when we saw the cusped towers of a cathedral against a hill and came into clean and elegant Burgos with its citified river between the high embankments, its lovely, unspoiled plazas and its odd-looking statue of the Bourbon Charles III. "On some happier occasion," Felipe said, stretching himself thankfully, flexing his stiff, cramped bones as he stepped out on to the pavement, "I would like to show you the cathedral."

"Isn't El Cid buried here?"

"He is, indeed. And his wife. And there are enough stained

165

glass windows, Flemish tapestries and ornate gilt to keep you gasping for days. It will have to wait," said Felipe in his decisive way. "It's coffee now. Ah, there's a bar."

We lunched standing at the bar, off churros, those curious curly fingers that tasted of nothing much more than oil and sweet batter; salami slices and fat black olives; wine, and coffee too strong for my palate. "What are you going to do when we get to Santo Domingo?" I asked. We had talked of many things in the car, but not that. I had sensed Felipe's need to cast his mind adrift for a while.

"We've got to find a family called Goizueta, haven't we?"

"And how do you propose to go about it?"

"How else, but through the church? In a Catholic country the priests know everyone. They will know who have Basque connections, too. Do you want another coffee?" I shook my head. "Then we'll be on our way." He paid and we went back to the car. We were nearing our journey's end.

"Do you suppose your father allied himself to these people simply because they are the most determined of you all?" I asked.

Felipe replied dryly: "I suppose that's the answer. If you could see no future but to bring down a Government, would you not choose to join the most discontented section of the community?"

And what now, I wanted to ask? What does one do with an anarchist when he has been dug out of his hole? Felipe was putting the car into gear. He turned to look at me, reading my thoughts with total clarity. "First, before he is an anarchist," he said, "Carlos is my father."

"Or was," I retorted softly, not wanting him to hold his hopes too high. He did not reply and I had to remember what he had said when I told him Ernesto had not pronounced Carlos dead. *"I know Ernesto. If he knew Carlos was dead, he would say so."*

We set out along the road to Santo Domingo. The air was cool, the sky bright blue. On this quieter road we passed peasants with donkey carts and the hills sprouted scrub oak, heather and bracken. "It's not Basque country," Felipe said, "but there is a fusion of people here."

"The peasants are all wearing berets. That's Basque tradition, isn't it?"

"It is, indeed."

We ran into the town and parked outside a parador. "This was an old monastery," Felipe said. "And that," he inclined his head towards a huge and venerable old building of honey-coloured stone, "is the cathedral."

"Where will you look for a priest?"

"It should not be too difficult. What will you do? Wait in the car?"

I said I would take a walk around the town, returning to the car within half-an-hour. I strolled down the ancient streets looking in shop windows that were closing one by one for the siesta, returned to the car, went off again, came back to the car, strolled into the rather dark lounge of the parador and eventually Felipe appeared. "There are five lots of Goizuetas," he said wryly. "If they're all asleep for the afternoon it is going to be a slow job. I've got their addresses, anyway. They all live in the town. There's only one thing to do, and that is to set about running up and down stairs in an effort to catch at least some of them before they finish lunch. Now there is no reason why you should have to accompany me. What would you like to do? I should think the cathedral is well worth an hour."

"Don't worry about me," I said. "I'll browse, returning to the car on the hour and half hour. If I am not here, look in the cathedral."

I stood watching him as he strode off down a side street, a paper with his list of addresses in his hand, and my heart was heavy for him, for who knew what might appear when the stone hiding Carlos was eventually upturned? I went through the door that led into the cathedral and was immediately startled by the sound of a cock crowing somewhere above my head. I looked up towards the rafters and there, to my astonishment, behind an iron-work grille were a cock and hen

167

in a coop that was gilded and decorated with carving and paintings. I blinked in disbelief. The cock crowed again and the pair eyed me curiously, perkily, with their beady eyes. I must have laughed out loud for a young sacristan came out from behind a pillar and smiled at me.

"Do you speak English?" I asked. He shook his head and I went on, wandering fascinated through the cathedral looking at the religious paintings, the iron-work and gilding. One or two black-clad peasant women knelt to pray and an old man sat with beret in his hands, gazing at the floor as though too tired to leave. I sat down in one of the pews to examine some wonderful pictures in relief of the nine Stations of the Cross. I must have been there ten minutes or even twice as long. It was cool and peaceful in the cathedral and I had nowhere to go. Then behind me I heard soft footsteps and the young priest was back with an older man, aquiline-nosed, with a fringe of grey-brown hair above the ears and bright blue eyes. He said: "You wish to know about the birds?"

I stood up, smiling delightedly. *"Gracias, muchas gracias,"* I said to the younger man who backed away smiling, and then to the older: "You are very kind."

He said: "Come with me," and led me across the worn stones to a semi-secluded area behind a pillar where we could see the birds. He pointed to them. "You are here with Don Lazaro?" he asked in a low voice.

I nearly jumped out of my skin. "I would rather you did not show any surprise. Listen carefully. There are people here who speak English."

In a very casual tone, speaking normally, he went on: "Long ago there was a hermit called Domingo de la Calzada. He built a hostel for pilgrims in this town."

His voice dropped. "Don Lazaro is looking for Carlos?"

"Yes," I replied, my heart beating crazily. One of the peasant women rose from her knees and walked past us, looking curiously into my face as she went.

The priest indicated the birds with a flick of one hand, saying: "A French family of pilgrims came to stay at the

168

hostel. The woman who managed it fell in love with the son. When the young man did not return her love she slipped a piece of silver into his wallet, then ran to the *alcalde* and denounced him as a thief. He was hanged on the gallows outside the town." His voice dropped again. "Does the son know about Zarraonaindia?"

I blinked. "Who?"

"The Basque, Zarra. Does he know?"

"He doesn't know anyone," I replied, desperately trying to keep the excitement out of my face. "Only one name—Goizueta."

A young girl came in from the street helping a very old and infirm woman. They came slowly towards us, then turned and went up the aisle. The priest nodded to them and at the same time again indicated the birds with a movement of his hand as he turned back to me. "Goizueta will not talk. It is Zarra you must see," he said, speaking in that same low voice.

"The father and mother," he went on loudly, "continued with their journey to Santiago where they confided their woe to St. James. On their way home they prayed beneath the gallows where the body of their son was still hanging. Zarra had charge of Carlos. But he has gone."

"Carlos has gone? Can you tell me where?"

A little group of men came in and the priest nodded to them, smiling. He was a magnificent actor. The cock in the rafters crowed again. The men went into the pews and knelt to pray. "We have many tourists asking for the story," the priest said, smiling calmly at me, then looking up into the hen coop. With a musing expression on his face he said softly, his lips scarcely moving: "There is to be a funeral this afternoon at five o'clock. If you will be here—" He broke off as the street door opened again and a young woman came in alone.

"The parents," said the priest in a clear, calm voice, "heard the boy say: 'I am not dead. God and his servant St. James have preserved me alive. Go to the *alcalde* and beg him to cut me down.'"

169

A little group of women rose from their knees, lit some candles, slid coins into the offertory box, and glancing curiously at us, went on their way with a smile from the priest, and a nod.

"The parents," he continued, "went to the mayor who was sitting down to a supper of two roast chickens."

His voice dropped: "If you sit in that seat over there, Signorita," he surreptitiously indicated a particular pew some distance from the door, "I will ask Zarra if he will come and speak to you."

His voice rose to normal cadence: "When the pilgrim's parents told their tale the mayor said: 'You might as well say these birds on the dish could get up and crow.' Whereupon both cock and hen stood up and the cock crowed. Of course, they rushed to the gallows and cut the young pilgrim down. Ever since, Santo Domingo town has kept two birds here in the cathedral in memory of the miracle. Five o'clock, Signorita. I will do my best." He inclined his head and moved away.

"Thank you, Father," I said gratefully, my head spinning, scarcely knowing how to look innocent and only as interested as a tourist ought to be. When the priest had taken leave of me I went to one of the pews and knelt down to say a little prayer for Carlos, and for Felipe. While I was at it I put in a word for Antonia. And Father Eladio. Then I went to the box by the door and, taking as many pesetas as I could spare from my handbag, I put them in.

21

THE HANDS ON my watch pointed to five, but Felipe had still not returned to the car. Excited, disturbed, I made my way into the cathedral and sat down in the pew the priest had indicated. Half-a-dozen black-clad women knelt in front of me. Suddenly the doors were flung open and I was startled to see an enormous, enthusiastic crowd of men come in at a cracking pace preceded by a workman in overalls carrying an effigy of Christ on the cross. Behind them a smiling young priest in white robes swung along lightheartedly in front of the pallbearers. The coffin was decorated with garish plastic flowers and it came without piety in a lively rush, on a platform that bounced irreverently on the shoulders of more overalled workmen all in high good humour. I gazed at it in mesmerised fascination, thinking inevitably of the black gloom that had hung over Antonia and Leo's double funeral in our English church less than a month ago.

When my first astonishment had subsided and the crowd, abandoning their party spirit, had dropped to their knees, I glanced round anxiously towards the door. It opened and closed continuously with the arrival of black-clad women who paused to dip their fingers in the holy water and to cross themselves. A man pushed through in front of the women, crossed himself hastily as he strode across the aisle, pushed clumsily past me, knocking against me without apology, forcing me to lean back and draw my knees aside. I shot him an indignant look as he knelt to pray.

He was a man of about fifty, lantern-jawed with an aquiline nose and brown hair. I could not see his eyes because he had covered them with his hands. He turned his head slightly in my direction, speaking in Spanish, praying I presumed. I straightened, glancing back towards the door, hoping I was not going to be shielded by this man when Zarra entered. He would recognise me by my pale hair, but I had no way of knowing him. Suddenly I became aware that the rugged, tough-looking man at my side was intoning English words among his Spanish prayers. I turned to him, startled, swinging my mind back as one does half-way through a sentence when one has half-heard the beginning. "You are listening?" he had said.

"Zarra?" I whispered. "You are Zarra?"

"Yes. He is at the iron works," the man said, his voice rising and falling softly as though intoning a prayer. "His name—Justin de Prideau." Automatically, I slipped to my knees, covering my face with my hands.

"Carlos? Carlos calls himself Justin de Prideau?"

"Yes. His brother gave him the name. There was an accident. He had a blow on the head. We found a doctor. There was a depressed bone in the head. From the blow, you understand. Some pressure on the brain. He did not remember who he was. The brother took him off to the hospital in Madrid for an operation, but we hear later he did not arrive there. The brother did not wish it. He gave Carlos a new name—Justin de Prideau—and took him to work at the iron mines. La Calahorra. Sierra Nevada. He is safe. Without the operation he does not remember he is *El Conde*."

I gasped with shock. And yet, I should be surprised! Ernesto has stooped to worse than that in the short time that I had known him.

"If you please, do not go until the mourners make it possible without being noticed. Tell the boy we wish him luck. But not to speak to me. Understand—not to speak to me."

I sat through that funeral in a kind of daze. The man Zarra edged a little farther along the pew so that we were separated. Two men came in late and knelt down between us. After a while I felt a tap on my shoulder and looked up into Felipe's bemused face. The funeral was in full swing. No one was likely to notice our departure but I felt it was better we should leave separately. I signed to him to go. I listened to his soft footsteps on the stones and two or three moments later, when the mourners rose noisily to their feet, I slipped out after him.

He was sitting in the car smoking a cigarette. He watched me with a puzzled frown as I crossed the street. I jumped in beside him. "Have you found out anything?" I noticed immediately that he looked infinitely depressed.

"They know what I am after. They won't talk. I suspect word went round like wildfire after my first enquiry. They're not taking chances. I should think it's all over Santo Domingo by now that I am looking for Carlos, but the place is shut tight as a drum against me."

"I've news for you then, Felipe. I have found out something."

"Marvellous girl. Tell me!"

I turned my head, glancing back and forth along the street. The passers-by looked innocent enough. "Shall we get out of here first? As you say, news of our arrival is all over Santo Domingo. And we've got to get back to Madrid, anyway."

"Don't keep me in suspense." He reached for the starter but did not press it.

"Come on, Felipe. It's better that we go."

Suddenly he had the car in gear and was shooting off down the silent street.

I did not tell him, not while he drove for he was too emotionally concerned for that. I persuaded him to keep driving until we came to a stretch of road a little wider than the rest and he ran the car half-way up the grass verge.

"Right! Out with it." He switched off the engine and

resting an elbow on the door frame, turned the full brilliance of his attention on me. "Right!"

"A priest came up to me in the cathedral, Felipe."

"Ah! I should waste my time battling with the Goizuetas!"

"Remember your grandmother telling us about the reports in the papers that Carlos was leading a band of anarchists somewhere near Burgos? Ernesto went to investigate."

Felipe nodded. "He found they were merely using his name."

"It was not so. Carlos was there. He was very much there. At some point—the man did not say Ernesto was the culprit— Carlos received a blow on the head. Afterwards, he did not remember who he was. A doctor saw him and sent him to hospital in Madrid, but unfortunately Ernesto took over and evidently thought it was too good an opportunity to miss— Carlos not knowing his identity—so brother Ernesto gave him a new name, Justin de Prideau, and took him off down to the iron mines to work."

"Ernesto keeps him there? A labourer? The priest told you this?"

"I don't know what Carlos does. The man did not say. And it was not the priest who told me. He said he knew I was with you, and told me to be in the cathedral at five o'clock when a funeral would come in. A man with one of those great long Basque names you mentioned—only he shortened it to Zarra—came in, pretending to be part of the funeral proceedings, and he told me the story. He was kneeling there when you came in, but he had moved away."

"Then why did you say we must leave? I could have talked to him." With a swift, striking movement he hit the steering wheel. "Damn!" One hand leaped towards the engine switch.

"No. That is what you must not do. He said, on no account were you to speak to him. Perhaps Ernesto has spies dotted around the area. There must be a reason for the Goizueta family not talking to you. They must be scared of retribution. Please don't go back, Felipe. Zarra didn't have to tell me anything. It was awfully good of him. We've got enough

174

information. You ought to be able to find a man with such a distinctive name as Justin de Prideau in or around the iron mines. What is there? Villages?"

He nodded. "Small villages. You're right, I suppose." He was looking at me, and his face softened suddenly. "He's alive. Carlos is actually alive."

I put a hand over his. An old man carrying a long stick and wearing a black beret and ragged working clothes came towards us chasing a little flock of pretty golden-haired goats, and round the farther corner came a black and white cow being driven home for the night. The sky was primrose pale with approaching evening and the sun had gone down behind a distant hill. Felipe took out a packet of cigarettes and lit one.

"My uncle has his own especial kind of luck, it seems," he remarked at last. "I've thought he wouldn't willingly kill a member of the family. He has been able to keep both my father and me alive all this time, and yet have what he wanted—the title and inheritance."

Silence lay around us. The goats and the cow had long gone past. Ahead, the scrubby green land rolled away to a distant stream. A church spire stood like a needle on a distant hill with the pink of sunset behind it. I said: "If you find your father you will, of course, take him to a doctor. Is it possible that a man could have pressure on the brain for twelve years, then have it lifted and become normal again?"

"Who knows?"

"I'll come with you to the iron mines, Felipe. But what are you going to do about your uncle? He has already offered to take you there. What do you think that meant?"

"It's pretty clear why I was not allowed to work at the mines, isn't it?" Felipe said grimly. "His offer to take me down could mean he planned to exterminate me in the presence of my father, or near. On his past record, I imagine that would appeal to Ernesto. So, if he finds we have been here—"

"Why should he find out? Those two men who spoke to

me were very, very discreet. They could not have been more so. And anyone who enquires will be told the Goizueta families sent you off with a flea in your ear. Why don't you use your second alibi, Felipe? Say you're going to Paris, then make a dash for the mines."

He squeezed my hand very hard indeed, then turned the ignition key and put the car into gear. "I'll do more than that," he said. "I'll get Ernesto to see me off at the airport, so he can be sure I've gone."

"And then come back?"

"No. I can stay in the Departure Lounge until the plane has left. Then—" He turned to me, his blue eyes glinting: "Can you drive?"

"Yes."

"Then you meet me in the car park and we'll go straight to Granada. We could be there before Ernesto can even ring Paris to check that I have arrived. He would have to give me a few hours to get in from Orly to Damian's flat. And anyway, why should I go direct to the flat? He need not necessarily have a check on me all day," said Felipe.

"The man Zarra didn't say Granada. He said 'the mines'."

"Yes. We go through Granada, then out beyond Guadix where the cave dwellers live and the Wild West films are made, and across the plain to the foot of the Sierras. If I can get a booking for an early flight to Paris, say eight o'clock," said Felipe putting his foot down hard on the accelerator, "we could be in La Calahorra by early afternoon."

176

22

WE WERE IN Madrid before dinner time, that wonderful, elastic Spanish dinner time that made travel so simple and problem-free. Felipe took me to an hotel near the Puerta del Sol and while I booked in he telephoned the airport. He returned triumphant to the foyer just as the boy was starting towards the lift with my bag. "That's settled," he said. "I am booked on a plane for Paris leaving at eight-thirty in the morning. Now, while you change—"

I suddenly knew I could face no more today. Within fifteen hours I had witnessed a death, driven over four hundred miles and with my senses tuned to the highest pitch, had my sympathies stretched like rubber bands until they could take no more. I stopped him with a lift of my hand. "Felipe, you have things to attend to this evening that have nothing to do with me. I am too tired to eat dinner, and if I am to be driving a strange car in a strange country at eight o'clock in the morning, I need to sleep now."

Felipe's well-cut mouth softened, and at the same time I thought I saw relief in his eyes. "You're sure?"

"Quite, quite sure. Do they have hot water in city hotels?"

"Of course," he replied confidently, as though there was hot water everywhere in Spain.

"Then I shall have a bath and go straight to sleep. You will visit your grandmother?" It was she who worried me most, though I did not know for certain whether she was

177

the tearing or the torn. Her total trust in her son Ernesto was a stone in my heart since I had heard of her love for Antonia and whatever the coming days were to bring I felt there could be little happiness for her.

"I will stay the night with *Mamita*," he said, making one of his snap decisions, "and ring Ernesto from there. I'll give him the opportunity to see me on the plane if he should so wish. I shall invite him to talk about the new job," he added sardonically. He gave me the keys of the car. "You will find the car park at the airport easily enough. Try to park in the second row beyond the gate so it will not be too difficult to find you. I will come out half-an-hour after the plane takes off. I won't say nine o'clock, because it may be delayed. You never know, Ernesto may be wily enough to hang around until it actually goes."

I slept like the dead that night. To give Spain her due the water from the bath tap marked C for *Caliente* came out very hot indeed. The bed might have been made of bricks or thistledown for all I noticed. I must have been asleep as my head touched the pillow. I was wakened by the telephone, a muted buzz close to my ear. Then traffic sounds muffled by the heavy city curtains and closed windows bore in upon my consciousness, and I opened my eyes to darkness, wondering where on earth I was, yet for all that with a feeling of foreboding as though part of my mind had jumped ahead to the day. I lifted the receiver, switched on the bedside light, grabbed my phrase book, listened to a polite Spanish sentence I could not understand and replied, reading: *"Gracias, Señor. Un poco de cafe, un poco de pan tostado."*

"Si, si, Señorita." Before I was properly dressed a young waiter arrived with the coffee and toast.

"Gracias, Señor." I was beginning to feel quite at home.

*　　*　　*

The city was more than awake. I hurried down the busy street, turned left at the Puerta del Sol, and checking on the

178

sketch map Felipe had given me, followed a long straight road, crossed a square, turned right and there was the car park where our Hertz car had spent the night. I nosed out into the traffic with considerable trepidation for the Spaniard, I had already learned, does not drive quietly. Most of them drove like Felipe and I had still to learn to stay on the right-hand side of the road. It was not so difficult once I actually found my place in the hurly-burly and, buoyed up by my own nervous excitement, I sped out without difficulty on to the airport route.

I ran into the car park at eight-thirty exactly, found a place in the second row from the gate, switched off the engine and settled down to wait.

I glanced swiftly down the lines of stationary cars but from where I sat I could see no Mercedes. My suitcase lay on the back seat. I reached across, opened it swiftly and took out a silk square which I tied over my hair. Then I found my phrase book and hunching down in the seat, set about learning some more Spanish phrases.

It must have been half-an-hour later that Felipe came striding between the parked cars. He was carrying a suit-case which he tossed into the boot, then slid behind the wheel. "Hello."

I smiled at him. "Everything went all right?"

"Fine." He smiled at me but I could see he was taut as a violin string and there were circles beneath his eyes. I felt suddenly guilty for having slept so well.

"Did Ernesto see you off?"

"He did. I had a feel . . ." Felipe stopped. "Okay, let's go." He switched the engine on, put the car into gear. "How's the petrol? We had better fill the tank right up." We moved out between the rows of parked cars.

I wanted to ask him what he had been going to say, but stopped myself. I searched the cars as we moved ahead. There were some Mercedes there among the Simcas, Fiats and other unfamiliar cars but none of them had a driver at the wheel. We came through the gate and swept round the airport structure, building up fast to Felipe's natural pace. There was a small car parked on the side of the road, alone. A man was behind the wheel, with dark hair, just as every man in Spain had dark hair but my heart jolted and I swung round in my seat. With nothing more than intuition to guide me, I found myself slithering up on to my knees and with sweat running down my back, I stared out of the rear window. The man's head had dipped as though he was looking in the glove box and I could not see his face. I am imagining things, I said to myself, but I knew, intuitively, that I had seen Ernesto in that car. I slid my feet to the floor and glanced up at Felipe's face. His chin was hard and high, his face pale and he was staring straight ahead with a concentration that had little to do with the job in hand.

He said in a queer, abrupt voice: "Do you want me to drop you off at Madrid?"

"That was Ernesto in the car, wasn't it?"

"Yes." Only that one word.

"You said you had a feeling, and then you stopped."

He took a hand from the wheel to brush across his brow. "It was bad judgment," he said, "going off like that. Too rushed. I had a feeling Ernesto smelled a rat. It was wrong from the beginning, or perhaps it was just that he knows me too well. His answer was too smooth, when I suggested he run me to the airport. Why should he run me to the airport?" Felipe asked himself savagely. "I never wanted him to do that before."

"But didn't you say it was the only opportunity you had to talk about the job in the iron mines?"

"Yes. Yes, I did, but that was wrong, too. If one out of two is playing a game, it works, but this time two of us were lying, and when both are lying, both can see. If I had genuinely believed he meant what he said about the mines I would have had my grandmother ask him over to her place last night. We would have talked about it as a family, with Pilar, my aunt, as well. Is he following?"

I turned to look out of the rear window. "No."

"He doesn't have to. There is only one road to Granada."

"But why should he know you are going there?"

"He doesn't necessarily know. Tell me, Suzanne, what you would do in his position, if it was not possible to kill me?"

"Move Carlos."

"It's obvious, isn't it? So, I have to get there before him. And he has a Mercedes, whilst I have a Simca."

"You drove out in the Mercedes this morning?"

He nodded. "It's somewhere around. The car Ernesto was sitting in belongs to Quiroga. He will have Quiroga parked somewhere out of sight in his Mercedes."

I jumped as though a bomb had gone off somewhere near. "That is why the car looked familiar! It was the one I saw getting out of the lane in a hurry near Father Eladio's house yesterday morning! Oh my God! It *was* him. It was he who killed the priest!"

"It had to be him," Felipe said, his matter-of-fact words whipped jagged with anger.

We had spun out onto the main route and were speeding back towards Madrid. I turned to look out of the window again. If Ernesto had to change over to the fast Mercedes, he was unlikely to be in sight, yet. "You haven't answered my question, Suzanne. Do you want to be dropped at Madrid?"

"There is only one answer, you know that," I said gently. "I want to meet Carlos. Did you think I would turn back now?"

"It's going to be dangerous. This is my particular Hell. You don't have to be involved."

"I may look frail," I said, "but as you said, I am really quite tough. Besides, when all this is over, I am hoping you will introduce me to one of those half-Arab, half-Andalusian horses you used to ride through the Sierra Nevadas."

"You ride?"

"Indeed." I flashed him a smile though I was far from feeling merry. "I didn't bring my gear, of course. Do they sell jodphurs in La Calahorra?"

"I doubt it very much. If it comes to anything so pleasant,"

181

opined Felipe with what turned out to be startling optimism, "we can always run over to Granada to do some shopping. Mountain villages," he added dryly, "are singularly lacking in fashion stores."

I looked once more out of the rear window. The road was flat behind, the traffic packing in thickly. There might have been a dozen Mercedes among the mass of vehicles that sped along in our wake. "There is no reason why Ernesto should race us to the mines," I said. "If I were he I'd have someone spirit Carlos off to a completely new area, being careful to leave no tracks."

Felipe did not reply. As we approached the city the traffic was building up noisily in the wide lanes. "You cannot go anywhere without leaving some sort of track," he said at last, then added thoughtfully as though speaking to himself: "Justin de Prideau, a Castillian who has lived twelve years in one of the tiny villages at the foot of the Sierra Nevada! There has got to have been a woman looking after him. And all Spaniards, but particularly women, are very family-conscious. I hold one trump card. I am Justin de Prideau's son. That has got to touch somebody's heart."

"If there was a resemblance, yes. But your grandmother said there was none," I reminded him tentatively, feeling a little afraid of the strength of the optimism growing in him.

"My grandmother hasn't seen Carlos for twenty-eight years. I am less worried about that than I am by the thought of driving this dreary little bus for something like five hundred kilometres."

It seemed a nice little car to me but I supposed that by comparison with the model lying broken in the gorge at Toledo it could be termed a dreary little bus.

He broke into my thoughts with one of those swift, decisive statements that were so typical of him. "I've a friend who lives pretty near here. I won ... der ..."

"What, Felipe?"

"I wonder if Garcia is using his Alfa Romeo?"

"Do people loan Alfa Romeo's?" I asked dryly.

"He only bought it after driving mine. I loaned mine to him for a weekend when I went to a wedding in Paris last year. It crosses my mind," said Felipe wickedly, "that, viewed from the right quarter, one could say he owes me a debt." Suddenly he was smiling, sitting up higher, squaring his shoulders. "And speed is not the only advantage," he went on. "Whoever looks out for us will be looking for a small black hired car. Uncle Ernesto will even have the registration number."

I felt an Alfa Romeo was going to be pretty obvious in a small Andalusian mountain village, but I kept my own counsel because it was clear he had made up his mind and I was glad to see his spirits high. I said with a nervous little laugh: "The thought of dashing three hundred miles with you in the fastest car I know frightens the wits out of me. Isn't there a speed limit on the main highways here?"

He turned his head slightly. "Don't worry that pretty golden head of yours," he said. "Do you know a better driver than me?"

"I think I know some more careful drivers."

"Because a man drives slowly, that is no indication that he drives well. I've never had an accident—" he grinned, "apart from diving into the Tagus."

"When you do things," I agreed meekly, "you certainly do them well."

23

GARCIA'S CAR WAS in the garage. We saw it through the open door as we spun into the courtyard of the house and I had to be glad for Felipe's sake. He left me in my seat while he went to the door. I saw a tall, motherly woman greet him and then they disappeared inside. I took out my phrase book and had learned three more phrases before he emerged. 'How much?' 'What does this mean?' and 'Please point to the phrase in the book'. Felipe came over to me with swift strides. A key ring dangled from his finger. "Would you like to drive into the garage as soon as I come out?" I nodded. "Leave the keys in it. Garcia will return it to Hertz at mid-day." He backed the long, low, powerful little sports car out, and I slid the Simca into its place, then picking up my handbag, jumped in beside him.

We were both so taken up with our own thoughts, me with my apprehension, he with his good luck, that we did not remember our suitcases until we had left Madrid behind and were sweeping across a great plain planted as far as the eye could see with green crops in ordered rows. "Felipe!" I exclaimed in consternation. "Our bags!"

That smile of his flickered across at me, casual, confident. "Garcia will find them and look after them. There's nothing you want, is there?"

"I suppose there isn't," I admitted, uncertainly.

"What does a girl need apart from lipstick and a comb?"

184

"You fantastic man!" But I found myself laughing, and he laughed with me. "I did have some roasted almonds I bought in Toledo. Since I cannot see you stopping for elevenses, we could have chewed them."

"Light me a cigarette, will you? That will take your mind off the almonds."

"No, I am damned if I will. You need both your hands." I leaned ostentatiously towards him, looking at the speedometer. The hands on the clock had spun up to a hundred and eighty.

"That's kilometres," Felipe pointed out. "Not miles."

On the road to Burgos we had been overtaken by all the fast cars and often by those frightening juggernauts, mechanical giant praying-mantis' from another world. Now we swept past them at immense speed and soon I found myself caught up in the excitement that came, inevitably, from split-second living. If Felipe drove at a terrifying pace, I had to admit he drove well and if he took risks I was not aware of them, or perhaps the taut urgency in him passed for a meticulous sort of care. We ate up the long, straight ribbon of road with the wind of our own speed screaming along the bonnet and the deserted cropland spinning away to be replaced by swamp land, stony earth land, some rivers that lay flat, stagnant and without beauty as though waiting for the summer sun to come and evaporate them from their dull world. There were no men working in the fields, no houses. We dashed by white villages from which, Felipe said, the workmen went out each day, and once a man in a cart drawn by two mules flashed by, the man dozing.

There were factories an hour later, and some tiny houses that Felipe told me could be covers for artesian bores. "The plain of La Mancha gets mighty hot in the summer," he said raising his voice over the muted roar of the engine. "Keeping the crops watered is a major operation."

"And I dare say it's freezing in the winter. Poor old Don Quixote! There's one of his windmills. Don't look, though," I added, my voice nervily sharp. "Keep your eyes on the

185

road." Above, the cornflower-blue sky was lively with a skirmish of cloud.

"You're not really nervous, are you?"

It was this sort of car that had killed Antonia. That had been what I was thinking all the time. Thinking of Carlos, thinking of Antonia, I had to think of that killer car. "No," I said. "No. And there are mountains coming up ahead anyway, so you will have to slow down."

Such optimism! The low, rough hills came racing towards us, attractive and wild, seamed with grey-green olives as neatly rowed as the crops of La Mancha plain, but untamed. We swept round a wide bend and there was a hill swathed in stripes of red earth alternating with the bright green of crops, a stream, a small vineyard coming into leaf and then the road dipped and we swept down into a gorge where a river sparkled over huge stones. We came up out of the gorge and swept across another area of plain. There was a town out in front, a mere huddle of tiled roofs yet, sand-pink and moss green.

"Do you want to stop? Coffee? Or a drink?" Felipe asked.

The excitement of the day had eaten up that small and very inadequate Spanish breakfast, but I knew the last thing Felipe wished to do was stop so I affected disinterest. "We may as well keep going now." He flung me a grateful look. The town tore towards us and I had a momentary pang of longing before it was too late.

I slept for a while then, an unquiet sleep full of the noise of the engine, and an awareness of hunger. I wakened as we swung round a sharp bend. A clump of cypresses swept by, some pines, a flash of golden broom and then we took a roaring dive into a twisting valley and out in front, to my horror, I saw an enormous truck slung half across the road, a small green car with the nose smashed up against the back seat and the doors stained red with blood, two police cars and a man in uniform transferring two very new-looking suitcases to his own vehicle. My own blood pulsed in my head and sang in my ears. I sank low in my seat, not

186

wanting to look. Felipe had, miraculously, slowed the Alfa to a mere crawl. Neither of us spoke. The police waved us on and the car gathered speed again, swinging round bend after bend with the fabulous gold of broom jutting out of the bank above and ragged birches with the pale leaves of spring standing on the slope below.

24

WE SWEPT THROUGH the straggly outskirts of Granada and turned east. Here, sandwiched between mountains and barely an hour from the Mediterranean, the early afternoon sun beat like a furnace flame. We passed small, poverty-stricken villages with broken-down houses where the women were washing household linen in fast-flowing streams, where donkeys stood tethered outside bars, idly flicking their long ears and swishing their tails against flies. We passed ragged, dirty children, naked children, a village idiot staring, some donkey carts laden with greenery, mulemen transporting their mysterious bundles. The road was good as far as Guadix. We crawled through the town, past small shops, a leafy park, tall, decaying buildings, squat modern ones.

Felipe drew the car in to the kerb. "Would you like to get out and see if you can find us something we can eat as we go along? You must be stiff, too."

"That," I replied as I tried feebly to lift myself out of the seat, "is the greatest understatement of all time. I doubt very much if I can stand up. And if I do, I shall probably fall over from sheer lack of food."

Felipe had the grace to look contrite. "You have been marvellous. If I ever get the chance I'll buy you the biggest, grandest dinner you have ever seen."

"And by the time I get it I'll be so hungry I won't be able to keep it down," I returned, thinking ruefully of the morning—Was it only six days ago?—when Perry Ballisat found me in Zocodover Square about to throw up. I opened the door, crawled stiffly out of the very low seat, and stood stretching myself thankfully on the pavement. The sun was stinging my bare arms and blinding my eyes. Felipe came round from the other side and handed me some peseta notes. "Sorry I can't go, but it would mean parking the car. If I stay with it I can move if the police bother me. If you find I am gone, wait here until I come round and pick you up."

I put my sunglasses on again. "What do you want?"

"Get what you like," said Felipe off-handedly, impatient to move on. "There is some sort of a bar on the next corner. You might find ham rolls or something like that, and some bottles of Fanta. Garcia has probably left a bottle opener somewhere in the car—I haven't had time to check—but have them opened anyway."

I found the bar, busy with chattering small dark people, Andalusians, as Perry Ballisat had said, heavily crossed with the Moors. They stood aside to make a track through to the counter for me, staring inquisitively at my fair hair, my white skin. There had been no time to consult the phrase book. *"Pan, por favor,"* I began, wondering nervously if a request for bread might land me with one of those great white loaves on the shelf. And then I saw some small, filled rolls ready beneath the glass counter. I pointed to them. *"Seis, por favor."* Felipe, I had no doubt, was capable of demolishing four and certainly I could put away two.

I ordered a milk shake. It ran down to my stomach and disappeared as though it had never been, leaving a silk lining on my parched throat. Guiltily, for the rolls were ready, half-wrapped in an inadequate little square of white paper. I ordered another. *"Otro, por favor."* Sloshing some more milk into the container, the man made a witty remark to the onlookers who had cleared a way round me and gone silent in their surprise. One of them, bolder than the rest, pointed to my waist then at the rolls and we all laughed. Business came to a halt as they closed round me, warmly eyeing my bare white arms, my fair hair, flatteringly eager to be friends. I drank the second milk shake swiftly, and this time I felt it filling the gaps, satisfying, comforting me. Picking up the rolls and bottles I extricated myself from my growing group of admirers. *"Adios,"* they called with charming regret, and I hurried back to the car.

"Here we are. Nectar from the Gods. Lemon Fanta and ham rolls." Then, as Felipe, with scarcely a glance at my booty, turned the ignition key I exclaimed: "But you must eat and drink something now. Please, Felipe."

His eyes met mine with a glimmer of a smile, impatient, apologetic, and then he switched the engine off again. He took a bottle from my hands and drank. "And eat one roll before we go on," I insisted, pushing it into his hands. "I've had two milk shakes and I feel a new woman. I say, they do go for English women in these parts," I told him. "It's very good for the morale."

He threw me a quick look, then ate his roll hungrily. I handed him a paper tissue from my bag. "I am sorry," he said abruptly as he finished.

"Sorry? What for?"

"I am not being an attentive companion." To my extreme surprise he put an arm round my shoulders. "You're lovely and you're wonderful, too, Suzanne. I want to tell you that, and I know I am using you. But it's because I need you. Can you take that as a compliment? The sort of compliment that is right for the moment?"

I was deeply touched and rather more shaken than I cared to admit to myself. "A girl likes to be needed," I said, speaking lightly over my emotions and then the moment was gone for a traffic policeman came walking towards us down the street and Felipe had the car started again.

"The road is slow from now on. I had a look at the map while you were shopping. It's bendy and unsealed. We've no chance of making any sort of pace." He took another roll in one hand and so we went on our way, crawling through the traffic then speeding out on to a sealed road lined with

190

square, white houses and tall trees. "This is where we turn off for the plain," Felipe said, turning down on to a loose metal road that dipped and curved through a startling, lunar-like landscape of weird, pale rock structures that rose like a stage back-drop for Snow White and the Seven Dwarfs in grotesque hillocks, misshapen, haphazard, rent with fissures and black with holes.

I blinked in disbelief. "They're houses!" I exclaimed delightedly. "The troglodytes! Look at the chimneys shooting up out of the rock and the grass!"

But Felipe had seen them before. "Sorry I can't stop. I'll bring you back some time." The road was twisting, the metal soft and loose. He was driving very carefully now. I leaned out of the window, startled, staring, and short, dark men and women stared stolidly back at me from their little square doorways in the rock as we ran by.

A group of black-eyed, black-haired, lively children dashed towards us, took a short-cut across a round grassy roof, splitting in the centre to avoid running into a smoking chimney, then hurled themselves after the car yelling: "*Pesetas, pesetas!*" I balanced the extra bottle between my knees and reached for my handbag but before I could open it we were gone from them up a steep little slope, round a sharp bend hedged in by more cave houses, and down a very rough slope into a dip.

"A lot of film people come here to make the Wild West films in the valley beyond," Felipe said, putting his foot down on the accelerator. "The local children have become accustomed to begging. I could do with another of those rolls." We swept up the next rise and suddenly we were on a crest from which we looked down a wide, flat valley on either side of which rose gigantic cliffs bleached beneath centuries of relentless sun, streaked iron-pink, slate-grey, white as chalk. Below and before them great sandstone structures reached towards the sky, nightmarish, grand and crudely lovely, stabbed with fissures black as night.

"It's truly wonderful," I exclaimed. "And oh yes, I would

191

like to come back. But Felipe, do stop and drink this other bottle now. That is something you really cannot do while driving and I cannot guarantee not to spill it on this rough road now the top of the bottle has been removed." I might have reminded him that he had been going to drive slowly but perhaps this pace we were now doing was slow to him. He did stop the car, but he did not turn the engine off. He emptied the second bottle, wiped a hand across his mouth, picked up a third roll from my knee and we were away again, sweeping round the next corner to a straight road with hillocks on either side and those strange rock houses set well back in grassy hills, thinning out to a straggle, until we left them all behind. Out in front now were the mighty Sierras, jade-green and grey, snow-patched at the summits, formidable, sky-high. "It's fantastic!" I exclaimed, over-awed. "Now I see why you wanted to work down here. The space! The emptiness!"

"Emptiness is great," replied Felipe between mouthfuls, "when you can come and go at will."

"You're thinking of Carlos?"

"Yes."

Carlos had to be a prisoner. We had both known that ever since Zarra had told us of his whereabouts, but we had not talked of it. The reality seemed too brutal. That a man should be imprisoned, somehow, for twelve years. And yet, Zarra had said he worked at the iron mines. Was that possible? To work with a companion watching every move? A guard? There were more unhappy connotations but neither of us wanted to face them. The blow on the head could have been very serious. I thrust that possibility aside as I had been thrusting it aside for a day and a night now. Time to face facts when we came to the end of the trail.

We sped along the soft grey metal road, dived down by a wide, dry river bed with leafy green poplars and silver-grey almond trees standing motionless in the flaming sun. Felipe was driving slowly now for the metal was loose, the surface very uneven indeed. We turned a corner and were briefly

192

hemmed in by tall forests of wild sugar cane. We passed a dark man on a mule, legs widely astride pannier bags stuffed with greenery. He gave us a nod and a friendly wave. Then we were up and away to cross a brown, stony hill green-cloaked in pines. The road rose and we climbed to our little horizon backed by the mighty Sierras and suddenly burst over the top to see spread out below us a fantastic great plain that stretched into the far distance and up to the foot of the mountains themselves, a brown plain, drenched in the green of wheat touched with early gold.

"I seem to have come through about four worlds in the past few days," I said, feeling a little numb with the shock and excitement of it.

Felipe said with a sharp lift to his voice: "You like Spain?"

"When my head stops whirling I'll think about it. It frightens me, that's about all I really know for sure. I think, too, I may be getting a new concept of life. I hate the poverty. I wonder how I will feel next time I buy a dress or a pair of shoes that are not really necessary."

"Spain is a land of contrasts," he said.

"And slow to learn. Or don't the people try?"

"I think we would try," he said after consideration, "if we knew where to begin. The Spaniard is a fatalist. It is said that the country brought a sad retribution upon itself when it expelled the Moors. As long as they were here making their contribution, Spain was king of nations but with their expulsion we started to go down-hill."

"That was a mighty long time ago," I found myself saying briskly, covering my thoughts for I was thinking that Felipe, who now said 'we' had always considered himself an Englishman.

"1609 saw the last of the Muslims; Spain went into a decline then and we've never managed to reverse it. I am not saying we don't try. Pilar does a lot of charity work."

"It's just a joke, though, isn't it, when you look at what we have seen this morning. I mean, pretty clothes worn at a First Night, and fêtes. Have you begun to wonder what

193

Carlos was about? What is a revolutionary but a man who wants something better for someone?"

"I know it sounds pathetic in the context of what we've been looking at today, but if we gave up the estate and all we possess, how much good could we do in a country the size of ours? What did Carlos do but bring himself down to the level of a peasant? Spain isn't going to blossom from the Pyrenees to the Sierras in our lifetime, no matter what anyone does."

"You said whatever Carlos has done, he is your father. Don't you think he might have been trying to do good?"

I felt, rather than heard him sigh. "We know so little about him. Do you see that mound ahead sprouting out of the plain?"

"Mound? I can see the Sierra Nevada. How could one fail? Those mountains fill the world. I suddenly feel the size of a peanut."

Felipe chuckled. "There is quite a hill this side of, and at the foot of the range. It looks like a pin-head at the moment, but it is a good-sized lump when one is close to it. There is a Renaissance castle on top, and out to the left, if you keep looking, you will see some grey humps which are the residue from the iron mines."

"We're nearly there?" My nerves began to tighten and involuntarily I turned in my seat, looking back along the expanse of dead flat road with the green-gold wheat on either side of it. "There is no one following."

"Good. We will be able to see any car now." And that was true. There was no hiding place on this vast and treeless plain. I closed the window for though the sun was scorching, an icy wind had come singing in from the mountains disturbing the wheat, so that it dipped and rose all round us like a silken sea. We spun across the plain, mile after mile of straight, rough road, the car jolting on its expensive tyres and eventually, as we drew nearer, the mighty castle did begin to take form, brown frowning walls and massive drum towers growing out of the bare round hill that jutted up

194

with startling suddenness from the plain in front.

"That is where the village is," Felipe said, "It's the most likely starting place on a search for someone from the iron mines."

"Is that where you stayed when you came here as a boy?"

"Yes. I told you about those treks through the mountains. One can ride more-or-less straight up out of that village. There is a track over the Wolf Pass—Puerto del Lobo—and it's a wonderful ride. You come out at a little village called Yegen which claims to have the finest water in Spain and the country beyond that is fantastic. Great red mountains and canyons. Ulysses is said to have visited there. I'll take you there one day." Felipe made me his absent-minded promise once again, his mind on other things.

25

As WE CAME nearer we saw the village itself packed tightly at the foot of the castle's hill, the houses jammed in upon one another hiding beneath slate-grey sloping roofs in a sort of meek obeisance to the grandeur above.

"What on earth is that fantastic castle doing in such a primitive place?" I asked Felipe in some astonishment. "Who lives there?"

"No one ever did," he replied. "Some mad Marquis built it for his wife but though he imported Italian architects and made it quite magnificent in the purest Renaissance style, she wouldn't stay there."

"I don't blame her."

"It is quite something with doors and balustrades exquisitely carved in the finest Carrara marble."

"What would she do other than sit staring out of the arrow-slits like one of Blue Beard's wives, waiting for someone to come?"

Felipe was not listening. He was peering through the windscreen as the car rounded a bend and turned into a rough and rather dirty village street. There were square-fronted houses on either side, a horse trough set back on a low bank, one of those bars with a bead curtain across its narrow door and a white-painted building bigger than the rest with wrought-iron work over the windows, a few window boxes with geraniums bursting out of bud, and a heavy, brown-painted wooden front door.

Felipe brought the car to a halt. "This is a *posada*," he said. "Let's see if we can raise anyone." He glanced at his watch. "Damn! Always the siesta hour. Anyway, let's try."

The heavy front door opened with creaking hinges onto a large gloomy area with a rough stone floor that smelled rankly of animals, of dung and earth. On the left hand side as we entered there was an open door leading to a stable and in the dim light from a low-powered naked electric bulb I could see two tethered mules munching straw. At the back of the room there was a stone water trough with a tap over it, and as my eyes became accustomed to the gloom I saw over to the right some steps leading beyond a rough curtain, and at the foot of the steps a gypsy family, the man asleep with a felt hat over his eyes, the woman huddled against him with her rags around her and a child curled up on the stones.

We tiptoed quietly past them, moved the curtain aside and went up some dark stairs, feeling our way in the gloom. They led to a square landing with half-a-dozen doors leading off it. One in the back corner was ajar. Tentatively, Felipe crossed to it and I followed. We looked into a spotless kitchen with a stove, a sink, several hard chairs, a wooden table and beneath the table on a spread sheet, a fat middle-aged woman curled up on her side, asleep. Felipe and I looked at each other with resignation and amusement. "Poor thing. We'll have to waken her."

He tapped sharply on the kitchen door and she lifted her head, eyed us, then rose without embarrassment to her feet.

While Felipe spoke to her, I went over to the window, looking out on the rough stone street, the shuttered houses opposite and beyond them, mesmerically, to the frowning castle standing guard over the little town. I could hear the muffled stamping of the mules in the stable below. The biting smell of deep litter wafted strongly up the stairs. There were flies everywhere, black dots on the white walls, on the windows, and silently moving through the air. I

197

brushed them from my bare arms and from my face.

The woman crossed to one of the closed doors and opened it. I saw a man lying half-clothed on a bed. She closed the door and disappeared inside. Felipe came across the landing to me.

"I say, they're a bit short on Women's Lib here, aren't they? He has a bed for his siesta." As soon as it was out I was ashamed of my flippant remark for Felipe was saying in a taut voice: "They know Justin de Prideau. She said her husband will take us to his lodging."

"Did you ask her if Ernesto, or anyone from Madrid, had been here?"

He shook his head. "I didn't ask because I don't want to rouse her curiosity. Any sort of car in a village of this kind would be known to be here, so someone will say so without our having to ask. Anyway, no one could beat our time," Felipe added confidently. "The telephone is our only opposition. The inn keeper may not know if Carlos has already been spirited away."

The door the woman had entered opened now and a small, thick, dark man with several days' growth of beard appeared. He nodded to us, pausing on the threshold to button his crushed shirt and hitch up a very worn and baggy pair of trousers. He had ebony black eyes and black tousled hair which he flattened with his hands as he came forward. He looked at Felipe with sharp interest and faint dislike, speaking rapidly and hoarsely in Spanish, then without waiting for a reply, signed to us to follow him down the stairs. I turned to thank the woman. *"Gracias, Señora."* She nodded, but her eyes were uncertain now and she did not smile. Once out in the street I glanced back up at the windows. She was standing there, looking after us, half-obscured by the curtain but not apparently attempting to conceal himself. Watching out of curiosity, I felt, but with something more.

"What is the man's name?"

"Aparicio."

"He's not very chatty, is he?"

Aparicio went ahead at a cracking pace down a slope and round a corner where chickens were bathing in the dust that lay among the stones in the dirty little lane, past a yard stacked with junk and timber, and then round another corner. Here was another of those white-painted, square-fronted *posadas* with the big, heavy front door. There was the same large stable entrance as before. Our guide stepped over the threshold and was swallowed by the interior gloom.

"Is he really here? Carlos?"

Felipe glanced down at me and a mixture of emotions flickered across his face. My own nerves were strung to breaking pitch. Was this really the end of the trail? We stepped tentatively over the threshold on to an earth floor. A moment later the light came on and I could see a manger at the back of the big, gloomy, raftered room. Two pretty little donkeys looked at us interestedly, their long, fluffy ears swinging as they shook the flies from their faces. Over on the right, bizarrely, for the smell of the stables was almost overpowering, we could see in the dim light from the single electric bulb a small, modern-looking white-painted kitchen beside some red brick stairs. The light entered the kitchen through a window that looked onto the stables and I could see, to my astonishment, a square refrigerator, a white enamelled stove and a group of large green wine bottles on a scrubbed table.

With a curt command in Spanish and a beckoning gesture, Aparicio, who was standing at the foot of the stairs, pulled aside a blanket serving as a curtain, then disappeared behind it. We crossed the intervening space and followed him. At the top of the stairs there was an enclosed landing without windows or light of any kind. He switched on another low-powered light and there was a table with a cloth of some thick red shiny material, and hard kitchen chairs standing round it.

Aparicio knocked on a door opposite. I looked round the landing room. There were some wedding photos. Grim-faced bridegrooms with their expressionless brides. They might have

199

been a century old. One armchair, and on the walls some brass pots and spoons. Felipe was speaking to the Spaniard. He nodded and Felipe turned to me. There was a curious little tugging at the corners of his mouth as though the strung nerves in him had lost the key to a smile. I reached for his hand and squeezed it. "Are you ready?"

He said: "As ready as I ever was. But I don't think I believe it. I feel as though I am going to wake up in a moment."

And that was how I felt, consumed with the unreality of the situation. Our man Aparicio opened the door quietly and touched a light switch inside. The naked bulb hanging from a black cord partially lit an enormous room so bizarre that I could only stand and stare. There was a bare wooden floor and from the ceiling hung half-a-dozen enormous hams. There were three beds, a green plastic bucket full of water beside which lay a towel and cake of soap, and over on the right a glassless window covered in wire netting through which came the distinct chick, chick of birds. In one corner there was a sack lumpy with grain.

This I took in at that first swift glance and then I was walking in a daze of sheer disbelief across the bare boards and I could see in the far corner another bed covered in a dark blanket and a man's head on the pillow.

"Justin!" The guide spoke hoarsely from the doorway. I stopped. Had Ernesto really brought Carlos to this? To the level of a muleteer? "Justin," our guide said again in his hoarse, grating voice. The man in the bed stirred, turned over, then sleepily pulled himself to a sitting position. There was another plastic bucket on the floor a yard away, another cake of soap and towel. I do not know why I was so conscious of this curious refinement. My eyes moved to the tousled, sleep-laden man in the white cotton vest who was looking from one to the other of us in such apparent surprise.

Aparicio, with a passing glance at me and a grunt for Felipe, left. Felipe was advancing slowly towards the bed, his body blocking my view of the man. I stepped aside to peer at him then paused, and suddenly conscious of the privacy of the moment, turned my back and went over to the netted gap in the wall. There, in a light well about ten feet square, was a hen coop with straw scattered about. Half-a-dozen hens and some small chickens were pecking at the straw. Behind me the two men were talking in Spanish and I found myself, weirdly, for I could not have understood a word, trying not to listen. I watched the restless brown chickens with a blank mind and my emotions shredded. I could not have said how long I stood there before I heard Felipe's footsteps advancing across the room. I lifted my head to look at him and found I could not see him for the tears in my eyes.

He said in a jolting, misshapen voice, as though wanting me to contradict: "It isn't him."

"How do you know?" I asked, my heart leaping, then plummeting, then leaping again, not wanting Carlos to come to this, yet wanting him to be found.

"I don't know," Felipe admitted. "And he cannot remember anything before he came here." We stood there in a stunned, bewildered silence, then: "He looks like what I remember of him," Felipe said in that strangely unfamiliar voice, "but it's not Carlos."

"Why would the man Zarra say de Prideau was Carlos' name, if it was not so?" I asked. "He seemed so eager to help. So plausible, too."

"Why, having heard the name, was it so incredibly easy to find him?" asked Felipe, his bewilderment going and sharp suspicion coming in to take its place.

"You mean—?"

"I mean we only asked once—in the obvious place, the *posada* that any traveller would stop at because it is there at the start of the village. And there was someone who broke off his siesta, if not affably, at least willingly. Perhaps it was too easy, like the Paris plane fiasco," Felipe remarked, still in that shaken way. "How could you know Zarra wasn't one of Ernesto's men?"

"He wasn't," I whispered heatedly, feeling the colour rush to my face. "I'd stake my life he was not. My life, Felipe."

After a moment's silence he said flatly: "Women's intuition is supposed to be better than men's. Come and talk to him. He speaks English."

I went hesitantly across to the bed. The man in it was unshaven, with perhaps three days' growth of grey-black beard and his dark, tousled hair was thick, streaked with grey above his forehead.

"Good afternoon."

"Buenas tardes."

I stared hard into his face, searching for some resemblance to Felipe, to Ernesto, to the Dowager Countess, and could find none. He did not have the obvious, high-boned look of an aristocrat. On the other hand, he did not look a peasant.

"I am afraid I speak no Spanish."

He nodded. "I speak English a little. I am sorry that I cannot get out of bed to talk to you. I have been ill for a week—more than that. A virus."

I sat down on the end of the bed thinking that he was far too modest about his English. He spoke it fluently and with confidence. "Tell me how you came to be here, Señor de Prideau, in this very primitive *posada*," I said.

"I am a working man," he replied, affecting surprise at my question. "I live here. I work in the mines."

"Where did you learn English, then?"

He shook his head. "I don't know. I do not know anything about myself before *El Conde* de Merito took an interest in me and gave me this job in the mines. You excuse my English. I do not use it much." He suddenly seemed to be straining after words as a man does when using a foreign language in which he has little practice. "You have come to tell me about someone called Antonia. Perhaps this is from the past I do not remember."

He nodded towards Felipe. "He asks if I am *El Conde*'s brother. Why should this be so? *El Conde* visits me whenever he comes here. He is kind to me, but what is this about my being his brother? I do not understand. Would *El Conde* allow his brother to work as a labourer in the iron mines?"

"How did you lose your memory?" I asked.

"An accident in the Sierras, perhaps. I do not know that either. I found myself here, in this village. The people were good to me. Friendly. They have taken me in and treat me as one of them."

"Why do you suppose *El Conde* de Merito takes such an interest in you?" I asked.

"I do not know. I thought, because I had no one. And I am often ill. It is my head. A head wound."

"Is it likely he would take such an interest in a lonely labourer if you were no kin?" I used the word 'kin' deliberately. It was not, I thought, a word a Spaniard with only a rudimentary knowledge of English would find familiar.

"I do not know."

The man looked down at his hands and with my eyes following his I saw his fingers for the first time. They were not the hands of a working man. The nails were clean and reasonably well cared for, the skin, though brown from the sun, was smooth. This man was not Carlos, of that I was suddenly and blindingly certain. Neither was he a labourer in the mines. I wanted to get away, out of this dark and squalid room, away from the lies and the strangeness to where I could think properly.

As though Felipe, too, had reached a definite conclusion, he moved with that quick impatience I knew so well. He said: "We must go now. Perhaps we can come and see you tomorrow when you are feeling better. We need to have a long talk. Meantime, we don't want to tire you."

"Why do you not bring your uncle here?" the man asked, and I saw, or thought I saw, a sly look come into his eyes.

"We may do that."

We said our goodbyes and went down the dark stairway in silence, through the rank-smelling stable area and out into the glaring sunlight of the dirty street. Felipe took my arm. "So?"

"He hasn't a workman's hands. And he isn't ill. His reactions are too quick. And he wasn't asleep when we came into the room, so he should have answered the knock. We must have been expected."

"Don't eliminate him!" said Felipe sharply. "Not entirely. Let's pause and think. Let's go over it. Even if there is a one per cent chance he is Carlos, we cannot leave."

"Without having the appearance of being a cultivated man, he could pass for Ernesto's brother," I said. "He doesn't look at all like you, but your grandmother said there was no resemblance. Of course there is no reason why your father would give an impression of being cultured after the life he must have been living, but somehow I felt there would be signs." Ernesto, for all his beastliness, had the unmistakable air of an aristocrat, and so had Felipe. This man, though indeed he had a good command of English, was from ordinary beginnings, of that I was certain.

Felipe said with a rough edge to his voice: "I know. I know. That man is not Carlos. I cannot pin down any particular thing. I didn't notice his hands as you did. But it isn't him."

"In the context of what is going on," I said, "it's feasible that he could be Carlos' guardian, put there as a stooge to hold us up until Ernesto can get here."

We halted in the middle of the dirty, stony, dusty street and stood facing each other, certain yet uncertain, panic-stricken at the thought of actually making a mistake.

A dog like the one I had seen at *El Regalo del Rey* with coarse, sandy coat and pointed nose came padding towards us. I said: "You saw him once, in partial darkness, twenty years ago. Can you remember, Felipe, really?"

"The curious thing," he said, "is that I feel certain I do. But more than that, I think I would know. I think there would be something to tell a man he was talking to his father. Something ..."

It was a frail thread of speculation.

"What are we going to do?"

There was a clatter of footsteps on stones and round the corner came two men in overalls. A woman called stridently from an upstairs window. Shutters were opened. The siesta was drawing to its close. "There are plenty of people in this village," Felipe said. "They cannot all be in on a conspiracy."

"I had a feeling that woman we first spoke to knew something."

"What made you think that?"

"I don't know. Intuition again, I suppose."

"I doubt if she would be of any use," Felipe said, "for she has a husband to deal with. Besides, if he has been bribed, she is bound to benefit. What would she gain by telling on her husband?" Some children came running round the corner and stopped to stare at us. They watched curiously, a little uneasily, as we approached, then turned and scurried away.

"I noticed a bar near the first *posada*," I said. "Let's go there and make enquiries."

We wended our way back up the street, turned the corner and I uttered a gasp of horror and amazement. The car had gone.

After the first shock subsided I said: "I'd opt for running back to that *posada* and walking right in on our friend without knocking. It won't take a moment and we're not going to find the Alfa in that time."

Two minds with but a single thought! I scarcely had the words out when Felipe was swinging me round. We bolted back the way we had come, clattering and slipping on the uneven stones and pulled up panting at the *posada* door. It was open now with light flooding the interior. A very old couple, perhaps not so old in years but darkly creased by time and hardship, were seated side-by-side on kitchen chairs inside the door, apparently impervious to the flies and smell, staring with eyes full of patience out into the blinding glare of the street. The woman held a small child on her knee.

The man noted our arrival with a turn of the head, a straight stare.

"Buenas tardes." We sped by, slipped through the curtain and ran up the stairs. Felipe crossed the landing at a run and without ceremony, so far had we convinced ourselves of the possibilities, flung open the door of the room and with a flip of a finger switched on the light.

The bed was empty.

26

I WAITED BY the water trough with the great mountains behind me, green, grey and patched at the summit with snow already dulled by spring's dust. Felipe went back alone to the *posada* outside of which he had left the car. What can one do without any knowledge of the language? All round me the village was coming to life. Women stood gossiping in their doorways, two old men, leaning on sticks, hobbled round a corner, chatting and gesticulating in the lively Spanish way. Two tiny donkeys came down the main street, their pannier bags heavily laden with that greenery I had seen them carrying so often today and which I assumed was the beast's own food. They ambled slowly past, leaving the aromatic scents of the mountain in their wake, a peasant woman in black with a black headscarf leading them.

I climbed the stone steps by the water trough and sat down on the dry grass. What on earth were we going to do without a car? Were there any police in this tiny mountain village? Any telephones? Was there a bus? A taxi? Was the whole village hand-in-glove against us? Did the dark innkeeper who had roused himself so reluctantly from his sleep know whom we sought? Did he see the man in the bed before turning tail? My mind was a warren of outlets and heaven alone knew which one we might pursue.

From the distance came the steady clip-clop of horses' hooves and then round the corner came two Spaniards riding tall, spirited beasts with prancing feet and necks arched. The riders, a man and a young boy, wore black sombreros and leather chaps, those apron-like shields that protect the leg and which I had seen in pictures of bull fights and Wild West films. They rode right up to the trough, eyeing me with calculated interest. *"Buenas tardes."*

"Buenas tardes." At the trough they dismounted, undid the horses' bits and led them to drink.

"¿Habla usted español?"

I raised a hand to stop him. "I do not speak Spanish."

"Eengleesh?" He was a good-looking man of about fifty, very short, not more than five feet four or five, with a fine head, a swarthy skin and coal-black eyes wrinkled smilingly at the corners.

"Yes."

He nodded. "I spik Eengleesh. Your are holiday?"

"Yes."

"You like ride horse?"

"Yes, very much."

"Mucho. Ah. I have stable. Good horse. Mountain horse. Arab-Andalusian. You like ride?"

How I would love it, under different circumstances! The horses looked wonderful. Finely built with slim legs, small, dainty feet and obviously very, very fit. Their coats gleamed like satin in the sun. "Is yours the only stable here?" I asked.

"Only stable? *No comprendo."*

Felipe had said he used to hire horses from a half-Mexican called Sebastian. This man, with his strutting style and swarthy look could easily be half-Mexican.

"Are there many stables here?"

"Many? No. One. Why you ask?" His black eyes flashed. "You no like my horses?"

"No, no," I assured him hurriedly. "I was wondering if you might be a friend of a friend of mine. He used to hire horses from someone called Sebastian."

The man's face lit up with a flame of delight. "I am Sebastian. You are sent to me?"

208

"No. But the friend who is with me has told me of you. He knew you more than twelve years ago. Felipe Lazaro."

"Ah! The boy Felipe!" His weather-beaten face softened as his mind flew back. He handed his reins to the boy and climbed the steps to stand beside me. "So, you know Don Felipe! He not come for long time."

"He is here. If you wait, you will see him." I scanned the rugged face anxiously. Interest? Friendship? I could scarcely doubt his genuine pleasure.

"Ah!" Sebastian exclaimed warmly. "It is long time I see him. Not since a boy."

"Do you ever see his uncle?" I asked. "The Count? *El Conde* de Merito?"

"Ah yes. You know *El Conde*?" Sebastian's smile went. "He visits the village, but I never see Don Felipe, not since he is a boy."

I picked a grass stalk, shredding it in my fingers. "Why does the Count come here?" I asked, trying to sound careless and sounding, to my ears, very curious indeed.

"Why? Excuse, I do not spik English *mucho*."

I shot him a suspicious look but he seemed to be genuinely puzzled. "*El Conde* comes here to visit a friend?"

"Ah yes. Not often. Yes, a man who works at mines and sometimes not well. Sick."

"Justin de Prideau?"

He nodded. The horses began to grow restive. The child spoke to Sebastian softly in Spanish. Sebastian went down the steps and took the reins of the lovely stallion. The boy mounted the mare and rode off down into the village. I rose from my dry grass perch and went to stand beside Sebastian, smoothing his horse's nose. The stallion raised his head, nibbling at my hands with velvet lips, friendly, gentle, but with flicking ears and lively eyes as though he was ready to be away across the plain with the wind behind him. A creature pattern of Felipe. I leaned my head against his lovely shining neck and he brushed my face, rolling his eyes at me as though we were in secret communion.

"I don't know Justin de Prideau," I said carefully. "Perhaps you could tell me what he looks like. Felipe is looking for him."

Before Sebastian could reply there were sharp footsteps on the stones over near the *posada* and I glanced up to see Felipe walking towards us. He saw my companion, did a double take and lengthened his stride, his face splitting into a delighted smile. "Good lord! That has to be my old friend Sebastian!"

The little man handed me the reins and strode to meet Felipe, clasping both of his hands, then thumping him on the upper arms. "Felipe! Felipe, *chico!*"

They talked happily together, then Sebastian turned to me, slapped Felipe on the shoulder and said: "You ask, what Justin de Prideau look like? Like him. Like Felipe!" He turned to Felipe with a puzzled smile, suddenly thoughtful. "He is relation? What you say, *bastardo?*"

We stood there in electrified silence. The stallion snorted loudly, flicked at some flies with his tail and took a step back towards the water trough. I went to him, holding the reins firmly.

"Odin! *Quieto!*" Sebastian said to him.

"He is a relation. Sebastian, have you seen my uncle *El Conde*, lately?"

"Lately?"

Felipe repeated the words in Spanish. Sebastian shook his head. "He never come to stables. I no hire horses. Sorry, Felipe. *El Conde—*" and then with many lively, angry gestures, he burst into a flood of Spanish.

"He says Ernesto ill-treated one of his horses, so he is not welcome at the stables," Felipe translated, and to underline his words Sebastian kicked the air and flailed it with one arm. "Cruel to horses."

Felipe turned to me with a grin. "Sebastian sounds like a friend, and just at this moment we need one. I'll talk to him in Spanish if you don't mind, because his English is a bit slow."

I nodded. "Go ahead. I'll look after Odin."

210

With a gallant gesture Sebastian took my hand and kissed it. "You ride Odin?"

"I'd love to." I led the horse away, so that Felipe could capture all the old charmer's attention. They seated themselves on the low stone wall by the water trough and I walked Odin a hundred yards up the road, then back again. They came to meet me.

"He says there's no transport here," said Felipe, "but he has a phone. We're going to his house. It's only a stone's throw away."

They went ahead, talking volubly, and I led the horse, frisking and dancing down a steep little lane that led away from the village towards a slope split up into market gardens. From a tall bank on the left hand side a stream of water leaped into the centre of the dust-dry road as though some irrigation channel had overflowed. At the bottom a small boy rushed out of a hovel with a hoe and began to build up a low wall to divert the water from the close-packed dwellings. Two dogs came over a low wall, eyed us suspiciously, then paused to drink. At the bottom of the lane we turned left and went through a little shelter of trees and there was a white-painted house, low-set and built round a courtyard. Vine trailing over wires to make a leafy ceiling reminded me of the Ballisat garden and I remembered with a pang that I had not been in touch. Perhaps I could telephone them now to tell them I was safe.

The boy ran out to meet us. He spoke to his father in Spanish, talking quickly and nervously, gesturing with his hands. Whatever he was saying, it was not good news for Sebastian grew excited, shouting back at him, raising his fist and bringing it down on his knee. The boy shrugged, unmoved, waiting with practised patience for his father's anger to subside.

Felipe turned to me, translating. "He says someone came this morning, hired two of his best horses and left word he won't be back for some days. Sebastian, as you will have gathered, is very displeased because he never hires to strangers for more than a day, but the man paid the stable-boy a lot of money. I gather Sebastian is going to have the boy's ears for supper."

Sebastian whirled round to me, the blood pulsing up in his neck and face. "You ask me about Justin de Prideau. This man who take my horses, he look after Señor de Prideau. Mystery man. I do not know him with horses. I do not hire."

Felipe broke in, his voice rough-edged. "What's his name? The man who looks after de Prideau?"

"Diego. You know him?"

"No."

Felipe spoke to the boy in Spanish. The boy ran back the way he had come. "He has gone to get the culprit." With a *"¡Pausa!"* Sebastian, who clearly did not trust the stable-hand not to run away, strode after his son.

Felipe said: "I am more than a little bit doubtful about that fellow Aparicio from the *posada* who took us to see the alleged de Prideau in bed. He says he didn't come into the room with us so he didn't actually see the chap's face, but he described de Prideau to me, and he described the man we talked to."

"It doesn't exactly tally with Sebastian's saying he looks like you," I replied dryly.

"No. It's totally unimportant in that context, but it does prove that Aparicio is one of Ernesto's men. Therefore, if Ernesto is keeping in touch, he knows we're here. At least, he will know just as soon as Aparicio can get to a telephone. That is, if Ernesto isn't already on our track. It's all pretty straightforward, isn't it! Carlos is here, living quite openly except that he is under surveillance all the time so that he cannot get away, and so that he can be moved fast whenever necessary."

"Do you suppose they have gone up into the mountains on horseback?" I asked in despair, my eyes going involuntarily to the great towering range at whose foot we now stood. "Why else would they want horses?"

Felipe looked grim. "The stable-boy may be able to give us a lead. If they have gone into the mountains, then I am going after them because it stands to reason Carlos would be taken to some mountain village to be kept out of the way until I've been disposed of. But it's not so easy to hide a man in such a place," Felipe went on, "because a stranger is a curiosity and so everyone knows he is there. Once one finds the village, one has only to question children."

Sebastian was coming round the corner of the building, his face as black as thunder, and a frightened-looking young man was hurrying reluctantly beside him. Sebastian burst into voluble Spanish and I could only stand back frustratedly, watching as Felipe and Sebastian shot questions at the boy and he supplied the hesitant, surly answers. It seemed, when the little drama was played out and the boy allowed to go, that we were indeed on the right track.

"De Prideau," said Felipe, translating, "has a constant companion who changes periodically. It is thought in the village that though de Prideau is a very mild man, it is possible for him to have fits, or even become violent, though no one has seen any of these things happen in the twelve years he has lived here and worked in the mines."

"That's Ernesto's cover? Medical supervision?"

"That's right. De Prideau is thought to be someone of fair importance but as Ernesto is interested, no one delves too deeply. Ernesto comes to visit him periodically."

"And does he really live in that squalid *posada*?" I asked, indignation rising.

"It seems so," replied Felipe, tight-lipped. "As a well-set-up gentleman, he would be too obvious, of course. And he would not be acceptable as a worker at the mines."

"No, of course. But what happened about the horses?"

"Emilio Diego is the man's name. He has been de Prideau's guard for some time. This morning, after Sebastian and his son left the stable, Diego came and offered a very large sum for the hire of two of Sebastian's best hacks. The stable-boy mistakenly thought Sebastian would be overwhelmed by the

213

sight of all that money—and I gather the boy was suitably rewarded as well—so he supplied the horses and worse, for another sum, the loan of a horse box."

"Where did he go?"

"No one knows. Sebastian says they didn't go directly up from here on the track that leads to the Puerto del Lobo—because that is where he and his son have been and he would have met them. Besides, he would not need the horse box. But as the box was returned only an hour or so later, I would hazard a guess that they drove over to Jeres del Marquesado, a little market town some distance west of us across the plain."

"What makes you think that?"

"Because the track up to the Puerto de Jeres starts from there. I know it well—at least, I knew it well as a boy—and I think I would remember it now."

"Who drove the horse box back? We could find out from him."

"As you can imagine, some stranger, who left immediately."

Dusk was coming down over the range and creeping across the plain turning the wheat to a lake of gun-metal grey. The sun was sinking low towards the horizon from a primrose sky.

Felipe said, making one of those split-second decisions that were so typical of him: "I am going to tell Sebastian the story as I know it, and ask him for a horse to go after them."

He understood. "What is the matter, Felipe? They are friends? These men, ¿amigos?"

Felipe's mouth turned down. "Not friends at all. Sebastian, can I trust you with a really big secret?" He repeated it in Spanish. The man nodded vigorously. "Sí, sí. Anything for you, Felipe. What has this thief to do with you? But first, come into my patio. We will drink some wine together for old times' sake. The many times we rode in the Sierras together. You remember my wife, Eulalia?"

We sat on hard chairs—I never saw a comfortable one in Spain—round a wooden table in a vine-roofed corner of the courtyard and the lovely Eulalia, plump with black silk hair dressed smoothly and turned up into a bun, poured wine for us into little glasses. Sebastian listened attentively to Felipe's story of Carlos' disappearance firstly from Toledo, then twelve years ago from Santo Domingo, and leaving out Ernesto's attempt on our lives, told the story factually and unemotionally, partially in English to include me, but translating as well, making certain Sebastian understood.

When he had finished the Spaniard asked simply: "What do you want of me?"

Felipe patted him affectionately on the shoulder. "You're a good man, Sebastian."

"You were always good with the horse, Felipe. Good to my horses."

"It's a big favour I am going to ask."

"You say."

"I want you to let me have a fast horse—"

"Two fast horses," I broke in, and he paused, turning to me with startled brows.

Sebastian laughed and lifting my hand from the table, kissed the fingers. "Ah, Felipe, you don't know the lady. I promise her my best, my own Odin." He turned his dark liquid eyes on me. "Great compliment, to ride Odin."

"Thank you, Sebastian."

"Suzanne, it's good of you," Felipe said worriedly, "but you've no idea what you're letting yourself in for. It's nearly eleven thousand feet at the top of the pass."

"I've quite a head for heights," I said in what turned out to be the most optimistic remark of all time. I had in fact been skiing once or twice but certainly not at eleven thousand feet or anything like it.

"Not only that, but it could be dangerous."

"Frankly," I replied, determined not to give an inch, "I think it's dangerous down here, cut off in the middle of nowhere with Ernesto on our track."

"I—I'll think about it."

"Don't bother. I am going. You promised me a ride through

215

the Sierras and I am not going to allow you to go back on your word."

"Some other time."

"This is a jolly good time. Look at Sebastian, he's falling apart laughing at our argument. You're not going to stop me, Felipe, so you may as well give in."

With a futile little gesture Felipe turned to our host. "Would you be willing to take a car round to Trevelez and wait there to see if your horses emerge? If the weather is bad, they may be forced down. And you are interested in getting your horses back, aren't you?" He had to translate then, to make quite certain Sebastian understood.

"I have a cousin in Trevelez. When do you want to go?" Sebastian re-filled our glasses. He was glowering, and those black eyes shot sparks. They reminded me, quixotically, that I had looked into Ernesto's dark eyes and found them as secret as a well.

"Is it too much to ask you to get out the horse box again and drive us round to Jeres del Marquesado?"

Sebastian glanced at his watch then at my thin cotton shirt and jeans. "The Señorita not right dressed for ride."

"If we go now, might we not find some shops open in Jeres?"

The two men tossed off their drinks. "Okay. Let's go."

27

SEBASTIAN TOOK ME shopping while Felipe dealt with the police. A pair of blue jeans and thick jumper, an ugly plastic anorak that was thin enough to roll up into a ball and tie on the pommel of the saddle, boots, a toothbrush and paste and a wonderful small sombrero. The sun in the mountains was dangerous, Felipe said, and no one ventured up there with an uncovered head.

Sebastian and I unloaded the horses outside a pretty white-painted *posada* with geraniums in the window boxes and that now familiar large wooden door that enabled one to lead animals in two by two. It was a very superior *posada* by comparison with the one we had visited this afternoon. The door led immediately into a small concreted hall where two mules were tethered and beyond that there was a big open courtyard, tiled and decorated lavishly with geraniums in scarlet flower. They stood in enormous pots round the walls, on shelves, and on the stairs that led up to a railed verandah encircling the upstairs rooms. There was a small palm tree in a large oil drum painted brown at the foot of the stairs, vines growing up the side, twining through the banisters and along the railings of the upper floor.

Sebastian led the way with Rosario, the big mare he had loaned to Felipe, and I came behind with Odin. As we were passing the mules Rosario lashed out with a hind leg and Sebastian called, too late: "Careful. Mares don't like mules."

In a desperate effort to separate them I lost my footing and slid back onto the tiles of the courtyard. A woman in an enveloping floral apron strode angrily forth in carpet slippers from the kitchen, waving a tea towel with all the drama and panache of a flamenco dancer, insulting us shrilly and volubly in Spanish. With consummate skill, Sebastian insulted her in return. Two mongrel dogs leaped into the fray, one from the street, one from the courtyard. Having recovered my balance, I drew Rosario as far out of the way and close to the smooth tiles of the courtyard as I dared, stroking her nose, trying to calm her.

It must have been a full five minutes before the noisy circus ended and the woman led the mules out into the street so that we could pass into the stable. *"Avaricia!"* commented Sebastian with disdain, tossing his fine head. "She get money from *personas* leave *mula* here to go to bars."

We watered the horses at a trough inside the stable door and filled the mangers with straw and barley Sebastian had brought in the little truck, then tied the beasts up side-by-side and put their tack over a saddle tree. Already three mules and a pretty donkey with long floppy ears were settled in for the night.

"I find you good hotel," Sebastian said as we washed our hands at the cold tap over the water trough.

"I really do not see why we shouldn't stay here," I told him, glancing in at the colourful courtyard as he tried to lead me away. I was desperately tired and had no wish to go any further.

Sebastian looked shocked. "You! English lady in *posada!*"

"Why not? Felipe says we must leave at five o'clock. I'll have an extra ten minutes in bed if I am on the spot." The excitements of the week, the unaccustomed travelling, lack of food and my recent illness were all beginning to take their toll. I was fine whilst walking but when I stood still my knees shook like jellies.

"Felipe would not have it. He is the son of—"

I raised a hand to stop him. "Felipe is first of all a sensible

218

man," I retorted briskly. I might have added that Carlos'
present position, if what we suspected was true, was not
exactly dignified. And Carlos was the Count. Sebastian
shrugged disapprovingly. "Besides, no one will think to look
for us here," I added. "And wouldn't you really like us to
keep an eye on your lovely horses?"

That brought a smile to his rugged features. "You are good,
Señorita." He raised my hand and kissed it. I went back to
the van for my shopping.

The Spanish woman, eyes still smouldering from the fracas,
met us in the courtyard. Sebastian asked her about rooms. She
led me up to the first floor past the billowing, luxuriant vines
that threaded in and out of the banisters and paused at a door
so low I had to duck my head to enter. The room was in
darkness and it smelled mustily of straw. She turned a switch
and that now familiar naked light bulb, hanging from a black
cord in the centre of the room, sprang to life.

There was an iron-framed double bed, a small plastic curtain
with blue flowers that seemed to be covering a tiny alcove, a
bar of criss-crossed wood with pegs for hanging clothes, a
statue of a sweet and placid Virgin in bright red and blue,
and four religious pictures on the walls. I could hear the
animals moving restlessly in the stables below. There was one
small, wood-framed window deeply recessed and covered by
green wire netting. Tentatively, I opened it while the woman
watched me in closed silence. Outside, there was a loft full
of broken chairs, old boots, piles of dusty rubble and tiles,
sacks lying empty, coils of wire, and a partially derelict
beamed roof. The plastic curtain gave up a low arch and
short, shallow tunnel that could have been a fire place, or even
an oven.

I put my shopping down on the bed. *"Baño?"* I asked.
"Ducha?" My work on the phrase book was beginning to
pay off.

She led me along the verandah to an enormous bathroom
with a leggy bath standing up to its ankles in water. I glanced
in what I hoped was a questioning and startled fashion at the

flood, then back at her, but she seemed unconcerned. There was a basin and an ancient lavatory emitting anguished, bubbling groans. There was one tap only. F for *frío*. I shivered.

Voices came up from below and looking down into the courtyard I saw that Felipe had arrived. "I have taken a room," I said, leaning over the banister to talk to him. "What do you think about staying here? I can even smell cooking. The thought of going out and looking for a fancy restaurant appals me."

Felipe's upturned face showed his lively grin. "Fancy restaurant? Where do you think you are? Granada? Madrid? Okay, it suits me to stay here. I'll talk to the Señora about food when she comes down."

We said a fond and truly grateful farewell to the kindly, concerned Sebastian and saw him off into the darkness with the loose-box trailing behind his little truck. He was going back to La Calahorra to spend the night, then in the morning he would drive in a great circle, via Granada, that would bring him back to that village called Trevelez, six to seven thousand feet up on the opposite side of the pass through which Carlos would have to travel if he had to emerge from the mountains on the other side.

"What happened about the car?" I asked when we were alone. "The Alfa."

"The police have been informed. What more can I do?"

"Did you ring Garcia?"

"And drive him mad with worry? No, I didn't," Felipe replied. "I left him in blissful ignorance. The car is insured, and whatever may go wrong, I won't see him out of pocket. But I did make a phone call." His eyes twinkled. "To my grandmother, to say I had arrived safely in Paris and naturally to enquire about my kind uncle who saw me off on the plane. It seems he suddenly decided to take off for the mines to make arrangements for a possible position for me. My grandmother seems to think she persuaded him to come down ahead to pave the way. A very clever fellow, Ernesto."

"Why are you looking at me like that, Felipe?"

He said thoughtfully: "I almost want you to say: If Ernesto is scudding round the mountains I think I will go back home. This is wild country, Suzanne, and you're involved with people who not only don't speak your language, but who don't think the same way."

"In other words, I am too much responsibility for you?" I looked him square in the eye, challenging him.

"Touché," he replied softly, and took my arm.

There was a trestle table in the courtyard from which we dined. Darkness had long since fallen and the Señora provided us with light from two neon bars strung precariously on thin wire hanging from the low ceiling near the entrance. We drank the local wine, rough to the palate and a lively tonic for our morale. The daughter of the house, a child of ten or twelve, served us with spinach omelette accompanied by tomato and cucumber salad while the rest of the family, three small boys and a baby, played on the floor nearby watching us.

The goat's meat was a shock, strong and tough, but it was surrounded deliciously by colourful vegetables in a thick gravy. Word must have gone round about the eccentric English couple for lively little groups of young people strode continuously through the outer door, crossed the courtyard to the kitchen, stayed a while then departed, eyeing us with friendly interest. An old man pulled up a chair at the end of the table and called for a drink. I left Felipe talking to him and went to bed.

I wakened at five o'clock. Below my room the animals were moving restlessly. The room was hot and dreadfully stuffy. I dressed hurriedly in the jeans and jumper I had bought the night before, put on the light mountain boots of suede and canvas that Sebastian had recommended, slid my lipstick into a pocket in the cotton shirt I had washed out the night before and managed to dry in the heat of my bedroom, and emerged with my new jaunty sombrero on the back of my head. Felipe appeared from the stable. "I've fed and watered the horses,"

221

he said after we had greeted each other, "and the Señora has breakfast ready."

"At this hour? I don't think I could."

"I think you had better try. We've a long way to go and since I want to use the saddle bags for barley we can't carry much lunch. The horses are doing the work, so they have first consideration."

"Of course."

I tried, but I failed. What the thick, milky fluid that passed for coffee lacked in taste, it made up in generosity, for the coffee cups were bowls the size of a soup plate. Owing to the early hour the rolls had been baked the day before, and I had more regard for my front teeth than to try to bite into them. I pulled the interior out with a fork and spread it with margarine and the honey that tasted of molasses. Concerned, Felipe went into the kitchen and persuaded the sleepy and somewhat displeased Señora to produce an orange and some rather old apples. I ate them hungrily.

The sun was not yet up as we led our horses into the square. The air was cold and I was thankful for the wind-proof jacket. We clip-clopped over a sealed road for about a mile, then turned in on a dry river bed. The sky by this time was lightening and behind us a pink glow showed the sun was on its way. On the river bank poplars, beech, and almond trees grew in profusion, and there were some great golden-faced sunflowers. Later the banks ran off into market gardens where beans and spinach grew, and small fields of wheat. There was sugar cane here and there, and green willow fronds that proved a great temptation to the horses who snatched huge mouthfuls as they passed by.

Half-an-hour later, as the sun began to rise, we turned directly in towards where the black mountains lifted into the sky. The long, rank grass and crops were heavy with early dew, and as the sun touched them sweet scents of herbs rose and the musky tang of the damp earth. Here we were able to canter for the first time. Odin, I already knew, was going to be a challenge to me. Sebastian had told us he fed his horses

222

ten pounds of barley a day and it told in Odin's dancing stride, his impatience with the bit, his lively leap at the sound of a goat bell or the chuckle of a jackdaw in a tree. He shied often and less, I felt certain, from nervousness than for the sheer excitement. Any excuse would do to leap in the air. Soon I caught his mood. With a firm hold on the reins and gripping the saddle close with my knees, I nudged him into a wild sort of canter that was rather a controlled gallop, down a narrow leafy track past fields where workmen were already, at this early hour, tilling the soil. Their singing sent Odin off into leaps of pretended surprise.

Felipe, whose Rosario was considerably better behaved, called anxiously: "Are you going to be all right?" and when I could I replied breathlessly: "Sure. He's lovely, but what a handful! I'll get my own back when we start climbing."

"Don't be too sure about that," Felipe warned me when we finally slowed. "These horses that are bred in the mountains can climb like goats. And they never seem to run out of sparkle. It's the Arab strain in them."

We passed a baby kid, new-born, bleating for its mother who had leaped to a low crag above, small cloven hooves ready, beady eyes startled. There were wild roses here of a delicate candy pink, honey-scented, and broom in showers of gold. Over in the east the sun rose and soon I had to remove the anorak. At the sound of the rattling plastic Odin went berserk, leaping up a bank, leaping down again onto the track, jumping in the air like a mountain elk. Felipe laughed delightedly. "I see you can stick on, even if you can't manage him, so I shall stop worrying. These horses know what they're about and providing you don't fall off you're unlikely to come to any harm."

"I hope you're right," I replied breathlessly. "I haven't lost my confidence—yet."

As we climbed higher the ground became more and more stony and the wind rose, murmuring in the thin stone pines. Often we paused, scanning the slopes ahead and behind but there was no sign of life. It seemed we were totally alone

223

with the birds and the elements. Silence lay all round us except for the occasional tinkling of a goat bell or the cronk, cronk of a raven as it flew purposefully overhead.

I removed my jumper and tied it up with the anorak on the front of my saddle. Behind, the great plain had come to golden life. Turning in the saddle I could see the grey mounds of the iron works over to the east growing smaller and smaller, the castle shrinking to a brown toy, and in the distance nine white villages with red roofs, sleeping. The sun was burning, the air growing sharp and thin. We rested our horses on a wide spur, loosening their girths and removing their bridles so that they could graze. They ate hungrily of the tough green grass and little bushes. A falcon swept by and disappeared beyond a rock ridge. Away in the distance, below one of those great clouds of formless snow, we saw some shepherds, thin sticks of men guarding small, white, legless oblongs that must be sheep, moving forward in a line. "I only wish we could meet some of them on the track," Felipe remarked. "They might give us some useful information."

"What do you expect Ernesto to do?" I asked, broaching the subject for the first time since last night when his potential arrival in Andalusia had been too much of a shock for open discussion. I suppose we had both recognised that there was to be no dispelling Ernesto by talk. We had carried our fears in private through the night, unallayed.

"I cannot worry about Ernesto," Felipe replied. "I cannot think at all outside of the fact that we must catch up with Carlos."

"You don't expect him to be up here? To follow Carlos? Or even to follow us?"

"It's possible, but unlikely. Having sent his henchmen off with Carlos into the mountains, why should he go as well?"

"I hate to strike a pessimistic note," I said, "but I can't help thinking that if he is quick and has enough smart assistants keeping an eye open, he will know we have flitted off with Sebastian in the truck, and with the horse box. After all, anyone could have seen us chatting at the water trough in La Calahorra."

Felipe gave me a droll look. "It doesn't help to put things into words. Of course I know. That is why I didn't want you to come."

28

As we rode higher, buzzards with golden necks and brown wings watched us frowningly from stony perches. The pines gave way to bare mountain covered sparsely in a tough green grass that fixed its roots tenaciously in what soil there was, thinly layered over rock and shale. I donned my jumper again for, although the sun was burning, the air was now extremely cold. The path was narrow here, often solid rock, but the horses' hooked shoes kept them from slipping. In places where it was very narrow, or very steep, we had to dismount and lead them. Sometimes we crossed where a landslide had peeled off all the small, rooted growing things and the track was a mere footprint wide so that I held my breath and my heart almost stopped from fright. By mid-day the villages down below had almost disappeared, a touch of thistledown on a grey plain.

"Stop a moment," I called to Felipe who was riding out in front. "These spurts of freezing wind are cooling me down a bit too much." I undid my anorak from the pommel. "Now, be a good boy, Odin," I said as I pulled it over my head. At the inevitable sh-crek of the plastic the lively stallion took a flying leap up onto the rock shelf above. By some miracle I kept my balance, turning away in a mindless panic from the almost sheer drop to a gorge thousands of feet below.

Felipe laughed. I think he was pleased that I rode so well. I put my sunglasses back on and tightened the band of the sombrero beneath my chin. "It's a great place for sunburn and sunstroke," Felipe called as I came down the sloping shelf on to the track again, "so for heavens' sake don't lose that magnificent hat."

He had scarcely finished speaking, and I turned to look at an eagle flapping by, uttering its plaintively angry mew, when a vicious gust tearing across the summit caught me at the wrong angle, hooked beneath the rim of my hat, and tipped it from my head. I swung round in a panic, leaped off my horse, threw my reins towards Felipe and dashed after the hat, scrambling across the rock and shale of the mountain-side as it raced ahead of me, a crazy black sombrero gone wild, leaping and scudding, dancing on the rocks and flying through the air. I did not hear Felipe's warning shout for the wind was in my ears. Perhaps a hundred yards from the track, the hat caught in a sharp little outcrop of rock and I fell on it, dragged myself to my feet, gave Felipe a victorious wave, and then, to my confused horror, felt my knees give way beneath me, felt my head go weightless. The entire mountain swept queerly upwards past my face, the trees, the shale, the rough, dry plants missing my eyes by a fraction as they raced by, and then a man on a mule, upside down, swinging past a tall thin shepherd and his absurd little line of oblong sheep.

I came to with Felipe holding my head between my knees. "Damn!" he was saying. "Are you all right? You can't run at ten thousand feet. Suzanne! Are you all right?"

I lifted my head. Tears, to my astonishment, were streaming down my face. "I'm all right," I replied shakily, "except that I can't get my breath, and I cannot think why I am crying."

His laugh was a little gust of relief. "It's altitude sickness. It takes everyone differently. I should have warned you. The shepherds up here never move out of a stately crawl."

"The horses!" I exclaimed, swinging round to look for them.

"They're all right. I've tied them together. They can't go far. Sit there quietly and I'll bring Odin over to you."

227

He did so, but my knee muscles would not work and I had to suffer the shameful indignity of being lifted into the saddle.

"We're nearly at the summit," he said. "You'll be all right when we get over the top and down the other side a bit. How do you feel now?"

"Great," I replied, feeling terrible, and hoping desperately that Odin was going to co-operate by not trying any of his jumping-jack tricks. Perhaps he, too, was feeling the lack of oxygen, for he went along quietly as we moved up the shale track to the summit, past the great dusty-white patches of winter snow where a great lone eagle swooped and soared, then onto a rock table-land where sleet cut at our faces and the wind beat against us with tremendous power. The horses, gripping the ground with their small, sure feet, forged forward with shoulder-thrust and heads low. The wind came in like a dagger from the snow on the various peaks around us, and the cold grey granite at our feet lay like a ragged scar left by a mountain wolf.

I will never forget that crossing of the summit, half-lying in the saddle with our heads to the icy wind and the air almost too cold to take into our bodies, freezing our nostrils and stinging our lips. I could see little with the sleet and snow on my sunglasses, but I had a strange, unsafe sensation of teetering irrevocably on top of the world, of being a part of the stainless blue sky where the lift of an eagle might take us to nothingness. The earth's pull, the safety one took for granted down below, had gone like a blow of thistledown.

Ten minutes of trial and testing, then we were over the top and suddenly the wind was caught, expelled by a thrusting crag. Felipe jumped down and threw his reins to me. "I'm going back to have a good look across the mountainside. We've got to stop here for lunch and to rest the horses so I'll just ensure we're not being followed." He returned a few minutes later, gave me a thumbs-up sign and mounted again.

We descended into a calm, green, basin-shaped valley where the hillside above was covered magnificently with great pin-cushions of lovely alpine plants, white, yellow, pink-flowered, a small miracle of beauty. The sun beat down through the thin air like a furnace. We stopped here and Felipe helped me off, for my muscles were still like jelly. "Sorry," I said, embarrassed and a little angry with myself for I am not a natural for the small, weak-woman stuff. I sat on a rock and removed my jumper and anorak while he removed the saddles and bridles. To my astonishment, he let the horses go loose and they fled with a thud and flurry of hooves, bucking and leaping like mountain goats down a curving green slope where the grass was like washed silk. They rolled on their backs, raced round in circles, shook themselves then set off at a trot for a drink. A stream cascaded in brilliant crystals through the wonderful rockery across the foot of the basin, to disappear round a jutting ferny ridge at the bottom.

"How are we going to catch them again?"

"No trouble. They're too far from home and too pleased with this basin after being confined to a stable or the dry grass of the plain. I have been up here many a time in the past," Felipe told me, "and we always let them go. They love the water and the damp earth. There is plenty of water from now on. Streams everywhere."

"It's positively Shangri-la, isn't it?" I asked, leaning over to touch a minute silvery plant with yellow flowers from which a wonderful aromatic scent arose. "I'd no idea this sort of thing went on up in the mountains! It must be a botanist's paradise."

He took out a cigarette and lit it, the smoke rising like a grey cord in the still air. But there was nothing relaxed about him. His eyes flickered towards the horizon and he scanned the slope ahead.

"It's so unbelievably silent," I went on. "No ants, no flies, no lizards."

"You'll see butterflies farther down," he told me, not knowing then that when we were farther down there would be something more diabolical by far than the transient beauty of a butterfly to take my attention. "When I was younger I

229

used to collect them. There is an Apollo with deep yellow spots instead of crimson ones."

Drunk with the beauty around me, a little dizzy from the thin air, I had lost any sensation of danger. I wanted to walk through the rockeries, stroking the tiny bright flowers, but a wavering in my knees warned me I would not get far. The giant pin-cushions billowed out above me, festooned in pink, blue, little red stars; at my feet were dainty white orchids the size of the smallest violet, ice daisies and saxifrage.

Behind and above us the great mountain summits loomed, splashed with aging winter snow. Felipe, following my eyes, remarked cryptically: "It's said there are bodies under that snow still—men who were caught by winter trying to cross during the Civil War."

I shivered and came back to earth. "It's a merciless land, Spain."

Felipe threw his cigarette away and said: "You must be starving. The Signora, for all her apparent disinterest, has done us proud." He brought out a pack of hard-boiled eggs, tins of squid and sardines, some tomatoes and a circular flat loaf. "I thought your saddle bag was full of barley for Odin and Rosario," I exclaimed delightedly, "and our lot was one light biscuit."

"Not quite. I'm sorry, but the bread is going to be hard. It doesn't last more than a day, and it's more than twenty-four hours old, now."

"I am hungry enough to eat Odin," I replied, "and far too hungry to worry about whether I lose my front teeth or not. At the worst, I dare say I can dip the bread in that stream."

"Indeed. You can drink from any of the streams in the mountains. The water is magnificent."

I reached for the butter and Felipe took my hand. "I'm glad you're with me." He leaned over and kissed me on the lips.

"I'm glad too," I said, my voice jolting a little and the

230

wild flowers disappearing into a glorious, hazy sort of mist of emotion.

"If there's danger—"

I stopped him. "If there is danger, we will cope as best we can." And then I saw what he meant and my blood froze. He had reached into his saddle bag with his free hand and brought out a revolver. "Felipe," I whispered hoarsely, "you wouldn't use it?"

"Everyone has a gun in Spain," he said, speaking lightly but not looking at me. "It really would not be sensible for two people to come over these mountains unarmed. Many, many people have lost their lives here. The Puerto del Lobo over there wasn't called Wolf Pass for nothing. There's many a traveller been killed for his lunch or his purse on this track, you know. I won't harrow you with the stories, but I know a few."

"But not now," I said. "It wouldn't happen these days."

He was silent, contemplating the dark metal of the revolver and with a feeling of strange emptiness, I remembered that I had wanted to telephone the kind family Ballisat at Toledo to tell them where I was, and that I was safe. I did not feel at all safe now, and I thought, inevitably, that if I should die here on the mountain no one would ever know what happened to me, and I wondered, now that my father and Antonia had gone, who would particularly care. I looked across at Felipe, sadly, thinking of Antonia who had known him for those few months, right at the beginning of his life, and wondered if today could be the end.

He mis-read my look. "Yes, it may happen still," he said at last. "Possibly to marked men. But we're marked men, Suzanne. I tried to warn you."

I nearly fluffed my lines. I nearly said: *We don't carry guns in England. I didn't expect it. I didn't know it would be like that.* And then I remembered the ordeal bean of Calibar, and Felipe's car going over the cliff into the Tagus, and I realised I had to be a right numskull if I thought any man in his senses was going to go after Carlos and his charge

231

in these mountains unarmed. "Of course," I managed to say lightly. "Of course, you would bring a gun. I just hadn't thought of it. If I had, I'd have asked you to bring one for me."

*　　*　　*

After lunch Felipe saddled the horses and helped me mount. I was still too weak to move at more than a very slow walk. I had taken my time going down to the stream for a drink, feeling as though some leaden weight was clamped to my knees. "You'll be all right when we come down a bit," Felipe assured me.

"I feel like an invalid. I am so sorry."

"Don't apologise. The track goes down steeply from here. You will suddenly notice the difference."

And I did. It was an hour later. All at once I was able to breathe again and my limbs felt as though they belonged to me and would work. I called out happily to Felipe riding in front down the rocky, shaly path, "I'm cured. I feel fine."

"Splendid."

After leaving the magic basin the ground had turned to rock again, but now there was more soil and there was grass. Totally recovered from my transitory mishap, my mind ran back, musingly, over what had happened. I had never fainted before and hoped fervently I never would again. The swinging rocks thrusting up at me, the life of the mountain missing my face by inches ... And then I remembered something that had been lying dormant in my mind during the time I had been more concerned with staying upright in the saddle, with not fainting again. Had I imagined I saw a man on a mule, alone? In the same context, I imagined I saw the shepherds with their sheep, but we had seen them some distance back. Were they still in sight when I fainted? Should I worry Felipe with something that had perhaps been a figment of my imagination? I glanced nervously behind, but there was no one in sight. And anyway, would Ernesto use a mule?

We were riding along a narrow path that rounded a green ridge, and because my mind was darting this way and that, confused, uncertain, I was caught unawares by the stupendous scene that suddenly unfolded in front. I reined in sharply, my thoughts teetering back to the present, my eyes starting from my head in sheer amazement. As far as the eye could see brown, grey, pink mountains billowed and surged to the south. Directly below, a narrow, deep valley rock-split, mis-shapen, twisted and turned and wound away into the distance. At the head, not far below us, there were scrubby trees, and at the bottom a lively, rushing stream, but farther down the valley widened, and there were rocks where cliffs fell sheer. In the far distance, a strange white cloud like a fat caterpillar.

"What is it?" I called, my voice sharp with fright, for unaccountably, I seemed to know. "What on earth is that? It's moving! It's coming this way."

Felipe turned in his saddle and when I saw his face my heart jerked with alarm. "It's coming all right," he said, "and it's coming mighty fast. It's cloud. The weather is breaking up down there and there's only one thing we can do. I know a shepherd's hut not far off the trail and not more than a half-hour's ride away. We'll make for that. Come on." He dug his heels into Rosario's flank. "We've no time to lose."

The horses moved off obediently enough down the slope on to a path that was dangerously narrow. We dismounted and I called to Felipe: "What happens? Does the cloud come up and fill the valley?"

"Keep an eye on it," he replied grimly. "You'll see. We'll be in real trouble if we're caught."

I thought of Carlos and his guard somewhere in front and wondered with alarm how far they had gone. Perhaps they were down in that silent, creeping cotton wool fog, already lost. We watched the cloud coming towards us, rising up the sides of the valley, inexorably blotting out the rocks, the green. Above and behind it, the sky was suddenly blackened

233

by a cloud moving over the sun. And then a wind came whirling in, clawing at us with freezing fingers, screaming round the crags. The horses walked with tails tight between their hindquarters, hunched with their misery, no longer pausing to snatch at the tufts of green that grew beside the path, hurrying, slipping a little, as though they knew the danger and knew, too, that there might be shelter ahead.

We came upon the shepherd's hut quite suddenly as we rounded a spur. A low, flat building made of the dark stones of the mountains with slate roof and shutters. There was a small building perhaps a hundred yards nearer to us that looked like a shelter for animals, and beyond the house another shelter much the same size. The path flattened out here and we spurred the horses into a canter away from the track and across the grass that spread out before the buildings. The valley had filled now, to the very summit of the ridges on either side with a terrifying, wedge-shaped solid mass of white cloud, and it was not creeping any more. It moved with the silent, sinister speed of a cobra up the sides of the valley, up to where the grass grew, and now it was swirling round us, rising above our heads, almost blotting out the buildings before we reached them.

I leaped out of the saddle and led Odin inside. Felipe followed close behind. There was a scuffling sound and I saw a donkey rising to its feet, looking at us with half-startled, half-friendly eyes. "There's a metal ring in the wall in front of you," Felipe said. "Tie Odin up there and take his saddle off."

I removed the bridle and uncoiled the snaffle-rope. "How long is this likely to last?"

"Heaven alone knows. Hours. Days. Not weeks at this time of year. If there is anyone in the hut, and I presume there is or the donkey wouldn't be here, he may be a weather expert. The question is, can we find our way that far now the fog has caught up with us? We're just a bit too late. Still, it's only a couple of hundred yards."

He was undoing the saddle bag and tipping the barley

234

into two careful little heaps on the floor or he might have seen the man come round the corner, gun raised. I opened my mouth to scream and received a stinging blow that sent me hurtling to the ground. Felipe must have lifted his head then. The man ground out an order in Spanish and as I crawled painfully to my knees I saw Felipe fling the barley in the man's face, saw his animal-leap, fast as a jaguar, heard the gun go off with a deafening crack, then the two men were writhing together on the ground with the horses stamping frenziedly, the shelter alive with their terror, only a yard away. The donkey made a coarse, jagged braying sound and I remember thinking: They're both going to be stamped upon! and I cried in a terrified but oddly calm-sounding voice: "Odin! Quiet, Odin! Quiet, Rosario! Quiet. Quiet!"

Odin reared, his front hooves hung grotesquely in the air, then came down with a sickening thud. The men seemed to rise together, then went over with Felipe on top. A curse, a terrified whinny, three pairs of animal eyes showing white in the thick, foggy darkness. A grunt, and then Rosario leaped forward. I leaped too, grasping the snaffle-rope, pushing my back against her side with all the strength I could muster, shoving her back, soothing words erupting from my dry throat in panic-stricken spurts. The animals seemed to calm a little, at least the panic seemed to go but they moved backwards and forwards, up and down, shouldering each other and the donkey as the men, with naked desperation, fought on the ground only a yard or so away.

And then I saw the gun. I leaped on it, picked it up and ran to the open doorway. "I've got the gun!" I shouted. "Tell him I am going to shoot, Felipe."

The man understood. Their grip on each other loosened and they fell apart. "Don't get up," I said, my voice sharp with terror. "Don't move or I will shoot you dead." I said that last phrase with such total conviction that I almost fooled myself, I who had never had a gun in my hand before and did not even know where to look for the safety catch.

It worked. My brave words worked. Felipe, who certainly

235

knew, leaped to his feet, whipping his own gun out, covering the man. "You're a magnificent liar," he said lightly. "If we hadn't had that talk at lunch I'd have believed you myself."

29

I TIED HIS hands together with the donkey's rope. This
shelter was obviously the little creature's home so he would
not run away. Felipe stood grimly over us, his own small
revolver in his right hand, the one I had captured held
loosely in the fingers of his left. "Are you quite certain it's
tight? Bring him over here while I check."

In response to my prod in the back the man Diego moved
sullenly forward. Clearly, he did not speak English. Felipe
spun him round, inspected the knot, then relaxed.

"*¿Es usted Emilio Diego?*"

He nodded sullenly.

"*¿Dónda está* Justin de Prideau?*" With an angry jerk of
the head, Diego indicated the direction where the hut lay.
"*¿Hay otra persona aquí?*"

"*No.*"

"Head him out the door," Felipe said to me. "He says
there are only the two of them there. I hope he tells the
truth."

Fog swirled whitely round us but we could see the track
—just. In any case, the ground was level here. We made
our way towards where we guessed the hut to be. I guided
Diego, with Felipe walking behind. There was no excitement
in me this time. No anticipation. I was too concerned with
my job of guarding our prisoner, and besides, had I not set
out to meet Carlos before? The knife edge blunts with rough

use. I will believe Carlos is here when I see living proof, I said to myself.

We were nearly upon the hut when its black form loomed up before us in the swirling mist. Diego led us to the door. "Hold him there while I go in," Felipe said. "We cannot be sure he is telling the truth." He opened the door very, very carefully. Diego said something in Spanish. Felipe pushed the door tentatively wider. Diego made an irritated sound and jerking his arm free of my restraining hand, he stepped inside. To my astonishment, Felipe allowed him to go. I did not know then, because I had not understood Diego's Spanish words, that he had said Justin de Prideau was tied up, similarly to him.

Felipe stepped through the door. A faint light, as from candles, showed. I do not know what made me turn my head. Some sixth sense, perhaps. It was as though a shadow passed through the mist nearby, and then there was a faint rattle of a stone. I swung round. I heard a cry of alarm, a snapped order, and knew that my dark ghost could be Carlos, making a getaway. I leaped after him, calling: "Señor de Prideau! Señor de Prideau!" My words were swallowed up by the fog. My feet made no sound on the grass and I could hear no sound in front. I kept running, blindly, and the fog swirled round me, then unexpectedly, out in front it cleared a little as fog will, and I saw the shadow of the dark form again, running.

"Señor de Prideau!" I shouted, "Stop. Stop. I am a friend." And in case he had forgotten English: *"Amigo."* He did not stop. Silently, like a black ghost, he kept running, fractionally outpacing me. And then the shadow disappeared and I spun round, directionless, suddenly panic-stricken in a tiny world of my own, silent, damp, unearthly white. "De Prideau!" I shouted desperately. "De Prideau!" My voice disintegrated into the droplets of fog and stayed with me.

Dear God! I had lost my quarry, and now I was lost. In which direction was the hut? I stood quite still, listening, straining my ears until they hurt. Perhaps I imagined it, but

238

I thought I heard just the tiniest sound. The sshh of footsteps on shale? I ran forward, and there, not more than a dozen paces ahead, the grass had given out and the shale and rock had taken over. I could hear sounds again, faint to be sure, but they could be the scuffle and scrape of boots. I ran as fast as I could, slipping and sliding amongst the shale and suddenly there was that dark figure again, melting away from me. I put on an extra spurt, breathlessly slipping and slithering. I fell to my knees, clambered up, lost him, spun round, darted forward, saw him again, and then, like a jack-in-the-box, he disappeared. I rushed forward and, too late, realised what his sudden disappearance meant. As my feet flailed the air I uttered a cry of horror and fell headlong, rolling over and over, grasping desperately at rocks and coarse plants that tore my hands, bumping and slithering uncontrollably; a jerk of agonising pain, numbness, a sort of awful resignation to a hurtling to nothingness over a cliff and then, with a resounding wallop, I came up against something hard and stopped dead.

I lay there on my side, half-stunned, the breath knocked out of me. My hand was in contact with wood, perhaps a tree, or tree stump. Some wonderful, benign growth had broken my fall. Tentatively, giddily, I began to pull myself upright. Nothing broken? I thought not. This thick jumper and anorak, the boots and tough jeans had indeed served me well. But I had lost Carlos. I jumped, then froze as a voice spoke in Spanish, not more than a yard away. My head came round like a rocket.

"English!" I said. "I am English. Señor de Prideau?" Balancing against the wood that had broken my fall, I turned myself round. He was there above me, looking down at me with Felipe's blue eyes. A big man in his shapeless anorak, with silver hair, a gentle face and that high-bridged nose, those jutting cheekbones that were a hall-mark of the de Meritos. If he had not looked like Felipe in his youth, then he had certainly changed with the years. "Thank God I've caught you," I gasped.

He smiled, his eyes puzzled. "I seem to have caught you," he said. "Who are you? Where did you come from? And why are you chasing me?"

"Come with me to the hut."

He drew back, sharp with suspicion. "If you are all right, I will go on," he said. "Are you sure you can stand?" I dragged myself to my feet. My bones were blessedly intact, though a pain as sharp as a knife shot through my ribs. "Now be a good girl," said Carlos, "and go back to your friend." With that he went sliding off down the cliff face, gripping small bushes and jutting rock pieces as he went.

I was after him, slipping and slithering down the slope. "Where on earth do you think you're going?" I called breathlessly, but he did not reply. He must have been accustomed to the mountains for his pace was better than mine, and he took chances. We skidded up against each other here and there, and once I grasped his arm, but he shook me roughly away. I had the advantage that he chose the track and I did not have to try a foot or handhold for safety. Where the cliff levelled out to a track he shot along it at a smart pace, then dived down again, until at last we came to a bed of smooth stones and I could hear the faint singing and bubbling of a stream. The fog was very thick down here and grey like a rain cloud. My hair and face were wet.

Carlos strode purposefully forward, his boots slipping among the clattering stones. Putting on a fast spurt, I slipped and slithered until I found a system of jumping from one square-cut, firm rock piece to another, and caught up with him. "Señor de Prideau!"

"What do you want with me?" he asked mildly, looking down into my face. I almost thought he seemed amused.

"I want you to come back. There is someone who wants to talk to you."

"Who wants to talk to me? Perhaps you will tell me his name." He did not slacken his pace.

"Felipe Lazaro."

"I do not know any Felipe Lazaro. And if he is a friend of that—that *diablo* Diego, then I do not wish to talk to him. Perhaps you know why I have been taken up into the mountains, and my hands tied, huh?"

"How could you be brought here with your hands tied?" I asked, gasping for breath, holding a hand against my aching side, tripping and sliding among the rounded, slippery stones again, half-blinded by the fog.

"You may know," he replied sardonically, "that I was not in a state of proper consciousness when I rode up here, and so I came of my own accord. In place of the drug I have been taking for my headaches, there must have been another. But the drug wore off. Perhaps it was the mountain air. And it would seem to me that Señor Diego has had the misfortune to lose his extra supply. But why does Diego tie me up, after three months of friendship? Three months of looking after me? Perhaps you can answer that question, English Miss."

"Yes," I said, breathlessly, dodging a rock and following Carlos up a little bank on to a steep slope that hung directly over the stream. I could see it now, dancing narrowly between high, jutting rocks, and leaping over a fall. "I think Diego brought you up here on the Count de Merito's orders."

He stopped dead and I bumped into him. He steadied me, staring incredulously into my face. "I will have you know, Miss, that the Count de Merito is the only friend I have. The only real friend. I owe my life and everything I have to him," said Carlos passionately. "It is he who supplies a companion for me. He made a grave error of judgment this time, with this bandit Diego."

"Why does the Count supply you with a companion?"

"Because he is a good man. A kind and compassionate man. He found me here, years ago, wandering after an accident, and took me under his care. You may not know," said Carlos, "but the Count de Merito is a very influential man round here. I suffer badly with my head. The Count pays for the visits of a doctor, and he provides a small job

241

for me for the times when I am well enough to work. So you see, young lady, I am unlikely to believe your story that Diego brought me up here on his orders."

I was too stunned to reply, so I did not.

The mist was thickening here, and darkening. I could not see the cliff opposite but I guessed it had closed in as had our side. If things became worse there would come a time soon when we would not be able to see at all. Carlos said, not unkindly: "If you must follow me, and I suppose you must now, follow closely for I would not like to leave a young girl like you alone on the mountains in such conditions." He stopped. "There has been a landslide here," he said. "We will have to go carefully. Perhaps you would like to take my hand. If we keep moving steadily, we will eventually arrive somewhere, for a stream has to come to the sea. If the fog lifts it will be easy, for in time there will be the lights of a village, but if it does not we will simply have to keep going. What is your name?"

"Suzanne Cole."

We traversed a rough stretch of cliff where there was no way of following the stream unless we walked in the icy water. There was no track either, so we moved slowly, hand over hand, grasping friendly little dry bushes whose tough roots were twisted tightly round the rocks and stones embedded in the cliff, finding footholds precariously on the rock face. We came out on a narrow path that led back to the valley for, as Carlos said, we must on no account leave our guide, the stream. "I once knew an Englishwoman," Carlos said.

My heart leaped. With tremendous discipline I made myself say casually: "What was her name?"

"You may think this sounds foolish," said Carlos, "but I do not know. I told you I had an accident and since then I have been unable to remember my past."

"You remember English."

He replied dryly: "As I remember Spanish. The Count visits me frequently and we speak English together so that I

242

may not forget it. Some day, who knows, my memory may return, and I may need it."

I was breathless again at Ernesto's penchant for taking chances. His delight in the razor's edge. His crazy sense of humour.

"Sometimes I have a flash of memory," Carlos went on, "but unfortunately when this has happened it has coincided with a return of my troubles. I have to be given drugs, and then the feeling of getting near to my past goes."

"The man who looks after you administers the drugs?"

"It has always been so. Diego is a male nurse."

"A confidante?"

He missed the sharp suspicion in my voice. "Of course we are friends—were friends," he amended, "this bandit and me." Carlos chuckled. "I would like to see his face when he finds the shepherd has untied me and sent me off down here to the river bed."

"Oh! The owner of the hut appeared?"

"And very angry he was," replied Carlos with satisfaction.

I wondered apprehensively, then, what Felipe's reception had been. If the shepherd let Carlos go, the chances were he was not going to give shelter to an imprisoned Diego, either. Of course, Felipe had a gun. Two guns, if that was any improvement. But everyone carried a gun, Felipe said, and so the shepherd might be armed as well.

A nerve began to thump mercilessly in my head. Drawing my thoughts painfully away from a problem about which I could do nothing, I said: "What happens when the Count visits you? Do you go out together? In public, I mean. Or does he visit you in your lodging?"

"You do not know that he is concerned with the castle?"

Ah! That made sense. Ernesto had to have glory. "He owns it?"

"Oh no. It is owned by the Government, but the Count has a certain responsibility. He arranges for the caretaking family, and he has a few rooms which he may use for himself, in return."

243

"So you sit around in splendour—" doors and balustrades of the finest Carrara marble, Felipe had said, "—like brothers?" I used the word deliberately, watching his face, but nothing showed.

"*El Conde* de Merito and I are very good friends," he said.

30

WE HAD BEEN walking for three hours but heaven alone knew how much distance we had made, for the winding track of the river we dared not leave must have taken us double the distance we would have travelled on the mule tracks. Suddenly it seemed that the valley must have widened for the fog was whiter, and though we could not see much more than before, the terrain was easier. We were able to walk on the banks of the stream, marshy land alternating with rocks, but there was often a wide, stony river bed blasted flat by the weight of the annual spring melting of the snows. I was growing desperately tired and very hungry. We came to a waterfall, and where the ground fell away on either side, we climbed the bank. There was a sheer cliff and we had to go higher still, and higher. All at once I realised that the leaden damp of the fog was lifting, the air was more clear. I was losing that frustrating sense of blindness. "It's clearing!"

Carlos replied: "There is a wind!" He lifted one finger, holding it high, then added: "Yes, a wind is starting. If it sweeps up the valley it will blow the fog away. You are tired?"

For answer I sank down on a rock. Oh, the relief of it! I was aching from head to foot. He said sympathetically: "You have been very tenacious, my dear. But then, you could not have gone back, could you? You would have been lost. Let us wait here for a while and see if that breeze is going to grow into a wind, because if it does we will be able to go up to the mule track and then the going will be very different. While we sit here, safely out of the way of Emilio Diego at any rate, perhaps you would like to tell me who is this Felipe Lazaro who is so anxious to interview me."

I had not wanted to tell him. I had felt it was for Felipe to break the silence of the past, but I felt assuredly, perching there on the sharp little rock with a scrubby bush supporting my feet and the fog billowing around us, lightening, thickening, waiting on the wind, that I held the moment in my hand. "Felipe is your son," I said, and looked up gravely into the blue eyes that were an imprint of Felipe himself.

"I have no son."

"You don't know what you have," I said. "You don't remember."

He sat looking at me, his face a mask, but he did not speak.

"I asked you if you remembered the name of the English-woman. She was your wife. Antonia. A fair-haired English-woman," I said, watching him closely, "with blue eyes."

At last he said, quietly and without emotion: "How do you know this?"

"Because she thought you were dead and she married my father. They are both dead, now. But Felipe, your son, is up on the mountain."

"Why, if this is true, was I not told?"

"Because everyone thought you were dead. They did not know that Ernesto, the Count de Merito, kept you hidden, and drugged, and guarded in a tiny village at the foot of the Sierra Nevada." I did not trust myself to say any more. Besides, I did not think it was my place to promote Carlos from a simple iron worker to a Spanish grandee. "It is said," I told him diffidently, "that you have a depressed bone in your skull and if that could be lifted—it is possible that a surgeon could do it—you might be returned to normality. You might even be able to remember. Your name is not Justin de Prideau. It is Carlos Lazaro."

246

He did not answer. We sat there side-by-side as the fog, thinning to a mist, swirled past us and around us, lifted and hung suspended on the air, then rose again. A freezing wind came flying up the valley, dancing around the crags and crevasses, sweeping the mist before it, lifting it until we could see the river below and the dark, threatening crags above. At last Carlos rose stiffly from his perch and held out a hand to me. "Come," he said, "we will find the track now, and it will be easier."

"You haven't answered," I reminded him, looking uncertainly up into his face.

"Because I cannot believe it," he said heavily. "We will see what my friend the Count de Merito has to say."

*   *   *

It was evening. The sun had gone down, the wind quietened, the valley was full of shadows. We had walked in silence up and down the narrow, rocky tracks, descending the mountain all the time, crossing and re-crossing the river bed on high narrow bridges, climbing over ridges where swallows wheeled and cactus grew along with thyme and lavender, cow parsley, oleander, and later, figs and almonds. I was dropping with exhaustion and Carlos knew, but he never slowed his pace. We came down a steeply zig-zagging path that led back into the river bed and there was one of those high, narrow bridges, higher and more narrow, it seemed, than any we had crossed before. It curved up from the rocky river bed, rising above a small canyon where the water splashed noisily into a huge black hole, then sped foaming over a fall.

"Be careful," Carlos said warningly as we stepped onto it, "for it is still very wet from the fog. It's quite safe, though. Animals cross these bridges."

I stepped gingerly on to it watching my feet all the way, trying not to look into the rushing torrent below, then gathering my strength, ran off the end. There was another ridge to cross in front of us and I remember thinking: Oh, no, I

247

cannot go a step further, and at that moment some movement drew my eyes to a clump of chestnuts not fifty yards away and there, to my utter disbelief, was Sebastian standing beside a mule, and Felipe standing beside him. I opened my mouth to shout but Felipe made a sign to me to be quiet, and to go on. Carlos had not seen them. He was walking ahead of me, head down, for he was tired too. Bewildered, I followed, then on a hunch, turned round, and sure enough hurtling down the track we had just left, too fast for safety, came Ernesto riding Odin, and behind him Diego on a horse I had not seen before.

I stood there, unable to go on, ignoring Felipe's urgent signs, for my legs would move only feebly, and then they stopped altogether. I think my mind stopped, too, and I stood there in a waiting vacuum. Waiting for the unacceptable, the unspeakable, to happen to all of us.

Ernesto was spurring Odin on and Odin, sure-footed and willing as he was, was slipping and slithering on the shaly track for he was being hurried at too fast a pace. Ernesto must have been wearing cruel spurs, for the stallion seemed to leap forward with an air of agonising desperation, to pause, then leap again. He was at the bridge, that very narrow, highly curving, slippery stone bridge that was built for people and mules and goats, and perhaps, taken slowly and with the utmost care, for horses on a leading rein. Odin stopped, his small, sure feet sliding in the loose stones. Ernesto lifted his right arm, flailing the poor beast with a stick he carried. Odin flung his head up. Ernesto spurred again, thrashed again, jerked the bit, and Odin reared, neighing a protest that was almost a scream.

Crazily, suicidally, I found myself running back down the track towards the bridge and as I did so I saw a figure dash from beneath the trees. Sebastian! And then my blood ran cold for I saw he held a gun in his hand. I heard his shout: *"Diablo!"* and some Spanish curses I did not understand. He was running, running ahead of me towards the bridge. Ernesto, too concerned with his fury, did not see either of us; I his quarry, Sebastian his enemy. He jerked the reins once more, and there was that terrible, heart-tearing cry from the horse.

Odin leaped towards the bridge, turned aside, reared, lost his balance on the loose stones and came down half over the bank where the crystal foam ran wild. Ernesto, losing his seat, was thrown towards the side of the rising curve of the bridge. He hit it and fell, a dead weight, into the rushing, foaming torrent below. I saw his body swing beneath the bridge and shoot through the foam, half-obscured, then with ghastly precision, one foot caught in a rock and he hung suspended for a moment over the waterfall with the waters leaping and foaming around him. Then he slid away and was gone. Felipe and Sebastian were already running, uselessly, along the rock-strewn bank.

Odin, whinnying with terror, was scrambling up the rocky slope, clinging with his wonderful hooked shoes, head thrust forward, every muscle in his body knotted tight and all his strength in his shoulders. Unheeding the slippery surface, I sped across the narrow causeway. Before I reached the other side the stallion was up, backing hurriedly off, trembling with terror, but unable to get away because his reins had caught round his forelegs. I ran to him and freed him. Farther downstream, on the opposite bank, the two men had stopped running. I put both arms round Odin's neck and buried my head in his thick mane.

* * *

So Ernesto, temporarily *El Conde* de Merito, died, and it was better that way. Better for Pilar, and Damian, and the Dowager. Better, too, for Carlos and Felipe, and me also, if it could be said that was important in the context, and I suppose it was, in a way, in the end. Sebastian and Felipe recovered his body but it took an hour or more of clambering over rocks and battling with the freezing waters of that murderous mountain stream. I rode Sebastian's beloved Odin on to Trevelez where his horse box awaited us and by the time he had made the long trip round the mountains to the village the other three horses were back in the stables. No doubt Diego, turning to race back up the mountain the way he had come, had seen Sebastian's hand on his gun and deemed it wise to make what reparation he could before disappearing. Anyway, to his credit he drove Rosario and the horse taken for Carlos, and Ernesto's mule ahead of him as he returned over the pass to La Calahorra. Ernesto's last act on earth had been an undignified one in Spanish eyes but he had been desperate, and desperation bears indignity well. He knew, because he had been careful to find out, that the weather might be bad on the southern slopes of the mountains and he knew a mule would pick her familiar way over any mule track. And these were mule tracks on which we rode, not horse tracks. The mules had been there since Spain began. But he saw the mists rising as he came, on the mule, round the ridge by the shepherd's hut, and he knew he was safe then to take the faster Odin.

Felipe guessed Carlos would make for the stream, and having run into trouble at the hut in the shape of the owner, thought fast, as he always does. He knew, as Carlos and I had not known and never found out because we were directionless in the fog, that the stream twisted and turned endlessly. He knew the going was so rough, he had a better chance of catching us by setting out on foot on the mule track. "I walked practically double to see it, like a tracker dog. Anything's possible, if you want to do it badly enough," said Felipe lightly. He beat us by nearly an hour to the bridge and Sebastian, worried about his horses, found him there, sitting under a wild chestnut tree waiting for us, knowing that in the time, following the zig-zags of the river, we could not have outdistanced him.

I was once again in the over-grown summer house, for the second time since I had hoped never to enter it again. Life is a perpetual facing up to things, Felipe had said. I had not thought of it quite like that, but assuming his words to be true

250

I set about facing up to the summer house. It was a fact that I nearly died there, but it was also true that it was here Felipe heard Antonia's story from my lips, and we became friends. This morning we had cleared the remainder of the cloying, suffocating vine. The seats, with their lovely creamy marble streaked with cinnamon and pink, scrolled and curved, looked magnificent. Not as comfortable as the old deckchairs we used in the Surrey garden, but there was little that was comfortable, it seemed, in being heir to an ancient palace. Marble garden seats were the least of Felipe's problems, now.

"How are your legs? Working again?"

"I'll admit to more-or-less total exhaustion," I said wryly. "I need a holiday to get over this holiday."

"I'll take you on one when everything's over."

"Oh! The promises you've made me!" I burst out laughing.

"This is real. How would you like to be the next *Condesa* de Merito? You can have a holiday for a honeymoon," said Felipe, and without waiting for an answer, took me in his arms. This time his kiss was a very long way from absent-minded.

"My God!" I gasped when I could speak.

"That's no answer to a proposal," he chided me gently.

"But F-Felipe," I stuttered, "I am the wrong religion and I don't s-speak Spanish, and my God! You wouldn't want me to live here—after all that's happened?"

"Why not?" he asked innocently. Those blue eyes that were once so coldly mesmerising, sent my heart into a series of somersaults.

"I couldn't be a Con—what did you call it? *Condesa*?"

"Why not?" he asked again.

"I'm English. I mean, I'm ordinary Eng—"

"No ordinary girl would do what you have done in the past week," he said, deliberately misunderstanding me. "Besides, as an English Countess I accede you might have to put your best foot forward, but as a Spanish *Condesa*—well, Pilar

251

spends most of her time at the hairdresser or the dressmaker or resting, so far as I can see."

"Catch *me*," I muttered. "I'll get this garden in order."

"That's my girl."

I heard the now familiar sound in the distance of the big door opening into the palace. We drew apart. I was still getting my breath back when Felipe, who had gone out onto the path, called: "Hi there, Ballisat!"

He came hurrying down the path, red-faced, worried, his dear, familiar, shambling self with his hair ruffled as normal and his clothes untidy. "Lord, but I am glad to see you, Suzie," he greeted me, clasping me to his big, soft front in a great bear hug. "Terrible rumours going round the town! I rang and the boy Alonso said you were here, so I came right up. What happened? What on earth happened, Suzie? Viola and I have been worried out of our minds. They say the police have been here all morning."

"They haven't been worrying me," I replied cheerfully. "For once I can say thank goodness I don't speak Spanish." I told him, as briefly and concisely as I could. "It's strictly confidential," I said. "There's a carefully censored version for the public and the police."

"And Carlos is actually in hospital now, and going to be operated on? Whew!"

"I spoke to the surgeon this morning," Felipe told Perry. "He seems to think an operation could work."

"He's going to get all his faculties back?"

"Who knows? We can only hope, and pray."

"What if he comes out—sorry to be so blunt—the same?"

"I would be very surprised if he did. He has been through a lot. You have to remember that if he is cured he will know the whole story, and that," said Felipe acidly, "is enough to sober anybody. Besides, we're not to know if he might not have quietened down much earlier if he had been allowed into Spain. What was there for him to do in the Basque mountains, but make trouble?"

We sat in silence for a moment in that very silent garden

that never seemed to get a breeze, our thoughts scattered. "Penny?" said Felipe.

"Oh dear." I wiped a tear away. "Half of me is up in that wonderful clear sky singing where the non-existent skylarks ought to be, the other half is scared to death."

"She is going to marry me," said Felipe, smiling. "Convince her it's all right."

I thought Perry would jump up and shout Congratulations! in that boisterous way of his, and give me another bear hug, but he just stared at me in silence for a long time. Then: "Yes, it's going to be all right," he said at last. "I was thinking of something that always bothered me about this place. It was given to one of your ancestors by a king?"

"Carlos V, in 1517." Felipe looked faintly perplexed.

"And for why?"

"In gratitude for services rendered."

"Rather dishonourable and infamous services?"

Felipe was watching Perry whimsically, a little non-plussed. "I suppose it was, when one comes to think of it." He turned to me. "Carlos V's mother, Juana la Loca, was the rightful queen, but Carlos wanted the throne and so he had her proven mad and locked away. Yes," he admitted, looking back to Perry. "I suppose it was not such an honour to have had a big hand in that."

"A black deed," said Perry solemnly, "has now been exorcised by what happened to Carlos and Ernesto, and to you, also, Felipe." Perry turned to me and winked. "I reckon you'll be all right, now."

Felipe was regarding him good-naturedly, and with respect. "It should take an American to point that out! I would not have suspected you of an interest in moral philosophy, Ballisat."

"Call me Perry. It was a shocking way for an ancestor to behave, and someone had to pay. But what is going to happen now? Ernesto's story was that the family would be in trouble politically if Carlos returned."

"That was so, when my grandfather was alive. But Franco

253

has pardoned his enemies. Besides, my redoubtable grandmother has already been in touch with General Franco, with
whom she is on good terms, and he had a great deal to say
about Ernesto's worthiness. Ironic, isn't it, but Ernesto did
what he thought was right, in the beginning," Felipe said. "He
liked being number one. That was where he fell down."

It was true that it could not be said he was wholly bad, but
the bad in him was shocking.

"And your grandmother? And the others?" asked Perry.

"It's up to my father," said Felipe. "We have told them
Ernesto met with an accident in the Sierras, which is true. If
Carlos recovers his memory, then he will decide what, and
how much, to tell. As for Pilar and Damian, they had no part
in the affair."

"Felipe, I've just remembered Garcia's car!"

"It turned up in Granada absolutely intact and without a
scratch."

"Thank heavens for that."

"It occurs to me," said Perry, "you're still missing the
marriage certificate."

"As a matter of fact, no. The solicitor received an envelope
from Ernesto only a few days ago. That gives rise, does it not,
to the supposition that Ernesto only found it a few days
ago. That he suppressed it in a moment of weakness and
might well have thought better of his decision a little later
had he lived. It was meant to be opened if Ernesto died, and
then Damian died also, without issue. In the present context
Damian felt that did not apply. It contained the marriage
certificate of Carlos and Antonia. Ernesto took it from the
chapel and made it safe for the future, should it be needed.
Perhaps," said Felipe magnanimously, "we should try to
remember that was one of Ernesto's last deeds."

"I have changed my mind," I murmured humbly, "about
wanting to be a Spanish *Condesa* one day. It is going to be
such a privilege that any of the hurdles I may have mentioned
seem to have faded to nothing. Thank you, Felipe."

"Thank *you*, Suzanne darling."

"And I'll thank you both to remember I am a very capable artist with a hungry family to support," said Perry immodestly. "Would you consider commissioning me to paint the bride?"

"And groom," I added. Felipe had come a long way in the past few days. From parador manager to heir apparent. It would be nice, I thought, to have his portrait on a palace wall.